THE DYSFUNCTIONAL FAMILY'S GUIDE TO MURDER

Kate Emery

THE DYSFUNCTIONAL FAMILY'S GUIDE TO MURDER

Alfred A. Knopf   New York

A Borzoi Book published by Alfred A. Knopf
An imprint of Random House Children's Books
A division of Penguin Random House LLC
1745 Broadway, New York, NY 10019
penguinrandomhouse.com
rhcbooks.com

Text copyright © 2024 by Kate Emery
Jacket art copyright © 2025 by Lila Selle

Penguin Random House values and supports copyright. Copyright fuels creativity, encourages diverse voices, promotes free speech, and creates a vibrant culture. Thank you for buying an authorized edition of this book and for complying with copyright laws by not reproducing, scanning, or distributing any part of it in any form without permission. You are supporting writers and allowing Penguin Random House to continue to publish books for every reader. Please note that no part of this book may be used or reproduced in any manner for the purpose of training artificial intelligence technologies or systems.

Knopf, Borzoi Books, and the colophon are registered trademarks of
Penguin Random House LLC.

Library of Congress Cataloging-in-Publication Data is available upon request.
ISBN 979-8-217-03016-3 (trade) — ISBN 979-8-217-03017-0 (lib. bdg.) —
ISBN 979-8-217-03018-7 (ebook)

Originally published by Allen & Unwin, Crows Nest, Australia, in 2024

The text of this book is set in 11.2-point Warnock Pro Regular.
Crime scene tape art by Prathaan/stock.adobe.com
Book design by Cathy Bobak

Manufactured in the United States of America
10 9 8 7 6 5 4 3 2 1

The authorized representative in the EU for product safety and compliance is Penguin Random House Ireland, Morrison Chambers, 32 Nassau Street, Dublin D02 YH68, Ireland, https://eu-contact.penguin.ie.

Random House Children's Books supports the First Amendment
and celebrates the right to read.

For Aggie and Christobel

CRIME SCENE DO NOT CROSS

1

THEY LOOK AT HIM LIKE THEY WANT TO KILL HIM.

This seems a little harsh, given Nick is already lying on a hospital gurney being fed into an ambulance, IV trailing from one arm. He doesn't seem like the kind of guy who intentionally screws up anyone's vacation. Aunty Vinka's latest (and hottest) new boyfriend is all dark hair, slow smiles, and cheekbones—he's part aging member of a K-pop band and part surfer, with shockingly green eyes.

"Sorry," Nick says, his perpetual grin finally fading into something closer to sheepishness. "I really thought I could catch it."

Aunty Vinka, who is definitely not delusional enough to believe she could catch a venomous snake using only a pair of kitchen tongs, smiles up at the nearest paramedic. Aunty Vinka smiles up at everyone: She's five foot nothing and likes to say my dad sucked up the entire height allocation in their family. "Can I ride with you guys to the hospital?"

The paramedic grunts, which I guess Aunty Vinka can

decode, because she climbs in, inadvertently (at least I hope so) flashing the family as she picks up the hem of her skirt, the silver charms on her anklet jangling.

"I'll call you when we get there!" she says, and the ambulance doors close before anyone can remind her that she can call all she likes, but we won't be picking up: There's no phone reception here at the family farmhouse. There's no internet, either, in case you were wondering how personally stoked I am to be here.

"I guess it's not his fault," Bec—Aunty Bec, I should call her now, for reasons I'll get to in a sec—says to Dad as the ambulance bumps off down the tree-lined driveway.

This is overly generous, because it really, truly *is* Nick's fault. Not the murder, which hasn't happened yet, but getting bitten by the snake. Turns out snake handling isn't actually "just a matter of confidence."

"Of course it's his bloody fault." Dad always says what I'm thinking and can't say. (Mum thinks he says what nobody should say, which might be why they're divorced.)

"He was trying to help," offers Shippy, who is Aunty Bec's (not so new, and not so hot) boyfriend.

"Help who—the snake? Mission accomplished."

"D'you reckon he was trying to impress us?" Aunty Bec says.

"What? Why?"

"Meeting the family, you know. He was probably nervous and wanted to make a good impression."

"I *told* him to put down the tongs," Dad says.

I'm not sure Nick heard Dad over Shippy whooping with

encouragement and Aunty Vinka shouting at him not to hurt the snake. If you're wondering why Nick wouldn't just leave the snake to slither back into the bush or call a professional, all I can say is: *Me too.*

"Let's go inside," Bec—Aunty Bec—says, sounding tired.

It's Aunty Bec, not Aunty Vinka, who you'd expect to have the hot younger boyfriend. Aunty Vinka is probably quite pretty, but most of the time she looks like she's recently escaped from a hippie commune (and not the kind with running water and yoga classes, but more of a make-your-own-compost deal). Aunty Bec, in contrast, is camera ready: all pressed clothes, swishy bob, and no visible pores. That's what makes it all the weirder that she's voluntarily tied herself to Shippy.

"I thought he had it," Shippy says, scratching at his floppy blond curls like someone whispered the word *nits* in his ear. "Just before it bit him."

"Another entrant for the Darwin Awards." Dad puts his arm around me as we head back into the farmhouse. "Do you think Vinka finds all these guys outside the lobotomy clinic, or is it just a coincidence?"

"Nick's a sweet guy, Andy, don't be a . . . jerk," Bec—Aunty Bec! Aunty Bec!—says, clearly remembering my presence and catching herself. She looks around for her son, Dylan, but he's probably in his room. Dylan's usually in his room.

We troop inside the farmhouse, which I probably shouldn't call a farmhouse because there's very little farming going on these days. When Dad and Aunty Vinka grew up here, Grandad ran cattle and sheep, but then the family moved to Perth and it became more like a vacation home, or a hobby farm at best. Grandad sold the last of the livestock before he and his second wife, GG, moved back here, but the name stuck.

It's still got that vacation-home feel: mismatched furniture, hand-me-down appliances, and the smallest TV you've ever seen in your life. GG talked about removing the wallpaper and painting the place when she first moved in, but somehow they never got around to it, just like they never got around to replacing the bed Grandad and his first wife, my grandma, had shared in the downstairs bedroom (um, creepy). That's probably why GG insisted on using the upstairs bedroom, even though Dad reckons she's taking her life in her hands every time she goes up and down the staircase Grandad built. Even when the whole place is clean, which it is right now because we're supposed to be driving back to Perth, it still looks grubby: There are stains on the wall that won't come out, and the couch is more patch than original material. I found mouse poo under my bed last night (or at least I really hope that's what it was, because the alternative is a rogue possum).

I want to ask Dad if people still die from snakebites (like middle-class people with vacation houses, not hikers lost in the wilderness with only a warm can of Coke), but is it too soon?

"So," says Aunty Bec, perching on the armrest of the couch, right over the biggest patch. "I guess we're not going home today after all."

"You guys can still go back to Perth," Dad says. "Ruth and I will hang around to see if Nick's okay, and maybe stick a pillow over his face if he's not, teach him a lesson."

Aunty Bec shakes her head. "Shippy and I drove down with Nick and Vinka, remember—my car's at the mechanic's. Couldn't leave if we wanted to." She says that like she wants to. "Do you think they'll let him out of the hospital today? I've got a meeting tomorrow."

"I doubt it."

"Great," Shippy says, flopping into the nearest armchair so violently that it rocks backward and almost tips over. "All chill and no Netflix." I'm not sure he knows what that phrase means. Also: gross.

Aunty Bec's reading the spines on the bookshelf. "Serves me right for forgetting my Kindle. These books haven't changed in twenty years: It's all Sherlock Holmes, Ngaio Marsh, and Agatha Christie."

She's right, but I don't care. I love murder mysteries, the higher the body count the better. You wouldn't think you could read a mystery more than once, but maybe my brain is defective, because I often forget who strangled so-and-so in the library or poisoned blah-de-blah in the conservatory. (I'm still not sure what a conservatory is, but they're constantly popping up.)

I love real-life mysteries too, and I'm pretty good at solving them. Sure, as a fourteen-year-old who's never lived anywhere but Perth, I only get to solve mysteries like the Mystery of the Weird Smell in My Bedroom (a moldy banana at the bottom of my bag) or the Mystery of the White Dots on My Black Skirt (a tissue in the wash), but they count. I'm sorry to brag, but, you see, it's going to be relevant soon.

"There's still the TV," says Shippy, who I am definitely not calling Uncle Shippy no matter what (he's not Dylan's dad so he's barely family anyway). "Right?"

"You could always catch the bus back," Dad says hopefully.

"I get carsick on buses and it's, like, four hours." Shippy brightens a bit. "Maybe I could check out the surf. Are there any old boards lying around here? Mine didn't fit on the car."

Dad shakes his head and doesn't point out that neither his dead-dad hobby farmer nor his elderly stepmother is likely to be a big surfer, which is uncharacteristically restrained.

Nobody has asked me how I'm feeling about any of this, which is annoying because I'd love to complain. It's not that I hate Dad's family: Compared to Mum's side, which is kind of a snooze (her only sister is a nun, and not the "How Do You Solve a Problem Like Maria" fun kind), they're good value, and Dylan is . . . I'll get to him. The problem is that tomorrow night I'm supposed to be watching a movie with my best friends, Ali and Libby, and if they do it without me, they'll probably bond over their mutual love of gore-free horror, and then the next time we have to pair up in PE, they'll choose each other and I'll be stuck with Viv, who will definitely want to do my personal astrology chart again.

The kitchen door bangs open and closed and in walks Dylan. He's missed the whole thing, which is classic Dylan, really. At the sight of us all he stops and slides his over-the-ear earphones down to his neck. Something that might be Finnish death metal blares out.

A word about Dylan, on whom Ali and I developed crushes

the summer he learned how to do something with his hair. It was awkward enough to have a crush on a family friend— Bec grew up around here too and stayed friends with Dad and Aunty Vinka when they all moved to Perth, so I've known Dylan my whole life. But it went full cringe about six months ago when I learned we're not just family friends but *related*. Turns out his mum, Bec, is the half sister of my dad and Aunty Vinka.

It's a whole thing, but the short version is that forty-something years ago my grandad had a super-sneaky affair with a woman he worked with, who put the resulting kid up for adoption. That much we know from a letter that surfaced after Grandad died. Turns out Aunty Bec's mum, who was *best friends* with Grandma, thought it was a great idea to secretly adopt the kid and not tell anyone. This bit Aunty Bec only found out after *her* parents were killed in a car accident and she went through their stuff.

The word you're looking for is: *yikes*.

Dylan looks at me and raises his eyebrows. He can't raise just one, like me, and I know it kills him. I shrug, not sure how to communicate the whole *Snake!* thing with just my face. Now that we're, what, half cousins, I haven't even noticed this trip that he's lost his curls (bad) and skinny jeans (good).

"What's going on?"

"We're staying another night," Aunty Bec says.

"Why?"

"Ask Nick," Dad says. That's when he gets a look like he's

just been told the toilet's overflowing and all the plumbers in the world are booked until Christmas. "Crap."

"What?" I ask.

"Someone's got to tell Gertie."

Anyway, that's how the whole murder-mystery thing starts.

CRIME SCENE DO NOT CROSS

2

BEFORE WE GET TO THE MURDER, THOUGH, YOU'LL HAVE TO MEET GG. (The nickname comes from her maiden name, Gertrude Goodwin, which is an amazing superhero name if only she had the inclination and a Lycra onesie.) Dad and Aunty Vinka have never been all that keen on GG, although they wouldn't say so. Aunty Vinka thinks Grandad moved on too quickly after Grandma died, and Dad once told me she has "bad politics." I've never been totally sure if they come here out of a sense of duty or to check on the house.

"I'll go up and tell her," Dad says, not moving.

"I can do it," Aunty Bec offers, also not standing up. "We've kind of bonded."

"Since when?"

"I had a conference in Dunsborough and stayed here for a week a few months back. After Mum and Dad died."

Shippy, slouched so deeply on the couch that his fading chest tattoos are visible, farts into the silence and I stand up.

"I'll tell her," I say.

"You don't have to do that, Ru," Dad says.

"I don't mind. I'm kind of bored anyway." (Do I just not mention the fart if nobody else is going to?)

"And you think she's the cure for that?"

"Andy," Aunty Bec says, but mildly.

"Race you, then." Dad takes off.

Upstairs, my victorious (but slightly puffed) dad raps lightly on GG's door, then doesn't wait for an answer. GG is propped up in bed, covered by her flowery pink quilt, and knitting something small and blue.

"Have you come to say bye before you hit the road?"

"About that," Dad says. "You're going to have to put up with us for another night."

"What?" GG's head jerks up.

"There was a snake in the garden."

"A snake?"

"Nick tried to catch it."

"Sorry?"

"With kitchen tongs."

"Oh. I heard some kerfuffle in the garden."

"He's gone to the hospital, so we're sticking around to make sure he's okay."

"You'll stay here?"

If you're thinking GG seems at best confused and at worst disappointed that her extended family will be spending more time with her—yeah, me too. Possibly I've been a bad almost granddaughter and not listened sufficiently attentively to her stories about her (dead) cat, her (dead) son, or her (dead) husband(s), but shouldn't she *want* to spend time with me?

"I'm sure Nick will be fine," I say, in case she's worried. I'm not actually sure Nick *is* going to be okay, because I always thought brown snakes were deadly. (That was the thesis of my sixth-grade report on Australia's deadliest animals, and I got two gold stars.)

"Is that okay?" Dad asks.

"Of course it is," GG says, rallying. "Do we have enough food in the house?"

"The pantry is stocked for the apocalypse," Dad says. "Were you a Scout, Gertie, or just a hoarder?"

"A Brownie," she says, although I think the question was rhetorical.

"Can I get you anything?"

"I'm fine for now. Just happy having a rest. Could I borrow your phone, though, Andrew?"

"There's no coverage in the house," Dad says slowly, like Gertie's losing it—which, if she's forgotten this basic fact, maybe she is?

"Telstra works now."

"Does it? I'm with Optus."

"Me too," I add, although nobody asked.

"Gertie," Dad says, "don't you have a cell with Telstra? Can I get it for you? And, by the way, what's happened to the landline?"

"The landline's broken and my cell's useless because I missed a bill."

"I can have a look at the landline, if you like," Dad says—

somewhat disingenuously, because he's the only person I know capable of making a broken phone worse. The one time I asked him to help install an app on mine he Snapchatted a random selfie, then reset the whole thing to factory settings.

"If you don't mind," GG says, and Dad looks immediately panicked. My snort is too loud, because he looks at me, either hurt or pretending to be.

"I think you're forgetting the summer I fixed the wiring for the downstairs lights," he says. What I *remember* from that summer is Dad getting first stuck and then zapped after attempting to get at the wiring by jamming himself into a crawl space under the wooden floorboards, which Grandad inexplicably built for Oompa Loompa proportions, but it doesn't seem polite to say so.

"Maybe later," GG says, letting him off the hook. "The boy next door can always take a look. He's handy."

"Do you want to come downstairs with us, Gertie?" Dad asks. "It's probably time for some lunch."

GG shakes her head, and Dad is out the door before she can find another DIY job for him to balls up. I start to follow him, but GG stops me. "Ruthie, can you do me a favor?"

"Can I get you a cup of tea or something?" Slowly I'm turning into every other woman in this family: offering tea just to avoid silence.

"No, I'm fine. I was just hoping you could get something down for me?" She points toward the wardrobe: a massively wide wooden thing that outlived Grandad and will probably see us all off, if only because nobody can figure out how to carry it down the stairs. "There's a box," she says. "Could you reach it for me? I'm just in the middle of a tricky bit." She raises the knitting in case I need proof.

"Sure."

The box is on top of the wardrobe, next to GG's old typewriter (which is the approximate size of a small car) and an old-fashioned suitcase. It's cardboard, with a fitted lid, and big enough to fit a bowling ball. (I really hope it doesn't contain a bowling ball.) Someone, presumably GG, has written *for M* on the side with a red marker.

"Where do you want it?"

"On the bed, please." It's lighter than I expected, but the reaching and twisting required to get it down still make me wince. "Are you okay?"

"I'm fine." I rub at my shoulder, embarrassed she's asking me if I'm okay and not the other way around. "I tweaked my shoulder at tennis the other day." *Wrenched* would be more accurate. "Do you need anything else?"

GG hesitates, but then she shakes her head. "I'll ask your father if I do." I'm not going to argue with that.

Downstairs, I head for the bookcase to grab an Agatha Christie or a Sherlock Holmes, undecided which pompous windbag of a detective I'm in the mood for. I've finished the book I brought with me for what was supposed to be a weekend visit, and I'm in the mood for a comfort read. Reading, eating, and going to the beach are really all there is to do down here, and I'm not a big beach person.

Dylan walks past as I drop into the couch. He looks at the book covers.

"You've graduated from Enola?" Dylan and I spent one

13

summer vacation here so obsessed with the Enola Holmes novels that we decided we were going to set up our own detective agency. Unfortunately, our first and last case, the Mystery of the Broken Window, was solved in under two minutes when we found a dead crow on the washing machine, and by the time the next summer came around, Dylan had moved on.

"Enola holds up," I say, and Dylan nods as he walks away.

I open *The Murder of Roger Ackroyd,* thinking not of Sherlock or Enola or even Dylan, but instead wondering about the box in GG's room and who *M* might be. I'll find out eventually, but it'll take a while.

3

AM I TAKING TOO LONG TO GET TO THE MURDER? I MIGHT BE TAKing too long to get to the murder. But without this helpful scene-setting you'd have missed the clues about who did it. Did you notice them? There'll be others.

For now, let's jump ahead to dinner and I'll try to be quick.

Dinner is what we're told is chicken casserole, and because it's from GG's freezer, I'm not supposed to criticize. It's one of those sticky nights where a thunderstorm threatens, so we're all a bit sweaty, and Dad keeps opening the windows to get a breeze through, then shutting them when someone complains about the mosquitoes.

Aunty Bec tries to make small talk with GG about the casserole—it's delicious! When does she find the time?—but GG puts an end to that by insisting she didn't make it. So far as she's concerned, it appeared in the freezer one day (information, by the way, she shares only after it's been defrosted, cooked, and partially consumed). I try not to think about the likelihood that it's been here since Grandad died a year and a half ago—a death in the family being the conventional time for people to turn up with foil-wrapped casserole dishes. If it's been here since *Grandma* died eight years ago, we're definitely done for, so best not to contemplate it.

"Does Mrs. Whatsit still own the place next door?" Dad asks, poking his fork into something unidentifiable and brown.

"She died. There's a young bloke there now."

"Ah, that's right, you said—the phone guru," Dad says.

Dylan, who hasn't touched his meal, appears with a stack of buttered toast and slides a piece onto my plate.

"In case you'd rather not die of salmonella," he whispers, and I'm grateful enough to not even mention that you don't get salmonella from food being in the freezer too long.

As the last of the casserole is being choked down (Aunty Bec) or scraped discreetly into the bin (me), Aunty Vinka arrives home in a taxi.

"Nick's fine," she says, before anyone can ask.

"That's great," Aunty Bec says. "Did they give him antivenom?"

"Not exactly."

"Is antivenom not the done thing?"

Aunty Vinka goldfishes her mouth, like she's not sure how to say the next bit. Even GG is paying attention. "The snake didn't bite him."

"What?" Dad says.

"The doctors think maybe he got stabbed by a bit of wire or even just a really sharp stick when he was trying to catch the snake." Aunty Vinka delivers this at 1.5-times speed.

16

"Are you joking?" Dad asks.

"It was an easy mistake to make. We all saw the snake."

"So why isn't he with you now?"

"There was an, uh, incident at the hospital."

"What do you mean?"

"Nick, uh, sort of tripped when he was mucking around with a soccer ball—"

"In the *hospital*?"

"—and fell down some stairs—"

Dad swears under his breath, but the way you do when you want everyone to hear you.

"—and broke his leg. Quite seriously, actually, Andy, so I hope you feel bad now."

"Don't be a—" Dad swears again, and this time I'm pretty sure I'm *not* meant to hear it, because it's the word that once prompted him to give me a ten-minute lecture on misogyny in rap music. Then maybe he thinks better, because he adds: "Sorry, Vinx."

"He'll be discharged in the morning. I was going to stay overnight with him, but those hospital chairs are bad for my alignment."

Having Aunty Vinka home and Nick definitely not dead lifts the mood, and after a glass of wine Aunty Vinka relaxes enough to offer a reenactment of the accident, which makes Dad laugh so hard he goes briefly nonverbal.

The mood is upbeat until the table is being cleared, when Aunty Vinka swoops in to take GG's barely touched plate.

"Have you had enough to eat?" Aunty Vinka asks.

"I'm fine."

"Is your stomach bothering you?"

"No more than usual."

"Do you want me to get your medicine?"

"No."

"Have you taken it already tonight?"

"I don't need it every night."

Aunty Vinka frowns. "Are you sure? I thought I saw on the box it said—"

"*Vinka.* It's fine."

"Gertie," Aunty Bec tries, a bit more gently, from the other end of the table. "I think what Vinka is—"

"*Rebecca,*" GG says sharply. "I'm not a child and I'm not senile."

This is more awkward than the time my computer science teacher typed in the wrong URL and our whole class learned what a foot fetish is. I look at Dylan, who is cheerfully eating toast and watching like this is *The Real Housewives of Dunsborough.*

"Does anyone feel like dessert?" Aunty Vinka asks too loudly.

"Is there any?" Shippy looks hopeful. "I could murder a crumble."

"It's not a restaurant, mate," Dad says.

"I just meant—"

"There's ice cream and I think I saw some chocolate sauce."

There's a round of "Yes, please" from everyone, including GG, who seems keen to bounce back from the awkwardness. It might take more than a bowl of ice cream, in my opinion, but what do I know? (Sure, I know who's about to die, but still.)

When I go to collect my ice cream, Aunty Bec and Aunty Vinka are talking quietly: a classic sign they might be worth eavesdropping on.

"... usually like that," Aunty Bec says.

"You don't know her like we do." Aunty Vinka pulls open a cupboard door and takes out a bottle of chocolate sauce, the kind that goes pleasingly hard when you put it on ice cream. "This is pure chemicals, you know."

"Jealousy is a curse."

"I'm telling you: Try vegan ice cream just once and you'll never go back."

Aunty Bec ignores that lie. "Do we push the meds thing?"

"Dad said she always dragged her feet. He used to put them into her food sometimes."

"Like, crushed up the way you would for a cat?"

"It's a liquid. But he was probably joking."

They finally spot me and hand over a bowl of ice cream, which I take, along with *The Murder of Roger Ackroyd*, up to my creepy-arse room while the grown-ups argue about whether to play the 1986 or 1991 version of Trivial Pursuit. Have I mentioned my creepy room? The entire house is a bit of a horror show at night, all wood paneling and mirrors with a perpetual film of dust, but only my room has an entire glass-fronted cabinet filled with eerie, faceless china figurines that definitely plot my demise the moment the light goes out. Possibly I need to stop watching horror movies. The figurines are a GG addition to the house, and, no, I don't know why she doesn't keep them in her own bedroom except that, presumably, they also horrify *her*.

I read until exhaustion turns all the *r*'s in my book into *n*'s, then lie in bed listening to the adults finish their game (pretty sure Aunty Vinka won because Dad seems *pissed*) over the distant rumble of thunder. The storm that's been promised for hours finally seems to have arrived. Footsteps go up the stairs and doors are opened and closed. Only when the house is quiet and dark do I realize what's keeping me awake: I need to pee.

"Don't even *think* about moving around when I'm gone," I whisper to the figurines as I pass. They don't answer, which, on balance, is a good thing.

The nearest bathroom is one floor up, one of many quirks in Grandad's questionable design skills, but when I get near the top of the stairs, a strip of orange light from under GG's bedroom door—and whispered voices—tell me she's still awake. I can't recognize the other voice, but they sound like they're arguing, which I guess means I'm going to the downstairs bathroom. (I could have saved some time solving the crime if I'd stayed to eavesdrop, as I'll eventually discover, but nobody's perfect.)

Apparently nobody in this house is asleep, because downstairs not only do I see the flare and fade of someone smoking in the part of the garden visible through the living room window (who *smokes*?), but I can hear the kettle boiling in the kitchen.

The bathroom mirror shows me the beginnings of a whitehead right between my eyes. I poke it a little in the hope it might make a satisfying mess on the mirror, but it just throbs beneath my fingertips and turns an angry red. Great.

The smoker is gone by the time I head upstairs, which is probably a good thing because the thunder has been joined by crackles of distant lightning, and surely rain can't be far behind. Two steps into my bedroom, I stop. Something is wrong and the room has rearranged itself in my absence. I must be tired, because it takes me an embarrassingly long time to realize I'm standing in Dad's bedroom, which adjoins my own. I start to apologize, then stop when I see his bed is empty.

Back in my own room I get into bed and finally fall asleep, listening to the rumble of the approaching storm. I wish I could say that the next thing I know I'm awoken by a scream—it would be more dramatic—but the truth is, nobody finds the body right away. We'll get there, though.

4

THE SCREAM IS COMING FROM THE TOP FLOOR OF THE HOUSE (told you we were getting there).

Aunty Bec, poised with a pan of scrambled eggs in one hand and a plate in the other, is the first to decide she's not imagining it. "What was that?"

There's the drumbeat of running feet and then Aunty Vinka arrives in the kitchen with her bathrobe flying open like it's a pair of wings trying to launch her into the air.

"Vinx, what—"

"It's Gertie!"

Dylan appears, looking like he might technically still be asleep. The gap between his T-shirt and pajama pants is a reminder of the foot he's grown this year. Not that I notice.

"Did you guys hear that?" he asks.

Dad puts down his coffee, ignoring Dylan. "Is the old duck okay?" He's aiming for casual but failing.

"No."

Dad follows Aunty Vinka out of the kitchen, and I hear their feet going up the stairs. Fast.

"What's happening, Mum?"

"Something to do with your, uh, with Gertie." Aunty Bec is struggling with what to call GG. Not to get ahead of myself, but that's not going to be such a big problem in a minute.

"Should we go up?" Dylan asks, and I'm not sure if he's asking me or his mum. He's definitely not asking Shippy, who's taken his breakfast of honey on toast into the living room so he can watch the cricket.

I'm on my feet. Maybe it's my fault for reading *The Murder of Roger Ackroyd* too late last night, but something is happening and I want to know what. My first thought is the snake Nick failed to catch—could it have gotten into GG's room?

Dylan's behind me on the stairs. "What is it?" he asks, like he can't see I'm two steps ahead of him.

I twist around, nearly missing a step. "Snake, maybe?"

"What?"

"The brown snake."

"How'd it get in the house?"

"I don't know!"

It's not a snake.

We reach the landing outside GG's room just as Dad comes out with a face that looks a lot like Aunty Vinka's did when she ran into the kitchen to blow our morning apart.

"Is it a snake?" I look down for a tail licking at the bottom of my leggings. I've always been scared of snakes. (I refuse to use the word *phobia*, because a phobia is an irrational fear, and it's perfectly rational to be scared of a venomous animal that could kill me with a nibble.)

"Ruthie, go downstairs," Dad says.

"What's going on?"

"Downstairs!"

"Dad!" This is so like my dad, treating me like I'm still the ten-year-old who was scared of *Star Wars*. Well, I'm fourteen and I've seen all the *Star Wars* movies, even the bad ones; I've kissed a boy (Jeremy, at a school party—it was so grim); I got my period; *and* I'm nearly as tall as Mum. Shakespeare married off Juliet at my age, although I guess that didn't work out so well for her. I don't say any of this, obviously, because how weird would it be to start shouting about my period right now?

"Where's GG?"

"Downstairs!"

Dad scoops me up and throws the top half of my body over his shoulder in a way I wouldn't have imagined he had the upper-body strength for. Is it possible he really does still think I'm ten? I have time to let out a yelp, and Dylan has to dodge my feet as Dad starts down the stairs.

Over Dad's shoulder, through the gap in the door, I can see GG's quilt on the floor next to—bizarrely—her old typewriter. I get a glimpse of a broken bedroom window and only have a second to wonder why there's a ladder propped against the frame.

"Put me down—you're hurting me." Technically I'm only at risk of death by embarrassment, but it works and Dad sets me down at the bottom of the stairs.

"I could do that all day once."

"Yeah, when I was two. Can you please tell me what's going on?" I try to rearrange my clothes, since the leggings I slept in have slid down and the T-shirt on top is bunched up. At least I put on a bra this morning or I'd never be able to make eye contact with Dylan again.

Aunty Bec chooses this moment to finally come out of the kitchen, a Band-Aid on one finger suggesting she was at least distracted enough by the uproar to burn herself on the stove, if not enough to actually stop making breakfast.

"What's wrong?" she asks Dad.

"I'm going to get the police."

"Should I come?"

"No, stay—Vinka needs you. I'll take the kids."

Dad doesn't pick me up again (he really does look quite winded—is he even doing cardio at the gym?) but heads for the front door, clearly expecting Dylan and me to follow, which we do, still wearing the clothes we slept in. Shippy looks up from the cricket (probably a tea break).

"What's up?"

"Gertie," Dad says. "Don't go upstairs."

"Why not?"

Dad shouts something as he snatches keys off the table with one hand and his phone with the other. My feet are doing their best to trip me as I follow Dad out the door. I've barely buckled my seat belt before the car is speeding down the driveway. Nobody mentions calling an ambulance, which is normally a good sign but right now feels like a very bad one. When I twist around to look at Dylan in the back seat, he's not even reaching for his own seat belt.

Uncharacteristically, I don't ask any questions as we skid over the gravel. Dad already answered the biggest one I had when he shouted to Shippy.

"It's a crime scene!" he yelled.

I've seen enough TV cop shows to know what that means.

5

GG IS DEAD. OBVIOUSLY. YOU DON'T GET SCREAMS AND THE POLICE and Dad cosplaying a fireman unless someone is dead. The surprising thing about GG being dead isn't so much that she's dead—it's been my experience that old people only have one trajectory—but the way that she died. I'm warning you now that it's not great, but it's also easier if I come out and say it, not talk around it like the police did when they interviewed me: GG was killed by being hit on the head with her improbably gigantic typewriter. Not the most obvious murder weapon, you might think, but right up there in the gruesome stakes.

By the time we're back from the police station, an ambulance has taken GG's body away and a detective has taken statements from all of the family. It doesn't look like the crime scenes you see on TV, where cops are swarming everywhere, dusting for fingerprints and rummaging through drawers. There's one sad bit of crime-scene tape across GG's bedroom door, and that's . . . kind of it? *Underwhelming* is the word.

It's a relief when the police leave in the afternoon so we can gather in the living room for cookies, tea, and wine for the adults. I don't bother asking if I can have a sip or explaining to Dad, yet again, how things work in Europe. Last time I tried, he managed, through his laughter, to tell me to start with Italian lessons. Aunty Vinka's the only one missing: She's getting Nick from the hospital (or so she thinks).

"This is the last of it," Shippy says, pouring a splash into Dad's mostly empty wineglass.

"That didn't last long."

"There's three of us drinking it," Shippy says defensively, and Dad is distracted enough, or on his best behavior enough, not to look at Aunty Bec's untouched glass. She's perched on an armchair, ostensibly reading a book but really looking at Dylan, who is also allegedly reading a book on the far side of the same couch as me. His earphones are on, but no way is he not listening to the adults. Just like me. "Plus, none of us are driving tonight."

"Or tomorrow," says Dad.

"What do you mean?"

"The police are going to want to talk to us again, mate. Didn't they ask you if you were sticking around?"

"Yeah, but—"

"I don't think they're going to be happy if we head back to Perth right away."

"They've already interviewed us."

"Come on, Shippy. We talked to that Officer Peterson—"

"Nicola's a detective, actually. Nice lady. Do they still have minimum heights for the police?" Shippy asks.

28

"—for, what, half an hour? Forty-five minutes?"

"I dunno about that."

Dad takes a sip of his wine. "Does that strike you as sufficient time to come to grips with a murder committed in the middle of nowhere with a house full of suspects?"

My eyes flick to Dylan, who's watching Dad intently. (Those earphones are connected to *nothing*.)

Shippy still doesn't get it. "What do you mean, *suspects*?"

"Come on, Shippy, you must have watched *Midsomer Murders* or *Broadchurch* at some point in the last twenty years?"

I wait for Shippy to fire back, but he just laughs, and the tension between him and Dad disappears like the wine.

"Do we need some more wine?" Shippy puts his empty wineglass down on the coffee table.

"Try the cellar—that's where the good stuff is," Dad offers. "Our dad used to stockpile brandy there, and there might even be a few bottles left, unless Gertie's been hitting it hard. Actually, I'll come with you."

"There's a *cellar*?" Shippy frowns.

"The *wine* cellar: It's just that big cupboard in the hallway."

"Can I have some?" Dylan asks, ostentatiously pulling off his earphones. (Impossible for my brain not to notice that, despite him not touching his phone, there's no sound coming from the twin speakers now hanging from his neck.)

"Uh, no," Dad says, giving him a *nice try* expression.

"I'm sixteen this year."

"Exactly."

"Mum?"

Aunty Bec's let Dylan have a drink at home before—he's

told me about it—but she shakes her head. "I'll make some more tea. Ruth? Dylan?"

I nod, more to get her out of the room than because I'm dying for another cup of tea, especially if she's going to use one of Aunty Vinka's tea bags, which smell like flowers but taste like hot water that only met flowers at a party once.

"Hey," I say, scooting closer to Dylan now that the adults are out of the room for at least as long as it'll take the kettle to boil. "What did the police tell you?"

"Same as you, probably. Mostly they just wanted to know what we did last night and if I heard anything. Mum was there the whole time."

"Do you know how she died?"

"Hit in the head, right?"

"Yeah, *by her old typewriter.*"

This is clearly new information to him. Dylan's eyes don't go wide or anything, because I'm really not sure that happens outside novels, but his nostrils sort of flare like he's sucking in a lot of air. "Did the police tell you that?"

"Only because I saw it in her room and asked them about it. Dad wasn't stoked."

"Why would anyone kill someone with a typewriter?"

I wait a beat for courage, then ask the question I was too embarrassed to ask the cops. "Could she have done it herself?"

"Bludgeoned herself in the head?" Dylan gives me just the kind of look I was hoping to avoid from the cops. "I don't see how. Mum told me someone broke in through the window."

The ladder. I didn't even think to ask the police about the

ladder I'd seen leaning up against GG's window. Enola would be ashamed.

"Why would anyone break in? It's not like she was rich."

Dylan quirks his mouth. "She was kind of rich."

"Hardly." I push at the rip in the sofa.

Dylan's look is pitying. "How much do you think this farm is worth? Mum says she's got, like, a whole share portfolio as well."

"Dylan." It's Aunty Bec, back with the tea I don't want. She has that parental trick of finding extra syllables in his name.

"It's fine B—Aunty Bec," I say quickly.

She puts the tea down. "Is there anything you two want to ask me about all of this?"

I look at Dylan, trying to gauge if there's a trap here. His face offers no warning, so I take her at her word.

"Was GG killed by someone who broke into the house?"

Aunty Bec looks alarmed by my question, but, seriously, what did she think I was going to ask about—the location of Grandad's pudding cups? "That's what the police seem to think," she says slowly, stalling.

"Was it a burglar?"

"I don't think the police know anything yet."

"But is anything missing? What is there to steal?"

Aunty Bec's face says she regrets opening this door and would very much like to slam it shut.

"Ruth, I really don't know. Maybe we should wait for Andy—"

"Did Gertie have, like, a hidden past that would give someone a motive for murdering her?" Dylan asks, and Aunty Bec and I both give him the same look. "Sorry," he says before his mother can get there. "You did say we could ask anything."

"I'm not sure I did."

"Ask anything about what?" Dad is back, a bottle in each hand. Beside him, Shippy is also carrying two, with a third cradled against his body like a newborn. Dad cracks one and pours himself a glass.

"Nothing," Aunty Bec and I say, super suspiciously.

Dad might not let it go except Aunty Vinka gets home right then and distracts us all.

"Where's Nick?" Dad asks, opening the front door before she can.

Aunty Vinka takes the wineglass, which was definitely not for her, and flops into an armchair. "It's a nightmare."

"Why? He didn't kill Gertie, did he?" Dad holds up his hands before anyone can say it. "Too soon."

"Nick's still in the hospital. Apparently he's picked up an infection."

"At the hospital?"

"He's going to have to stay in for a day or so."

"He's having a bad week. Not Gertie bad, but not ideal."

Aunty Vinka waves her hand in front of her face like she's dispersing a bad smell. "Don't even start, Andy. This one isn't his fault. But I'm sure he'll be fine. I got him some essential oils to complement what the doctors are doing and they seemed to make him calmer." It's a mark of how serious the situation is that Dad doesn't even touch that. "Honestly, it was more stressful talking to the police."

"What did you tell them?"

"Who?" Vinka is clearly distracted.

"The cops."

"About what?"

"About everything." Dad holds his arms open. "About what happened last night. About, you know, *whodunit.*"

"What?" Shippy's head jerks up.

"*Andy.*" Aunty Vinka nods at me, and I get that feeling you get right before someone sends you out of the room. Luckily, Mum, who would definitely be telling me to go upstairs right now, isn't here. (I knew that divorce would come in handy one day.)

"Ruth's already been interviewed by the police. She knows what they are investigating." Everyone looks at me, like I'm supposed to say something.

"Yeah, I know GG was killed," I say, trying to look like this doesn't thrill me just a little. I've read a lot of murder mysteries (too many, a child psychologist might suggest) and I've seen stories about real-life murders in the news (my parents' fault for making me watch the news with them every night), but the idea that GG has been murdered still doesn't feel real. It can't—otherwise, shouldn't I be weeping in a ball right now? "There was a ladder outside the window," I say. "That must be how they got in."

"I think it was left out in the garden by the guy who fixed the roof last month," Aunty Bec offers.

"It's the typewriter that I don't get," Dylan says. "Why hit someone with a *typewriter*? How would you even be sure it would kill them? You'd have to use so much—"

This time Aunty Vinka actually pokes Dad, right in his side. *"Andy,"* she says, and I know Dylan has ruined this for me.

"Ruth, your loving aunt makes a fair point. Maybe this *is* an adult conversation. Why don't you go and have a shower before dinner or something?"

"I don't need a shower."

"Have a bath, then. There are some fancy bath-salt things in the cabinet."

I don't want to go because I know the adults are going to talk about GG and I'm going to miss everything. But if I stay, I'm pretty sure they're not going to talk about GG at all. It's all very *Catch-22* (a book Dad bought me that I couldn't finish, although, if he asks, I loved it).

"Is Dylan allowed to stay?"

"That's up to *his* mum."

Aunty Bec shrugs. Well, this is unbelievable.

"Fine." I slide off the couch and take another cookie. "I'll go." I stomp down the hall to the bathroom, get the bath started, then (obviously) sneak back like I'm six again and trying to catch Santa on Christmas Eve. I know, I *know*, eavesdroppers only hear things they don't want to hear, or however the saying goes, but this is a real-life murder mystery happening in my house, and if Dad thinks some fancy bath salts are going to distract me, he's kidding himself. (I *do* like fancy bath salts, though—he knew what he was doing there.) For once, luck is with me: Apparently, someone's been redecorating, and the big standing lamp that usually lives in the corner of the hallway on the far side of the stairs has been moved closer to the open kitchen door for no reason I can see. Under normal circumstances a lamp would offer bugger-all cover (exactly how skinny do you think I am?), but this is one of those boxy, full-length things, and if I crouch, there's a chance it might hide me if someone decides to come and check on the bath situation.

". . . not about fascism. It's a murder investigation. It takes more than a couple of hours," Dad is saying. Don't ask me how they got onto fascism in the thirty seconds I've been gone.

"They should be out there, looking for the person who did it," Shippy says, his words getting sloppy around the edges.

"As far as they're concerned, *we* probably did it." Dad shuts everyone up with that.

"What do you mean? Someone *broke in* through a window. There was a ladder," Aunty Bec says.

"Right." Dad puts a whole lot of weird mustard on that single word, hitting the *t* with the enthusiasm of Mrs. Labouchere, my choir teacher.

"Why would they think we . . . anything to do with it?" Shippy asks, his voice muffled (smart money says he's going back for another drink).

"Great point, Shippy. It's not as though one of us could possibly have slipped out of the house in the night, propped up the ladder, hit Gertie over the head, and made it back to bed before morning, is it?" I can tell from Dad's tone that he's building to something, preparing to Make His Point. This is helpful for me because his voice is getting louder.

"I don't think—"

"I'm sure the police think it's far more likely that a stranger happened upon this remote farmhouse and decided that, rather than break in at ground level, he was going to break into the window on the top floor for no obvious reason and with no obvious motive, just on the off chance there might be untold riches hidden under the bed."

"*Andy.*"

"Given we'll inherit now that Gertie's dead, I'm sure the burglar theory is where the police are going to be focusing their investigation."

"Are we allowed to be discussing this?" Aunty Vinka says.

But Aunty Bec is talking now. "Hypothetically, I suppose we did all have a motive, but why would any of us need to use a ladder and smash the window?"

"I wouldn't worry, Bec. You had the least motive out of all of us."

"What do you mean?"

"Gertie's biggest asset is this place, and that's being split between me and Vinka. We went through all this with Dad's lawyer after he died."

"Bec didn't tell you?" Shippy reenters the chat just when I'm starting to think he passed out.

"*Shippy.*"

"Bec, what is he talking about?"

"Gertie told Bec she . . . getting an equal share," Shippy says.

"What?"

"Didn't she?"

"You . . . tell them?"

"Mum, what's he talking about?"

"Bec?"

"Should we be talking about this?"

Are you following this? Me neither. *I* should at least be able to tell who's saying what, because I know everyone's voices, but, honestly, I kind of tune out while trying to digest what Shippy's just said: I definitely heard the words *equal share*, which would mean... well, what would it mean? I should probably be listening if I want to find out. I tune back in when Aunty Bec starts talking and everyone else shuts up for two seconds.

"Gertie and I had a talk," Aunty Bec says. "She told me that now that I'm part of the family, she changed her will to split the estate evenly. She told me it's what, uh, your dad. Our dad. What he would have wanted."

Gertie changed her will just before she died? This is a big deal. I don't really believe in using exclamation points ever since my English teacher once told me it was like laughing at your own joke (turns out she was quoting someone else), but if I did I'd be using them here! Like this!

"That's great," Aunty Vinka says, too late to pass off as a spontaneous reaction. "You *should* get an equal share, Bec. Just because you're a half sibling doesn't mean anything."

"Of course you should," Dad says quickly, probably annoyed he didn't get to say it first. "I'm just confused about why Gertie didn't tell us. Or why you didn't tell us."

"I was going to. I didn't realize it would be an issue quite so quickly."

"That's great," Aunty Vinka says again, too loudly. "It's not like any of us would ever challenge the will anyway." The words *challenge the will* do a lap of the room.

"Did you tell the police about the will?" Dad asks.

"No, I didn't think about it. Why?"

There's another silence, and if these guys don't stop it with the awkward silences and the long, uncomfortable pauses, my bath is going to flood the entire house and I won't be held responsible. At the same time, I get it. I mean: Would *you* want to be the one who points out to Aunty Bec that the police need to know that she's just added herself to the list of people who had a motive to kill GG?

"Where are you going?"

"I need some water. Anyone else?"

At some point in my adventures in eavesdropping I've crept out from behind the lamp so I'm nearly standing in the kitchen door. Hearing Dad's footsteps, I have just enough time to spring back behind the lamp before he comes into the kitchen. I should go. But if I leave now, I'll never know what else the adults are thinking. Dylan could surely be persuaded to tell me later, but he'll miss the nuance. Dad won't tell me anything; he'd be happy if I believed GG was just taking an extended nap.

The fridge door opens with the *suuuuck* noise it always makes.

"Did Gertie take her meds last night?" Dad calls through to the living room.

"No, remember it was a whole thing," Aunty Bec shouts back.

"Did she change her mind, though?"

"Why?"

"There's some missing."

More footsteps. I'm tempted to shut my eyes, which is ridiculous, because I'm not a four-year-old playing hide-and-seek.

"Two doses are missing," Dad says.

"Are you sure?" Aunty Bec asks.

"The packet hadn't been opened last night. Now there's two gone."

"So I guess she took her meds after all?" That's Aunty Vinka, who doesn't sound bothered. I'm inclined to agree with her. It's not going to make a difference to Gertie now whether she did or didn't take her medicine.

"She's only supposed to take one of these a night, so even if she did, where's the other one gone?"

"One?" Aunty Vinka says sharply. "I'm sure it was two."

"I see where you're going, Andy, but Gertie didn't die of a drug overdose," Aunty Bec says.

"It just doesn't make sense."

"I think we should leave it to the police," Aunty Bec says, "and forget this whole Poirot-in-the-drawing-room performance."

"What?"

"Poirot. You know how at the end of every book the detective gathers all the suspects together and does the big reveal? Isn't that what you're aiming for, Andy?" I never knew Aunty Bec was a Christie fan too. Maybe everyone is secretly a sucker for books in which a seemingly inexplicable murder is solved by a smug know-it-all detective at the end. (I really hope *you* are.)

"I don't think I could pull off a mustache."

"I'll say," Aunty Vinka chimes in.

"You know what I mean, though," Aunty Bec continues. "This playing-detective stuff. It's going to be a long few days if we're all sitting around here accusing one another of murder."

Spoiler #1: It's going to be a long few days either way.

Spoiler #2: I get to the bath before it overflows, but I won't be so lucky next time.

6

IN THE MORNING I GO FOR A RUN TO GET A PHONE SIGNAL, PAST GG's window, where cardboard covers the broken panes and the ladder is gone. The garden beds are churned up, and shards of glass in the soil catch the morning light. A long strip of police tape has become detached from the side of the house and is flapping around like a seagull with a broken wing.

My phone is full of texts from Ali and Libby asking for any updates on GG's death and reassuring me that the movie was kind of bad so I didn't miss anything. I give them the headlines: no updates and still no idea when I'll be home. Neither of them is on their phone, apparently, so I hang out for a bit, swishing through my recent photos to delete the bad ones, just in case Libby wakes up or Ali risks a glance at her contraband Android. By the time I've consigned ten hideous selfies to the trash and changed my phone background to a photo of nearby Yallingup Beach (Dad took me our first day here, before things got weird), nobody has replied, so I jog home.

Dad's not impressed by my morning's activity like I expected, but rather pissed off that I didn't tell him where I was going. He reminds me that *a woman has died.* The word *woman* makes GG sound so young, like someone with a job and plans for Saturday night. I think up some comebacks in the shower, but by the time I'm wrapped in a robe and headed up to my room, I've conceded he might have a point.

Upstairs, I find Dylan sitting on my bed, paging through a paperback, and I let out a little yip of surprise, grabbing on to the cords of my bathrobe to make sure it hasn't swung open. If you think I'm being paranoid, then let me suggest that *you*, unlike me, have never answered the door to a delivery guy while wearing only a robe. (No, I don't want to talk about it.)

"Hi."

"Hey." He swings his long legs off the bed and straightens up, raising the book I've been reading. "How's this?"

"Good, but, you know, I've read it before. I finally read the Naomi Novik series you were banging on about last time I saw you."

"And?"

"So good. I kind of hated the end, though."

"I forgot you hate happy endings."

"Was that ending even happy?"

Dylan looks around the room. I should probably tidy up just a little bit. My weekend's worth of clothes appear to have been breeding, and the babies are half-empty teacups.

"Why is your room so much bigger than mine when I'm older and, like, a foot taller?"

"You are *not* a foot taller."

"Why do you want to embarrass yourself like this?"

Dylan stands up straight and I shuffle in so our backs are together, keeping an iron grip of terry cloth the whole time. Obviously, I don't notice how he smells because *we are related*, but is that . . . licorice?

"Inches," I say, "mere inches."

"Half a foot, then. Still doesn't explain why I got screwed on the room."

"Is this why you're here? To guilt me into swapping? It's not going to work."

"I dunno, how long has *this* been going on?" He points up at the overhead light, which, now that he mentions it, is flickering. Probably the same mouse that's been crapping under my bed has gotten into the wiring. "Maybe I got the better deal? At least Gertie's ghost isn't trying to communicate with me in the creepiest way possible."

"Way to go dark, Dylan. Just turn on the bedside lamp instead if it's going to give you nightmares."

"The lights *and* these creepy little demons?" He taps the glass that stands between me and the horror figurines, and I wonder if it's too soon to suggest they get boxed up, along with some of GG's other things. "I take it all back. Let me keep my cupboard, Uncle Vernon, please."

"I know, right?"

Dylan is still looking at the figurines. "Do you think they run around at night when you're sleeping?"

"Shut up. Also: Get out. I need to put on some clothes."

"Wait." He reaches out and actually grabs the end of my bathrobe cord, then drops his hand when he realizes what he's caught. A red blotch appears on his neck. "Can we talk about what's going on with, *you know*. Everything."

"GG."

"Yeah." Dylan runs a hand through his hair, and in the old days this would have caused a bundle of curls to tumble into his eyes, but now it just messes up his hair a bit. A retrograde step, that haircut, even if he's almost making it work. Ali will be bummed. (*I'm* bummed.) "What do you think happened?"

Nobody has asked me this obvious question I've been waiting for. Now that it's here, though, it scares me. I stall.

"What do you mean?"

"Do you think it was a stranger who broke in and attacked Gertie?"

"I guess."

Dylan doesn't say anything else, just lets the silence sit there, expanding to squeeze all the air out of the room. I hate it when he does that.

"There are a few things I don't get," I say, cracking like a suspect in a cop show who needs to move the plot forward.

"Like what?"

Am I doing this? I guess I'm doing this. I blame my reading habits. When all you read are crime novels, everyone seems like they could be a murderer. Or a detective. Dylan and I are still too close together, so I take a step back under the guise of retying my robe and perch on the end of the bed. Dylan sits back down too, right on top of the old T-shirt I slept in last night. I hold up a finger.

"Why would a burglar come to this house in particular?

You can't see it from the road, and it's not like farmers keep a lot of cash and valuables lying around, even if this was still a proper farm. The most valuable stuff on a farm is, like, the land and the equipment, and that's all gone except for the old tractor in the shed. GG doesn't even have any livestock for a cattle rustler to steal."

"Does anyone *rustle cattle* these days? What movies have you been watching?"

I keep going with finger two. "How did they get here without anyone hearing a car—"

"There was a storm that night," Dylan interrupts, unhelpful with his logic. "The thunder was pretty loud in my room." I ignore him.

"—or seeing the headlights or anything?" I stick up my thumb, just to keep things fresh. "Why did they use a ladder to get into GG's room instead of breaking in downstairs?" Do I need to mention I'm now sticking a fourth finger up or have you got it? "Why was there glass on the *outside* of the window if someone broke in?"

"Was there?"

"I saw some on my run." I'm not finished. "If they did break in to rob the place, why kill GG at all instead of just running away?"

"Do you thi—"

"Why was some of her medication missing? Who was smoking in the garden the night she was killed?"

"Ruth, I can't keep up."

"Isn't this what you wanted?" I could really do without Dylan looking at me like *I'm* the psycho here when *he* ambushed *me* in my bedroom.

"It is. I just, sorry, I forget what you're like sometimes." He reaches across the expanse of the bed like he's going to pat my arm or something, then changes his mind. "It's good—this is why I wanted to talk to you."

I relax into the bed, trying not to think about the bathrobe thing. "What do *you* think happened, then?"

"Obviously, I don't know anything."

"Hence my use of the word *think*."

"I agree with you. It's weird that anyone would break into an old farmhouse, unless maybe they were looking for something specific?"

"Like what?"

"Maybe Gertie had a secret stash of cash or jewelry or, uh, a piece of priceless art?"

Dylan looks like he's waiting for me to take the piss (and I really do think about making a joke involving the creepy figurines being wildly valuable collector's items), but I'm mostly pleased he's taking this seriously. It makes me feel less weird for not being curled up in the fetal position, like I'm probably supposed to be. Is it normal for a teenager to be talking about her step-grandmother's death like it's a true-crime podcast? I've done a few of those Are You a Psychopath? online quizzes and they all say I'm okay, but at times I wonder.

"I don't know if I see GG as an international jewel thief."

"It wouldn't have to be international. Australia has diamond mines."

"Even so."

"What did she do before she met your grandad?"

I try to put together the bits of GG's life I know about. The puzzle is embarrassingly small, the kind of three-piece wooden puzzle you give a two-year-old. "She worked in agriculture, and she must have had some money because she drove a fancy-looking convertible when she and Grandad started going out. But, I dunno, who would have known about any of that?"

"Maybe she had a secret husband she left for your grandad, who came to seek his revenge?"

"He's your grandad too," I remind Dylan. "But, no, her first husband died."

"A child, then, angry at her mum for pissing away her inheritance on a run-down farmhouse?"

"It was a he, and he died too."

"Or is that just what he wants you to think?" Dylan taps his head and I roll my eyes like this isn't fun.

"Also, *did* she ever spend any money on this place?" I eyeball a long crack in the wall. "I feel like we're getting off topic."

"Has your dad said anything to you about any of this?"

"Not really."

"I thought your mum would have scheduled a Zoom counseling session to Talk It Out by now."

"I don't know if Dad has even told her yet. She's in the middle of nowhere in Tasmania on a hike with Brian." Brian is Mum's new husband, who is dull but otherwise fine. "What's your mum said?"

"She says it's going to get messy."

"What does that mean?"

"That it's complicated, I guess."

"Those were her exact words: 'This is going to get messy'?"

"Something like that."

"Do you think she knows something?"

Dylan looks directly at me, decoding my question with the ease of someone who has known me for too long. "I'm pretty sure she didn't bash Gertie over the head with her typewriter, if that's what you mean."

"Wow."

"You asked."

I consider it. Aunty Bec doesn't seem like a psychopathic killer, but in books it's always the last person you'd suspect. Although, technically, the last person I'd suspect is myself, so by this logic I guess I did it. (This is not a confession, and while I'm at it, the fact that I'm reading *The Murder of Roger Ackroyd*, a mystery in which, famously, the narrator is the murderer—sorry for the spoiler—is not a clue or anything, so just calm down, although, also, good on you for noticing.)

"Did you see anything on the night GG died?" I ask, thinking of the smoker in the garden, Dad's empty bed, and the conversation I overheard in GG's room.

"Not anything weird." Dylan shifts uncomfortably on the bed, then pulls my sleep T-shirt out from under one thigh and chucks it at me. "How long do you think we're going to be here?"

"Like, here in the house?"

"Yeah."

"A couple more days, I guess."

Dylan makes a noise like his footy team has just lost in the dying minutes of the grand final.

"Why do you care so much? At least we get to miss school."

"There's nothing to do here, that's all."

"Like you have things to do in Perth."

"I have things to do."

"Yeah, right." I look more closely at Dylan. "What is it? What's so important you're not stoked to get an extra-long weekend?"

"Don't do that."

"Do what?"

"Make lucky guesses like you're a psychic at a town fair."

"What fairs have you been going to that have psychics at them?"

"Look, I know you're going to roll your eyes, but it's the school ball on Friday."

"And you're going?" Dylan and I aren't as close as we were, but I know him well enough to be confident that wearing a suit and dancing to music that doesn't involve someone screaming directly into a microphone about their PERSONAL PAIN is not his idea of a fun night.

He looks shifty. "Lisa wants to go."

"Oh." Lisa is Dylan's girlfriend. I've never met her—he doesn't bring her to family stuff—but I've seen her on Instagram, with her bad hair extensions. "Do you *want* to go?"

"Sure." He's about as believable as an actual psychic.

"Are you guys . . . okay?" This is fifty percent me being caring and fifty percent nosiness, because I've had my suspicions for a while about Dylan's girlfriend (and this is *not* about my historic crush, if that's what you're thinking). I may not know Lisa, but, like I say, I know her social media. Until recently, her content has been faux artsy stuff: pictures of trash in the lake, videos of her and her friends mucking around, heavily filtered photos of her and Dylan squinting into the sun. The past few months, though, there has been a growing number of increasingly thirsty selfies, Dylan hasn't shown up in forever, and the comments have been . . . interesting.

"We're fine. I just want to know when we're going to get out of here." Dylan's voice is flat. He does not care for this line of inquiry, and I let it go.

"You can get out of *here*—here being my bedroom—right now so I can get dressed."

Dylan looks like he wants to say a thing, but he swallows it and stands up. "Have fun with your creepy dolls."

"They're figurines."

"They're going to watch you get dressed."

He's halfway to the door when we both hear a car engine. Nick? The police? The murderer come to turn himself or herself in?

"It's probably just Shippy," Dylan says.

"Did he go out?"

"Yeah, Mum's been freaking out."

But it's not Shippy.

7

IT IS, RATHER, THE BEST-LOOKING MAN I'VE EVER SEEN IN REAL life. He's standing in the kitchen, awkwardly holding an open cardboard box in his arms. This guy looks like a contestant from *Farmer Wants a Wife* but one of the rare hot ones, not the bros who are just a nice pair of arms. He's wearing jeans, a checked shirt, and dusty boots, looking like a Google image search for *Aussie farmer*. He's not wearing an Akubra Cattleman hat and that's a relief, not just because it'd be dorky as hell, but because he's got thick dark hair it'd be a shame to squash. He must be a stickler for SPF, because he lacks the deep tan of most country people, but it works.

"G'morning, sorry to drop in like this out of the blue."

Aunty Vinka and Aunty Bec are standing in front of him, both looking a little stunned. Dad, drinking coffee at the table, meets my eyes and rolls his just a little bit as I sit down next to him, grateful I took the time to get out of my robe and pull on a T-shirt dress. Up close I can see the box in Farmer Guy's arms is full of what looks like a week's supply of fruit and veg.

"I'm Vinka and this is my, uh, Bec."

"You must be Mrs. McCulloch's relatives."

"Yes?" Aunty Vinka says, like she's not sure.

"Sorry, my name's Sasha." He shifts the box to hold it against his body with one hand and extends the other to shake my aunts' hands, one after the other. "I heard about what happened to Gertie, and I thought you could do with some supplies, if you're sticking around." He nods at the box in his arms.

"That's so thoughtful. Thank you."

"I'm sorry to hear about Gertie's passing," he says, so formally I want to blurt *it was probably murder* to shock him, or maybe just to get him to look at me. He's older than me, obviously (not a huge market for fourteen-year-old farmers, so far as I'm aware), but not as old as Dad or Shippy. In his twenties, maybe?

"How did you hear about what happened so fast?"

"Everyone sort of knows everything in the country. Also, I have a friend who's a cop."

Sasha shifts the box with a grunt and Aunty Vinka notices. "Sorry, you can put that on the table."

"Thank you."

Dad doesn't get up from the table or put down his coffee, but he gives Sasha a slow nod of greeting.

"I'm Andrew."

"Sasha."

"Did you know Gertie well?" Dad asks.

"I live nearby, so I did some work for her sometimes when she needed a hand."

"You're the young guy she mentioned—you bought the farm next door?"

Sasha looks disconcerted by the idea that GG's been talking about him, but after a beat he nods. "Yeah." The smell of him is filling the room, earthy and maybe just a tiny bit like manure, but the way manure smells when you go to a riding stable: wholesome and fresh. Actually, it's entirely possible the smell is coming from his boots and quite literally *is* manure.

"That's so good of you," Aunty Vinka says.

Dad, at least, remembers my existence. "This is my daughter, Ruth, and my nephew, Dylan."

We both mumble something that probably starts with an *h*. Sasha doesn't shake my hand, but he gives me a big grin that would definitely convince some wannabe reality star to move to an isolated farm in Western Australia for him.

"What do we owe you?"

"Nothing. I just wasn't sure if you'd be able to get out to the shops with everything going on."

Nobody mentions that GG's cupboard and freezer are stocked like she was an apocalypse prepper. Which . . . maybe she was? I haven't seen any signs of a shotgun collection or a water purifier, but I haven't done much in the way of snooping. Maybe she was part of an apocalyptic prepping group and one of them lost their mind and crept up to her window one night and . . .

"How long are you sticking around here for?" Sasha asks, and the grown-ups all swap looks.

"We're not sure," Aunty Vinka says. "My partner had an, uh,

accident and he's in the local hospital here, so between that and the police investigation, we might be here for a few days."

"Well, I'm nearby if you need anything. The farm's tricky to get to—few too many gates—but I can give you my phone number."

"Our phones don't work here," Dad says.

"What about the landline?"

"Broken."

"Gertie's cell, too?"

"Some issue with a bill, apparently."

"I forgot about that. You know you can get reception further out in the paddocks even if you're not with Telstra, right?"

"Yep, that's what we've been doing. Can we—do you want a coffee or anything before you go?"

"I don't want to trouble you."

"It's no trouble."

"Then, sure. I've got fifteen minutes before I need to be anywhere."

Dad makes the coffee while Aunty Bec and Aunty Vinka settle in to interrogate our hot neighbor. They wouldn't put it that way—they'd say they're just being polite and making chat—but it's an interrogation. I don't mind. I'm grateful. I mean, this hottie just turns up out of the blue and he lives next door *and* none of us have ever met him before? Hello, prime suspect, so nice to meet you. All I'm missing is a motive, and how hard can that be? Maybe *he's* a secret prepper too and the two of them—

"How long have you lived next door?"

"Not long, but my family's been in the area for a while."

"Do they still live nearby?"

"No, I'm afraid they've all passed away."

"Sorry."

"It's hard work, farming." Sasha meets my eyes and smiles, and I can't not smile back, even as I'm now a little fixated on the idea that his entire family could have died in some kind of horrific farming accident. I sense, rather than see, Dylan looking at me.

"It sure is," Dad says, like he doesn't spend his working days in an air-conditioned office arguing with people who are paid to stop politicians telling anyone what they really think. He hands Sasha a coffee without asking if he wants milk or sugar.

"We're going to be making funeral arrangements soon," Aunty Vinka says, which is a thing I haven't thought about. "I don't really know who Gertie was close with in town. Is there anyone you think we should reach out to?"

Sasha looks like he's considering it.

"There are probably a few ladies in town she was friendly with," he says eventually. "I can't remember their names off the top of my head. I'll have a think, though."

"Thank you."

"She used to go to the library," Aunty Bec says. "She was friendly with one of the librarians. Laura, I think?"

Sasha nods slowly. "Laura, yeah, that sounds right."

More silence, during which surely everyone is secretly doing the same thing I am: mentally tallying up the list of people who would come to *my* funeral. My family, that's a gimme.

Ali and Libby, too. Tanya from tennis. Sam, who I almost kissed at a party once, might come out of some weird sense of obligation or guilt for turning his head at the last second and mumbling "Maybe not, hey?" Mum and Dad's friends, probably. It's a small list, but it sounds like I might be ahead of GG, numbers-wise.

When I tune back in, Sasha is finishing his coffee and saying his goodbyes. Numbers are exchanged, some more thank-yous handed out, and he's escorted to the front door without me even getting a chance to ask where he was the night of GG's death and whether he was aware of any priceless artworks/jewels/uncut gems she might have owned. I do get a good look at his profile, though.

Aunty Vinka walks him out to his car and comes back in pretending to fan her face.

"Wowza," Aunty Bec says.

"I *know*," Aunty Vinka says, and the two of them collapse into giddy, uncharacteristic laughter. "So hot."

"Mum!" Dylan gives her a disgusted look and then gives me one too, which is unfair.

"Someone get that guy on *Farmer Wants a Wife*," Dad says.

"That's what *I* was thinking," I say, and this time Dylan's look is maybe a little more justified.

"Hey, Ruth," Aunty Bec says, maybe sensing her son's growing discomfort and keen to change the subject, "you haven't seen Shippy this morning, have you?"

"No, why?"

"He was gone when I got up, that's all."

Apparently, this is news to Dad. "Where is he?"

"I have no idea, that's what I'm saying."

"Reading Tolstoy in a field somewhere, do we think?"

"*Thanks*," Aunty Bec says, making it sound like a slap. "Your car is missing too," she adds, and that makes Dad's head jerk up.

"What?"

"You did tell us yesterday we could use it if we needed to go into town. I suppose Shippy took you at your word."

"I was talking to *you*."

"I can't really imagine where he'd need to go so early. It's not like he brought his surfboard."

"Library?" Dad says, overly committed to his bit.

"I can't decide whether you two genuinely don't get along or if you're going to run away together when my back is turned," Aunty Bec says.

"The latter, definitely. Have you seen his guns?" Dad flexes his own biceps. It's a bit tragic.

"He didn't leave a note?" Aunty Vinka asks.

"No."

"I'm sure he'll turn up," Dad says, as though Shippy is the missing half of a pair of socks.

Shippy does turn up, by the way, just not quite as anyone expects.

8

YOU'LL RARELY FIND ME COMPLAINING ABOUT A LACK OF SHIPPY in my life. Under ordinary circumstances I regard Shippy the way I regard a mosquito bite: annoying without being dangerous. Or maybe he's more like my Spotify subscription: a small price to pay for something I like (in this case Aunty Bec and Dylan).

And yet. By mid-afternoon, when he still hasn't come home, I am distinctly unsettled. The whole household feels on edge, even Dylan, which I can tell because he's curled up on a chair in the living room with the rest of us, instead of locked in his bedroom listening to Scandinavian rockers work out their trauma.

"At what point do you think we call the police?" Dad quietly asks Aunty Bec, who has started a thousand-piece puzzle on the coffee table. Clearly, she's settling in for the long haul.

"What do you mean?"

"About Shippy."

"I don't think they take missing-persons reports seriously before forty-eight hours or something."

"That's a myth."

"Still."

"It doesn't strike you as being a little . . . suspicious?"

The grown-ups are sprawled out over the living room. Dad is surrounded by a stack of DVDs, VHS tapes, and old board games he found in the cupboard. For the last ten minutes he's been counting pieces inside the box for Risk, for reasons best known to himself. I'm in the nearest armchair, ostensibly still reading my book, although obviously mostly eavesdropping.

"What do you mean?"

"Bec, you don't find it strange that the morning after our . . . stepmother is murdered, Shippy does a runner?"

Aunty Bec pauses in her separation of the puzzle's edge pieces to give Dad a *really?* look I feel from across the room. "He hasn't *done a runner,* Andy, and please stop talking like you're in a noir film. I'm sure there's a perfectly rational explanation."

"Like what?"

"He might have gone for a . . . look around the farm."

"In my car?"

"So he's gone into town."

"All day?"

"Dunsborough is a vibrant regional community," Aunty Bec tries, and Dad snorts. "Okay, but you know Shippy—he's probably off at the pub with someone he just met."

"Let's examine the facts. Fact one: Shippy disappeared mysteriously in the night."

"He didn't disappear. He's just . . . not here."

"Fact two: He stole my car and didn't leave a note."

"Borrowed."

"Fact three: Gertie was murdered—"

"*Andy.*"

"She was, though." Everyone goes quiet for a minute, but Dad's never been able to let a silence sit for long. "I hate to state the obvious, but what do you think the police are going to think if they hear your boyfriend has disappeared right after our stepmother was brutally murdered?"

"Vinx, can you step in?" Aunty Bec appeals to the figure swathed in a caftan on the nearest armchair, who's been mind-melding with her crocheting through all of this.

"I hate to say it," Aunty Vinka says gently, the same way she talked to Grandad when he was almost dead but not quite and the same way I once heard her talk to a dog in the street, "but it is pretty odd behavior."

"There's a big gap between odd behavior and murder suspect, but don't mind me—I'm going to drive out to get some service and see if Shippy has called." Aunty Bec stands up and tosses her head so her bob swishes around her face. I wonder if my hair would do that if I took a photo of Aunty Bec to the hairdresser. She has to pause her attempt to storm out to borrow Aunty Vinka's car keys, which is embarrassing for her.

Dad keeps going once she's left, because of course he does.

"What do you think, Vinx: police or no police?" he asks while Aunty Bec is probably still clicking in her seat belt.

Aunty Vinka makes a *yuck* face. "Should we call the police on Shippy, you mean?"

"Not *on* him, exactly. Just . . . about him."

"Oh, in that case I'm sure Bec won't care. Just explain it that way."

"Shut up."

"Anyway, that's not the real question."

"It's not?"

"The real question is *why* would Shippy kill Gertie? He might have some, uh, problematic views on immigration, and the less said about his aura the better, but he doesn't strike me as a psychopath."

"Money," Dad says. "Bec will inherit one-third of the estate."

"Money, though." Aunty Vinka shakes her head. "It's just *money*, isn't it?"

"Vinx, that's almost as dumb as the time you claimed not to know what Facebook was. This property has got to be worth a couple of million."

Aunty Vinka just frowns at that and goes back to her crocheting. "Although," she says, almost as an afterthought, "he only inherits if he stays with Bec, right? So why would he disappear?"

She's got a point.

"Maybe Shippy has a secret." I don't realize I've said this out loud until the others go quiet.

"Ruthie?" Aunty Vinka's head jerks like she's forgotten I'm sitting *right here*, not hiding, exactly, just . . . turning the pages of my book very, very quietly. "Honey, this isn't really a conversation for kids. Do you and Dylan want to go for a walk or something?"

"You let me watch *Talk to Me* when you were babysitting," I remind her—a little disloyally, since that was supposed to be our secret. "Do you really think this conversation is more traumatic than that?"

"It's so important to support Australian cinema," she says, avoiding Dad's eyes. "But, Andy, maybe we should stop talking about this in front of the kids."

"Hold on, Vinka, I think I heard Ruthie say something about Shippy's dark secret." There's a smile licking at Dad's lips.

"I didn't say *dark secret*."

"What do you think Shippy's not-so-dark secret is, then? Tell us about his beige mystery?"

Even Dylan is looking at me now, and I can feel all the blood in my body trying to force its way out through my cheeks.

"I don't know what it is, but maybe GG was going to expose it." Dad and Aunty Vinka exchange a look, and for a moment I think they're going to send me up to my room, but Dad grins at his sister, and while I can see her teetering, she just shakes her head and doesn't tell me to go away. Adults are more fickle than the face recognition on my phone. I keep talking, fast as I can without being weird about it. "Maybe it's a secret he couldn't risk being exposed."

"What kind of secret?"

"Something that would make Aunty Bec dump him so he'd miss out on the inheritance. He's, uh, secretly married."

"I don't know if that's a turnoff for her," Aunty Vinka murmurs.

"He's got three secret kids."

"Getting warmer!" Aunty Vinka says, and has she been . . . drinking?

"What happens next?" Dad asks, encouraging me.

I sit up straighter in my chair and put my book down, enjoying the attention but also aware that the timer has started on how long I can get away with this. "GG pulls some 'you tell her or I will' stuff—classic mistake. Shippy freaks out and hits her over the head with, uh, an old typewriter for some reason. Then he sets up the ladder and smashes the window to make it look like a break-in."

Mentioning the actual murder sobers everyone up. I'm about to mention the hot neighbor, Sasha, while we're on the subject, and see if anyone else thinks he might have had a motive to kill GG, but Aunty Vinka gets in a question first.

"Why the typewriter, though?"

I think about it, the way I'd think about a math problem or how to handle a situation where Ali and Libby want to wear the same dress to the same party and neither of them has a plan B (not a hypothetical situation, since that did actually happen last year when John from school had a party in a fairly transparent attempt to hook up with Kym, which, FYI, did not go well, although that was not the fault of my dress solution, which was perfect). "He never meant to kill her," I say. "It was a crime of passion, and the typewriter was right there, I guess."

"It wasn't really, though; it was up on Gertie's wardrobe. Why not use that hideous cat statue next to her bed or a lamp or something?" Aunty Vinka points out.

"It shouldn't have even been in her room," Dad says out of nowhere.

"What?"

"The typewriter. You know she loved that thing."

"She told me it was worth a lot of money," Aunty Vinka says.

"I once tried to type on it, and she gave me a ten-minute lecture about the lack of typewriter ribbon still available in the world," Dad says.

"What do you mean it shouldn't have been in GG's room?" I ask, not quite ready to be edged out of the conversation.

Dad starts to pile the Risk pieces back into the box, not bothering to keep them separated by color, so you can tell that he's Going Through Something.

"Gertie asked me to take it downstairs," he says.

"What?"

"The typewriter. The night she . . . died, she asked if I could take it down for her. She didn't say why."

Aunty Vinka lowers her crocheting. "Oh, Andy."

"She asked me at dinner, but I just . . . forgot about it. I got distracted and then I had to . . . make a work call"—he glances at me, his cheeks going pink for a moment—"and it slipped my mind."

If you're hazy on the timeline here, the important thing to note is that GG asked Dad to take down the typewriter *after* she asked me to fetch her that cardboard box. If I hadn't been such a baby with my sore shoulder, would she have asked me to get the typewriter as well? It's not a nice thought, so I chase it away and focus on the obvious thing here.

"Dad, are you saying she asked you to take the typewriter down and then that night someone killed her with it?"

Dad looks guilty. Not *guilty* guilty, like he's the one who hit GG with the typewriter, but guilty like someone who might have forgotten his teenage daughter is in the room.

"I know what you're thinking, Ruthie. But life isn't a detective story: Coincidences do happen."

"Okay."

Silence settles, and we all get back to whatever we were pretending to do until at some point Aunty Vinka throws down her crocheting and goes upstairs. Only a couple of minutes later . . .

"*Andy!*"

Dad's on his feet and out of the living room before I've registered that it's Aunty Vinka's voice coming from upstairs.

"Should we—" Dylan starts to ask, but I'm already tripping over my feet to follow Dad.

When Dylan and I make it to Aunty Vinka's bedroom, she and Dad are looking out the window. I come up behind them but can't tell what in the back garden has so captured their attention, unless you find a lemon tree particularly shocking.

"What is it?"

"Vinka thinks she saw something," Dad says.

"I don't *think* I saw something. I *saw something*."

"Sorry. Vinka saw something. Which has since disappeared."

Dylan and I scoot closer and I scan the view. There's the lemon tree (still boring), the fence (ditto), and beyond that the paddocks.

"What did you see?" I ask Aunty Vinka, who sighs so hard her breath mists up a bit of the window.

"I saw someone out there, in the garden," she says, pointing. "Near the tree."

"There's nobody there now?"

"I only looked away for a second and they disappeared."

"Let's look outside, then," Dylan says. "Quick, before they get away."

"Mate, I'm not sure—" Dad starts to say, but apparently nobody in this family walks anywhere anymore because Dylan's out the door. He's fast, but we catch him outside just as he gets around the side of the house.

"Dylan, slow down," Dad puffs, sounding pissed off in a way that makes me think he might have noticed how entirely *un*-puffed his fifteen-year-old nephew is.

"If there's someone out here, we need to catch them."

"If there's someone out here, it might be the person who killed Gertie. You kids should go inside."

"It *might* have been a bird," Aunty Vinka says, smoothing down the caftan that's turned into an air balloon. *Good of you to tell us now,* I think but do not say.

There's nobody in the garden. Or, if you want to get technical about it, there's nobody but the four of us in the garden, and we're not suspicious. (Are we?)

When we've all confirmed a lack of intruders (or birds), we head back inside together. I'm part relieved not to have to confront a possible murderer, part disappointed not to have learned anything new, and just a tiny bit concerned Aunty Vinka might be losing it. I'm so distracted I trip on a power cord trailing from the lamp at the bottom of the stairs and nearly face-plant into the railing.

"Steady on," Dad says, catching my elbow. "One body is

enough for the week." Most of the time I wish Dad would stop treating me like a kid. This is not one of those times.

It's unfortunate that, at no point during this ill-advised mission, did I stop to consider why someone might be prowling around the house and what they might be looking for. Perhaps, if I'd had a proper look around, I could have saved us all a lot of time and energy. Certainly, nobody else would have had to die.

9

THE THING ABOUT FAMILY VACATIONS IS YOU'VE GOT TO BE PREpared for the fights. It doesn't matter how many of you there are, how big the house is, or even how much you all like each other: Sooner or later someone will have a fight with someone else. Wait long enough and it's entirely possible that *everyone* will have a fight with everyone else.

When Dylan and I fight, it's not even about the murder.

We're in my bedroom, officially just hanging out but unofficially comparing theories. We're both suspicious of Sasha: Dylan because he's too good-looking (he doesn't say that, but I know) and me because it's easier to think about a stranger killing GG than anyone in our family. Even so, it'd be easier to pin it on Sasha if GG had been killed with a shotgun or a spade or, I don't know, run down by a combine harvester. A typewriter is such a weirdly specific choice of weapon that it feels personal, especially after Dad's revelation (if it is a revelation) that GG asked him to move it only hours before it was used to kill her. Is it possible GG wanted the typewriter moved because she was scared of it, or is that the kind of thought you have right before you get committed to a mental-health facility?

"Who else is on the suspect list?" Dylan asks when we've run out of possible motives for Sasha to be the killer. He flops back on his elbows, knocking my book off the bed with one long arm. He rolls over, exposing a slash of stomach I don't even notice, picks it up, and scans the cover. "This is the one where the narrator did it, right?"

"No spoilers."

"You've read it before. You've probably read it three times already."

"Just because I know the ending doesn't mean I want to *know* it."

"You're so weird."

"Hello? That's why you adore me."

"That's true." I'm waiting for the joke that doesn't come, and instead, when I look at him, he's just looking at me.

"Do you want to talk about a fictional murder in a book or do you want to talk about the actual murder that happened *under our roof*?"

Dylan concedes the point with a head tilt. In the days of the long hair, that head tilt made his hair fall into his eyes in a way that briefly inspired Ali and me to write some pretty gushy things in our journals. Now that he's my cousin (*half* cousin, and technically in Western Australia you can marry your cousin—don't ask me how I know), maybe I should be grateful for the buzz cut (although it does, now I'm looking closely, make his eyes look even bigger).

"I asked the question," he says. "Who's on your list?"

I open the notes app on my phone to the list I've made, headlined SUSPECTS. He reads it, looking first confused and then amused.

"You're really putting yourself down as a suspect?"

"In the interest of fairness."

"And me?"

"See above."

"And your dad?"

There's a moment where I could tell Dylan that Dad wasn't in his bedroom that night, and I think about it. But, really, what am I saying—that he was briefly out of bed at some point? He was probably in the bathroom. Or getting a drink of water. He might even have been smoking in the garden, if he's been keeping a secret nicotine addiction from me. Regardless of the fact that I dutifully thumbed his name into my phone, I *know* Dad could never have hurt GG, just as surely as I *know* that I didn't do it. I don't *think* Dylan did it, just like I don't think Aunty Vinka, Aunty Bec, or even Nick or Shippy did it, but it's not the same.

"In the interest of fairness."

"Statistically, it's most likely to be a man," Dylan says.

"Only one of those has mysteriously disappeared in the night."

"So . . . Shippy?" Dylan doesn't look as troubled by the idea that his mum's boyfriend might have murdered someone as you'd think.

"The thing nobody seems to have thought of yet is that Shippy is just as likely to have become the murderer's latest victim as to be the murderer himself."

"You think Shippy's dead?" Again, Dylan's face doesn't reflect great shock or alarm at this idea.

"When people go missing in books and movies, they usually wind up dead. That's how the police know they're dealing with a serial killer. This is a classic act-two second murder."

"You are aware this is real life, Ruth?"

"Even in real life people do sometimes get killed. Like in this house, for example. Plus, I know Shippy is Shippy, but is he murderer material? Sexual-harassment scandal, absolutely. Light embezzlement? Aggressively on-brand. Murder? I don't know."

"What is *light* embezzlement, exactly?" Dylan asks, looking like he's thinking about smiling. I ignore him.

"Let's think about this logically." I take back my phone. "What are the established facts?"

"We're really going to Miss Marple this?"

"And you pretend you're not a Christie fan."

"Christie who?"

"The established facts of the night," I continue. "GG was murdered on Sunday night. She was wealthy."

"Rich," Dylan corrects me.

"What's the difference?"

"Rich people don't talk about money."

"I don't think that's true."

"Whatever," Dylan says. "She had money."

"And our parents will inherit it."

"And Vinka."

"And Shippy. What's your point?"

"There might be other things going on. If Gertie had money outside this place or if she borrowed against it, someone else might have had a motive we don't know about."

"So, the motive is money?" I say.

"It's the obvious one."

"I agree."

"Why's Nick on your list?"

"Everyone's a suspect."

"But he was in the hospital."

"Only with a broken leg. He could have snuck out, called an Uber, come here, killed GG—"

"Sorry I asked."

"—and got back to the hospital without anyone noticing he'd gone."

The door opens and I yelp, but it's only Dad with a mug of tea and a plate with two chocolate cookies on it. He clicks on the overhead light, then stops so abruptly when he sees Dylan that the tea sloshes over the rim of the mug.

"Sorry, mate, didn't know you were here. Ruth, I thought you might want some tea?"

"Thanks." I quickly click my phone to turn the screen dark.

"The kettle's just boiled if you want one, Dylan."

"I'm good," Dylan says, although I'm not a hundred percent sure Dad was offering. I take the mug, the plate, and then the opportunity.

"Hey, Dad, what time did you go to bed the night GG died?"

"Ten or ten-thirty, I think. Why?"

"Were the others in bed?"

"Heading that way, but why?"

"Did you check on GG before you went to bed?"

"Yeah." He gives me a look that says his patience with this interrogation is over. *"Why?"*

"Just asking."

I wait for Dad to mention that he got out of his bed for some reason, but he's frowning at the flickering overhead light.

"How long has that been happening?"

"Um, I dunno. A day?"

"This house is falling apart."

Once Dad's gone, I pick up my phone and type: *Dad first to bed at 10/10:30 p.m. GG alive and well.*

Dylan leans in to read the screen. "You're taking his word for it?"

"What?"

"That Gertie was still alive when he went to bed."

"Yeah."

"Just saying."

"What about you?"

"What about me?"

"What time did you go to bed?"

"I went to bed at eleven."

"You went to bed before I did."

"I went to my *bedroom* before you."

"What were you doing?"

"In my... bedroom?" I hate that this makes me blush and I double hate that Dylan sees it. "What do you think? I did some yearbook stuff, listened to some music, turned out my light at eleven. Like I said."

My mind hooks on what's probably an irrelevant detail. It's like that. It can't help itself. "*You're* doing yearbook?" I'd be less surprised if he'd announced he's marrying his biology teacher. Dylan looks... cagey.

"Are we going to talk about murder or yearbook?"

"How can I possibly solve the Mystery of GG's Death when the Mystery of Why Dylan Is Doing Yearbook is right here in front of me?"

"You're getting weirder."

"Just tell me why."

"I'm community minded."

"Are you, though?"

"I love my school?"

"Do you?"

He makes a sound like a bicycle puncture and I know I've got him. "Okay, I'm helping a friend."

"Who?" Then I get it. "Lisa."

"Yeah."

"So, you're doing your girlfriend's homework? That makes so much more sense."

"It's not like that." But the flush in Dylan's cheeks tells me it kind of is like that.

"I'm just glad you guys are okay."

"What does that mean?"

"Nothing."

"It's not nothing. What do you mean you're glad we're okay? Why wouldn't we be okay?"

This is the moment I should stop. I could make a joke and change the subject. But I've never been good at keeping out of other people's business. I have a bad feeling this is going to be like that time Ali was missing twenty dollars from her locker, and then our friend Shannon (who is no longer our friend Shannon) had money for the cafeteria even though she never has money on a Tuesday, because she gets paid for her deli job on Thursdays, and all I did was *mention* it to Ali, and then *boom*, and, really, couldn't I have let it go?

I've learned nothing because I say, "I just noticed some guy on her socials, and I wasn't sure."

"What guy?"

"The guy on her Instagram."

The train is rolling out of the station, and even if I wanted to leap out onto the platform, it's too late. Or maybe that's a bad metaphor. Maybe the train is rolling but I'm on the tracks and there's no chance to get out of the way. Out of my own way. Wait, am I the *train* or . . . ?

"What are you talking about?"

I pick my phone up off my bedside table, then put it right back down when I remember there's no internet. This is going to be harder without visual aids.

"You know I follow her on Instagram and TikTok, right?"

"I didn't even know you were *on* TikTok."

"I lurk." I sound defensive. I hate sounding defensive. "You don't know what I'm talking about?"

"I have no idea what you're talking about."

Am I going to do this? I'm going to do this. "She's just been posting a lot more thirsty selfies than usual."

"What does that even mean?"

Dylan is online enough to know exactly what *thirsty* means, but I indulge him anyway, somehow already regretting every moment of this conversation, even the bits that haven't happened yet. "She's been posting pics and videos where she looks super hot."

"That's what everyone does. That's what social media *is*."

"That's a very reductive view, but put that to the side for a moment. Lisa, historically, hasn't posted thirsty selfies and now she's posting lots. Exhibit A. Exhibit B: A guy called PandaBear02 has been liking all of them."

"Who the hell is Panda Bear-oh-two?"

"That's his social-media handle."

"I didn't think his parents, Mr. and Mrs. Bear-oh-two, named their kid Panda."

"His real name is Paul and I think he's a senior."

Dylan's face does a thing, like maybe that name and my single-line description aren't completely unfamiliar to him. I do the classy thing and don't ask him if he knows a Paul who's a senior and has been creeping around his girlfriend. "How do you know that?"

"The *internet*, Dylan."

"Heaps of random dudes follow Lisa on social. Some of

them are weird and creepy. Her DMs are a toilet," Dylan protests.

"It's just that whenever he comments—which he does all the time—Lisa likes or replies to his comments. She doesn't do that with the other weirdos."

"Okay."

"And when I set up a fake profile so I could follow Panda-Bear02 on Instagram, I—"

"Wait, really?"

"—I noticed that for the past couple of months, he's been doing a lot of vagueposting of, like, a photo of a sunset with 'thinking of her' or something super cheesy like that. Kinda creepy, too."

"Says the stalker."

"And *then* a week or two ago he posted a photo of a girl, shot from behind, like you couldn't see her face. But she had long brown hair."

"Lots of girls have long brown hair. *You* have long brown hair."

"It's really more of a lob, but thanks for noticing. So this Panda—"

"His name is Paul Rainbow," Dylan says abruptly, red blooming high on his cheeks.

So he knows. Or if he doesn't *know*, he at least knows who Paul is, which might mean it's all aboveboard and Paul is Lisa's gay friend or her brother or, hell, her gay brother. Dylan's face, though, doesn't look like Paul is Lisa's gay brother.

"Paul Rainbow sounds as made up as PandaBear02."

"I know."

"Who is he?"

"He's a friend of Lisa's."

"Okay."

"Because girls aren't allowed to have friends who are boys?" Dylan's voice has gone all spiky, and those big eyes, so soft ten minutes ago, are half concealed by lowered eyelids. He slides off my bed, and I have to stop myself from telling him to tie up his loose shoelace. *Pick your moment, Ruth, pick your moment.*

"I didn't say that." I'm trying to work out how to articulate what it was that made me suspicious, but Dylan will have me institutionalized if I try to explain how PandaBear02's use of the baby-seal emoji conveyed a romantic vibe. "I was just being nosy. I'm sorry."

"You're not being nosy; you're going full Jane Marple."

"I knew it—I knew you were a superfan." It's my effort to change the topic, and it almost works. Dylan's mouth, halfway curled around an insult, closes and opens again.

"Everyone knows Miss Marple."

"People have heard of Miss Marple; they don't know her first name is Jane."

"Whatever." Okay, so it didn't work. "Why are you prying into my life? You don't even *know* Lisa."

Now my cheeks are red, like we're passing the embarrassment back and forth between us. "Can we forget I said anything? I'm an idiot. You know this."

Dylan is halfway across the room, shoelace flapping.

"Whatever. I'd better go and do some more of my *girlfriend's homework.*"

"I didn't—"

"Tell me when you've worked out who did it in the library with the candelabra."

He's gone before I have time to point out that a *candelabra* does not appear anywhere in the game of Clue.

10

I WAKE UP TO A HAND OVER MY MOUTH, AND MY FIRST THOUGHT is that the killer has come back for me. My second thought is that GG wasn't killed quietly in bed—she was on the floor next to her bed, like maybe she tried to fight back or run away, and am I seriously going to go more quietly than an old lady? Nope. I open my mouth as wide as I can and bite down on as much soft flesh as my teeth can find. The hand disappears and so does my readied scream.

"Dylan, what the *hell*."

"I didn't want you to shout or anything." Dylan is whispering, and I automatically drop my own voice to mimic him.

"And you thought the simplest way to achieve that was to play at being a murderer in a house where someone was recently murdered."

He holds up his hand. "Mistakes were made."

I sit up in bed. The light coming through the window of my bedroom is the watery evening kind, filtered through old-fashioned lace curtains that would be fluttering very prettily right now if there was any kind of a breeze.

"What time is it?"

"I don't know. Five?"

"Did I fall asleep?"

"You were out of it. I did knock."

"Why?"

"I guess you were tired."

"No, why did you knock? Why are you here? Why are we whispering?"

"I came to say—well, never mind, and then I heard them." Dylan points at the window and puts his finger first to his lips and then to his ear. I stop trying to talk and listen instead, pulling the edge of the curtain back enough so I can see the tops of two heads.

"So?" I whisper.

"They're talking about Shippy," Dylan whispers back, climbing onto my bed without asking, jamming his body up against the window on the opposite side from me, and sticking his head through the curtain.

Possibly I should give him a hard time about his tantrum. Or maybe I'm supposed to apologize for fairly transparently suggesting his girlfriend is cheating on him. As a compromise, pretending neither happened works for me. Repression gets such a bad rap when, in my experience, it can be super useful.

"Who's out there?"

"Your dad and Aunty Vinka."

What are they doing? I mouth more than say.

Instead of playing at mime, Dylan leans over and puts his mouth on my ear—I'm talking lips on lobe—so he can whisper directly into it. His breath raises hairs on the back of my neck. "Trying to fix the sprinklers."

My dad is from the Call a Plumber school of pipe repair, and Aunty Vinka's idea of home repair involves a smudge stick, so this is out of character. I push my face close to the open part of the window and see Dad regarding a couple of bits of pipe as though they've personally wronged him.

"Does this attach to this bit, do you think?" He taps one against the other. "Why is everything held together with electrical tape?" Then he answers his own question. "Dad."

I lean across to Dylan but stop short of tasting lobe. Now that they're talking about the sprinklers, I don't think we're going to pick up a clue unless it's about my grandad's shoddy approach to home repair.

"What did they say about Shippy?"

"They decided to call the cops," Dylan whispers back. "Your dad wanted to call tonight, but Vinka said we should wait for tomorrow."

"Who won?"

The rise and fall of Dylan's shoulders says he doesn't know.

In the moment of silence a sentence from below carries clearly—"What about the kids?"—and we both lean back toward the window.

"They do seem to be taking an unhealthy interest in this. It can't be good for them."

"Ruth's like a dog with a bone with this stuff. She doesn't

let things go. She'd make a great reporter, actually," Dad says, which is one of the nicer things he's ever said about me. Is it possible people say nice things about me when I'm not around all the time?

"Maybe you should take her back to Perth?"

"Now that Shippy's gone missing with my car, I'm not sure how I'd manage that one. Silver lining: At least we know Nick couldn't have done it. Shame. I'd quite like to see Nick charged with murder. I don't trust anyone that handsome."

"Five minutes ago you said if anyone in the house did it, it was Shippy," says Aunty Vinka. I look at Dylan, checking for a reaction, but his face is as blank as a Hollywood star being asked about war in the Middle East.

"You agreed," says Dad.

"He's got such a . . . aura. I know you don't . . . in these things, Andy." Aunty Vinka's voice goes in and out, like she's moving around.

"Because they're made up, Vinx."

"But it's true. I warned Bec but she didn't want to hear it."

"She and I are aligned on that. Oh, bloody hell, check it out: There's a pen holding these two bits of pipe together."

"What do we do with that?"

"Hear me out on this, but could we just . . . add more tape?"

There's a long pause.

"Screw it, why not?"

There's no talking for a bit, and Dylan and I look at each other, not wanting to say anything in case we're overheard. When Dad speaks again, his voice has gone serious. I don't know if it's the kind of change Dylan would notice, but it's obvious to me. "What do you make of Gertie's missing pain meds?"

"What do you mean?"

"Well, where did they go? Can you put some more tape here?"

"Does it matter? Gertie didn't die of a drug overdose."

"It's odd, though."

"The idea that anyone could kill a living thing is odd to me." Aunty Vinka is sounding pensive.

"I'm begging you: Don't make this about veganism."

"I wasn't going to. Hey, careful with that thing."

"There's nothing you want to tell me?"

"What are you saying—argh!" I risk a look to see Aunty Vinka bent over, grabbing her hand. "It's okay. I just stabbed myself with that bit of wire."

"You and Nick make such a great couple."

The front door bangs and there's a crunch of gravel.

"How's it going out here?" Aunty Bec asks.

"We were talking about Gertie's missing meds," Dad says, not wasting time on small talk, which, as an eavesdropper with a slightly stiff neck, I appreciate. "You didn't see anyone take them?"

"Of course not."

"Speaking of suspicious characters: Any sign of Shippy?"

"Has it even occurred to you that Shippy might be a second victim?" Aunty Bec says. "One person has already been killed in this house. Why not two?"

Finally, someone is on the same page as me. I elbow Dylan, who mimes being sick.

"Why's my car missing, though?" Dad asks.

"Shippy took it to meet the killer," Aunty Bec says, but flippantly, not as though she believes her boyfriend is really dead.

"Why?"

"Or the killer came here, killed Shippy, *and* stole the car."

"Then how did they get here?"

"Who?"

"The killer. If he—or she, let's not be sexist; I'm sure women make great murderers too—drove the car away after killing Shippy, how did they get here in the first place?"

"Can we drop this?"

"Sorry for trying to argue that it's more likely your boyfriend is a murderer than that he's dead. Which would you prefer?"

A few moments later the front door slams.

"Andy."

"Too far, I know."

Dad and Aunty Vinka trudge inside, and Dylan and I sit back from the window.

"Was that worth waking you up for?"

It was, but why would I let him know that when his ego is already so very robust? Instead I ask the question he dodged earlier. "Why did you come up here anyway? You never said."

Dylan shakes his head, uncrossing and crossing his long legs awkwardly, an adolescent Bambi. "I went for a walk and called Lisa."

"About Paul What's-his-face?" Why am I pretending I can't remember his name? On my deathbed I'll remember the name Paul Rainbow.

"She said we should talk when I'm home. I think you were right."

"Oh," I say. Then: "Sorry."

"It's okay. I guess things have been a bit crap for a—" Dylan stops talking.

"What?" But then I hear it too: tires on the driveway. I look out the window. Then, without waiting to see if Dylan is behind me, I run out of the room and down the stairs.

Everyone else is outside when I skid to a stop behind Dad to stare at the same thing they are: the car pulling in beside the house. Our car. The engine cuts off. The driver's door opens and Shippy, a little red in the face and chapped on the lips, gets out.

"Hey, guys," he says. "You won't believe the day I've had."

Then the passenger-side door opens.

11

SHIPPY'S BACK, BUT HE'S NOT ALONE. I GUESS I GAVE THAT AWAY already. The guy climbing out of the car is tall, skinny, and maybe around the same age as Shippy. I don't know, once grown-ups hit thirty, they all start to look the same to me until they make it to fifty.

"Hi, I'm Rob."

Social conditioning coaxes a *hi* or *hey* back from each of us, all too polite to say what we're really thinking, which is some combination of (a) Who are you? (b) Why are you here? (c) Where has Shippy been this whole time? and (d) Do you know you've got a bit of something green in your teeth?

Aunty Bec is first with the hugs, arms snaking around Shippy despite several pretty suspect stains on his T-shirt. She's last with the hugs too, because nobody else goes in for one.

"Where have you been?"

"This is Rob," Shippy says unnecessarily. Then, when nobody says anything, he adds: "What are you all doing out here?"

Dad does an actual facepalm, something I thought was reserved for emojis.

"Why don't we all go in for some tea," Aunty Bec says in a voice that would make me want to change my name and move to Bali if I was Shippy.

"Lovely place," Rob says politely as we're herded into the living room. "Do you all live here? How many acres is this? Do you run cattle?" Nobody answers this slightly frenetic and frankly pretty weird jumble of questions. Rob and Shippy take a seat on the most comfortable couch, flanked by Aunty Bec, who keeps looking at Shippy like she thinks he might disappear again and she's not sure whether to hope for it.

It's a nice novelty to witness Dad's anger without being the target of it. I'm not a teenager who gets into serious trouble—I've never had detention and I'd have to have sex before teen pregnancy became an issue—but I'm still pretty much constantly getting told off for some minor infraction, from failing to stack my bowl correctly in the dishwasher (I know what you're thinking and the answer is *I have no idea*) to reading too late in bed. (Aren't parents supposed to be catatonic with joy if their kid puts down their phone long enough to read an actual book?) Dylan perches on the arm of my chair and tilts in.

"Who's Rob?" he whispers, as though I've been privy to a briefing session he blinked and missed.

"I don't know him," I whisper, but too loudly, because the room goes silent just as I say it. Nobody says anything, but Dad covers a laugh with his hand, Rob's ears go sunset pink, and I die of embarrassment (so you should know that the rest of this is being narrated by my ghost).

"So," Aunty Bec says, coaxing a sentence from that one word. "What the hell?"

"I know," Shippy says, grinning like he doesn't realize everyone in this room was within touching distance of ratting him out to the cops as a possible murderer half an hour ago. "Crazy day, right?"

"Where. Have. You. Been." Aunty Bec articulates each word like a series of slaps, and only now does Shippy realize how seriously the vibe is off.

"I went out for a surf," he says.

"A surf?"

"The swell was unreal."

"But—" Aunty Bec hesitates, like she's trying to find the biggest *but* in what he just said. She makes a call: "Your surfboard's in Perth."

"First day of the trip I got talking to Rob in town when you were in the bakery. He said he could hook me up with a board if I needed it, but I didn't think we'd be here long enough." Shippy grins. "Only remembered this morning and thought I'd try my luck." Everyone looks at Rob, who seems to be a step ahead of Shippy and ducks his head apologetically. "I thought I'd be back hours ago."

"You didn't wake me up to tell me?"

"I texted."

"No, you didn't." Aunty Bec takes a deep breath. "I didn't have any messages on my phone, and I went out to the bloody paddock—and got bitten by a bull ant, by the way—to check."

"I did."

"Show me your phone."

Aunty Vinka comes in with a tray full of mugs and everyone takes one, even though the tea is gray and smells like a full dishwasher before a cycle.

"The message didn't send," Aunty Bec says, shaking her head at Shippy's phone. "Did you try to send it when you were still here?"

"Yeah."

"The here where there's no phone reception?"

"Oh." Shippy gets it. The scary thing is, he's a civil engineer: People rely on this guy to keep bridges from falling down.

"Why were you gone all day?"

Shippy's face relaxes, as if he thinks the hard bit is over. He has no idea. "The surf was unbelievable, so I did wind up staying awhile. Rob was getting out at the same time, so we went for a coffee and grilled cheese that, seriously, took like twenty minutes."

"Great coffee, though," Rob chimes in, doing his bit for the Dunsborough Tourism Board, I guess.

There are still some unanswered questions—Why is Rob here? What happened to the rest of the lost time? Is it possible Shippy has some kind of hidden depths that enable Aunty Bec to put up with . . . the rest of it?—but Rob reminding us all of his existence seems to prompt Aunty Bec into some knee-jerk civility.

"Do you live in Dunsborough, Rob?"

"Just in town for a surf," Rob says. "It was my birthday last week, so, you know, bit of a present to myself."

"He's been sleeping in a friend's van," Shippy adds, "so I told him he was welcome to crash here for a day or two."

Everyone cares way too much about what this complete stranger thinks of us to react openly to this, but Dad reaches out a hand to crush Aunty Vinka's shoulder and Dylan bumps his knee against me. (I can't look at him.)

"If it's okay," Rob chimes in, possibly correctly interpreting the silence.

"It's fine," Shippy says.

"You'd be very welcome," Aunty Vinka says. "We *are* hoping to head back to Perth in the next day or so, though."

"That's seriously so kind," Rob says with an easy smile. "Is it just you guys in the house? I think you said the other day it was your . . . stepmother's house, Shippy?"

Dad is having none of this cozy Welcome to the Family business. "I still don't understand why you were gone all day."

"That's the wild part," Shippy says, clearly loading an anecdote. "We had our coffee and food and, okay, we might have had a brownie too." He glances at Aunty Bec. "But when we got back in the car, the tire was flat, totally blown. Must have picked up a nail on the drive from the beach, because there was a big one just sticking right out of it."

"And it took you all day to change the tire because . . . ?" Aunty Bec presses.

"No spare." Shippy looks at Dad. "What's the deal with that?"

"Andy, you don't have a spare?" Aunty Vinka says, distracted.

"My missing spare tire is not the villain here," Dad says. "Roadside assistance exists, people."

"What did you do?" Aunty Bec's voice sounds a little gentler, and maybe she's not going to straight-up murder Shippy in front of us, which is a shame, if only because it really would help clarify the question of whether anyone in the house is capable of it.

"By the time we figured all this out, the coffee shop had closed—it's run by one of the local guys, and we told him the surf was great, so he shut up to hit the beach. Total own goal."

"Our bad," Rob agrees cheerfully.

"I figured we'd hitch a ride into town to see if we could find a garage or something. I tried to call, but, you know."

"No reception," half the room choruses.

"Exactly. After about twenty minutes of guys just cruising past me in their SUVs, this one guy stops and offers to help. Turns out the bloke is a mechanic—can you believe it? He insists on taking us back to the garage and sorting us a spare tire. Then, of course, Yusef—that's the guy, great bloke—suggests we go for a beer, and we can't exactly say no after he's helped us out. We might have had a few too many because Yusef got a bit messy and I wasn't sure he should drive, so we had a meal to sober up and a few coffees and then he drove us back to the car and we were on our way."

Shippy shrugs.

"You do realize we almost called the cops?" Dad says.

"What for?"

"For *you*."

"Andy, I never knew you cared."

"You disappeared the day after Gertie was *murdered*, Shippy. That's the sort of thing that the police usually like to know."

"Did you say *murdered*?" Rob asks, looking startled, but he's top of nobody's priority list right now, so I'm not sure anyone else hears him.

"You thought *I*—" Shippy doesn't finish the question.

"Nobody thought that, honey," Aunty Bec says quickly, and do you think she knows she's lying?

"You can't seriously—"

"Sorry, who's been murdered?" Rob asks again, sounding genuinely alarmed but not yet loud enough to break through the others' bickering.

"We did kind of think you'd done a runner, mate," Dad says, and it's possible he believes he's helping. "But it was a working theory. We weren't quite ready to knot the noose."

"Bloody hell," Shippy says.

Aunty Vinka stands up. "Sorry to interrupt this . . . whatever it is, but I'm going to head to the hospital. There's a chance Nick could be released tonight, and if not, I said I'd take him a change of clothes." (I'll tell you right now: Nick's not coming home tonight.)

"I should probably think about doing something about dinner," Aunty Bec says with the intonation of someone who's just announced an impending pap smear. She doesn't move.

"Let us handle dinner tonight," Shippy says, pausing for a round of applause that never arrives. "Rob, you were talking about that laksa you learned to make in Vietnam—you must be a decent cook?" It feels a little optimistic to imagine GG might have the ingredients for a laksa kicking around, but I'll let Shippy handle that one. "How about it? We can whip up something, I'm sure?"

"Uh, sure." Rob stands up. "And maybe you can fill me in on what's been going on here? Sounds like you've had a big week."

Shippy shakes his head. "You've got no idea, mate. There was a break-in and Bec's stepmom—the woman who owns this house, actually—got killed. You know what? I could really go for a carbonara."

I get a glimpse of Rob's face as Shippy leads him into the kitchen, and he looks like he's the one who got bashed on the head by a typewriter, although whether it's shock at the fact that he's agreed to stay in a house where a murder just took place or shock at Shippy's indifference, it's hard to say.

"Where is he going to sleep, do you think?" Dad asks Aunty Bec, nodding at Rob. "Your bed? Cozy, but you could make it work."

"We can make up the couch."

"It's a shame Gertie's room is a no-go: a free bedroom just sitting there."

"Andy, you've got problems."

"*I* wouldn't sleep there, but"—Dad drops his voice—"does Rob strike you as the kind of guy who's never slept on the mattress of someone recently deceased?"

"It's still a crime scene. Go grab some clean sheets from Gertie's room, though. They're in the wardrobe. Top shelf. Try not to touch anything."

That's when I see my chance and nudge Dylan so hard he slides off the armchair. He looks up from the floor resentfully, and I definitely don't laugh.

"We'll grab the sheets," I say, jumping to my feet and yanking on Dylan's elbow to pull him up.

"You don't have to do that," Dad says.

"It's fine."

Dad's expression crosses the line dividing curiosity from suspicion.

"Andy!" Shippy shouts even though he's just one room away. "This pinot's okay to go in pasta sauce, right?"

"Okay," Dad says to me, leaping toward Shippy and the open wine bottle in the kitchen with the vibe of a mother rushing into a burning house to rescue her baby. "Thanks, I guess." Dylan and I are out the door before Dad can grab the knife from the hands of a red-eyed Rob (so on-brand for Shippy to make him cut the onions) and use it on Shippy.

"What's this about?" Dylan says, nearly crashing into a lamp as I drag him up the stairs.

"Obviously, this is our opportunity to search GG's bedroom without anyone busting in to ask what we think we're doing."

"I'm pretty sure the cops have already done that."

"Yeah, but there might be a clue only we would understand."

"Such as?"

"I don't know—we haven't found it yet."

"Flawless logic."

Being inside GG's room again is creepier than sleeping in a bedroom full of faceless dolls. There's no dark stain on the floorboards, the broken glass from the window has been swept up, and the bed has been stripped. But the gloom in the room is real, thanks to a square of cardboard taped over the broken window, and it doesn't entirely go away when we snap on the light.

"Okay, Enola, where do we start?"

"The wardrobe?"

Dylan starts pulling out drawers while I reach for GG's dresses and coats, passing one after another between my hands as I go through the pockets, with no idea what I'm looking for. Nothing that I find (three tissues, a pencil, one single gold earring) strikes me as being *a clue*, but I lay them out on top of the bare mattress anyway because it's always the seemingly innocuous stuff that winds up being important, isn't it?

"Is it weird for me to be going through her stockings?" Dylan asks, holding up a single stocking, the nude kind with a black seam. "I feel like a pervert."

"They're stockings—don't make it weird. This stuff will all have to go to the secondhand shop or the dump or something."

"What's that got to do with it?"

"Someone's going to have to go through it all."

"You could pull off these stockings," Dylan says, waving one of them at me. "You've got a retro face."

Because I don't want to interrogate what Dylan might mean by "retro face," I focus instead on dragging over the stool from GG's dressing table to stand on so I can look on top of the wardrobe. Dust lines show where the typewriter that killed GG used to live. There's the suitcase I noticed last time, plus a few old shoeboxes tucked toward the back: One contains stacks of photos bound together with elastic bands, another has three pairs of old glasses, and the third has a bunch of old chargers. There's no sign of the big cardboard box, the one that was apparently *for M.*

"What's wrong?" Dylan asks, having presumably gotten a good look at my face.

"There was a box," I say, slowly because I'm trying to think and talk at the same time, which is always a tough proposition. "GG asked me to get it down from the wardrobe the night she died. Now it's gone."

Dylan shrugs. "Maybe the cops took it?"

"I guess." I don't really get why the cops would take one box over all the others. "It said 'for M' or something like that."

"Who's Em? Emily?"

"No, *M* like the letter." The box might be nothing, but I can't let go of the idea that its absence matters. In front of Dylan, though, I play it down. I'm not sure why. "Have you found anything good?"

"A bunch of personal papers. Plus the warranty and instructions for everything Gertie ever bought."

"Seriously?"

"There's a receipt here for a toasted-sandwich maker she bought in the nineties. She didn't even live here then. At some point she packed this receipt and brought it with her."

"What about the secret drawer?"

"What's the secret drawer?"

Classic Dylan strikes again. Do I have to do everything myself?

The door to the bedroom opens and Dad comes in with a glass of wine and an air of triumph I don't care for.

"I knew it," he says.

"What?" But I know what he means: GG's papers are

everywhere on the floor around Dylan, I'm rummaging through her belongings, and there's absolutely no sign of the sheets we're ostensibly here to collect. The only way we could look more guilty would involve a bloody knife and a headless corpse.

"The moment you offered to help, I knew you'd be snooping."

"We're not snooping." Dylan would be more convincing if this defense wasn't delivered while clutching the toasted-sandwich-maker receipt.

"Sure. And Shippy's one of our leading thinkers." Dad nods at the papers. "What did you find?"

There's a moment when I could tell Dad about the box. I don't, and like all good ideas unacted upon, it passes.

"Nothing," I say after a pause that Dad would probably find more suspicious if his glass wasn't half empty.

"A lot of papers," Dylan says, pulling Dad's focus. "Most of it is junk, but there's her birth certificate, marriage certificates, that kind of stuff." Dad crouches down next to Dylan and I see his eyes flick to the wardrobe's ornate carving of a bird, which marks the secret drawer I never got a chance to tell Dylan about. It's still closed.

"We'll be down in a sec," I say.

"Guess again. Grab the sheets and head down. I'll tidy up so the cops don't realize you've been up here trying to do their job for them." In case I've missed the point, Dad reaches up to the top shelf of the wardrobe and pulls out an unfitted white sheet and a pillow that's slightly yellow around the edges. Dylan gets a tartan blanket and pillowcase, and the two of us walk to the bedroom door as slowly as it's possible to do while still meeting the definition of walking.

"Wait, Ruth," Dad says as I go through the door, waving for Dylan to keep going. He steps out onto the landing. "How are you feeling about all this?"

"I'm okay. I mean, it's awful, obviously, but I'm okay." What I am is trying not to look over Dad's shoulder at the wardrobe's secret drawer. How could I not think of looking there right away?

"You know that the police are going to find out who killed GG."

"Who do you think did it?"

Dad blinks at the question. "Probably some career criminal who was looking for money or jewelry."

"Right." I hate that Dad can't be honest with me the way he can with Aunty Vinka and tell me what he's actually thinking. But I can't say that, so I settle for something I can say. "Where were you?"

"What?"

"You weren't in your room the night GG was killed." Dad gives me a look I don't understand, which is weird because I'm usually fluent in Dad. "I didn't tell the police."

Dad opens his mouth and then shuts it again, a couple of times, like my old black moor fish before the cat killed it. "I was just checking on GG," he says. "You haven't been worried about that, have you?"

"No."

"Because there's absolutely nothing to worry about."

"I know."

I really *don't* know. If what Dad's saying is true, it must have been his voice I heard talking to GG when I was on my way to the toilet. But his is the only voice I think I would have recognized, even at a whisper through a closed door. And if it *was* him, what were they talking about like that?

"I know you love mysteries, and I love that about you, but this is real life, Ruth. It's a lot more boring than a book. It can also be more dangerous, which is my way of saying that I don't want you doing anything stupid."

"Like what?"

"Like searching Gertie's room for what I imagine you would call clues."

"That's not—"

"Somebody killed Gertie, honey. This isn't a game or a story. You need to leave this to the cops."

He waits for me to agree that he's right, of course he's right. I wait for him to stop treating me like I've only recently gotten the training wheels off my bike.

"I'd better get these sheets downstairs," I say.

Dad goes back into GG's bedroom. He's very clearly up to something, but aren't we all? I watch through the gap in the door as Dad bends over in front of the wardrobe, his body obscuring the secret drawer he is obviously sliding open. It can't entirely obscure the flutter of the paper he pulls free.

I hurry down the stairs before he can catch me, wondering not just what Dad has found (and how I'm going to get a look at it) but what has happened to the box that GG was so keen to see the night she died. Probably, if I was paying attention, I might have a pretty good idea about that already. Considering Dad was bang on when he accused me of looking for clues, you'd think I'd be slightly less hopeless when it came to spotting them. Still, I bet you haven't figured it out yet either.

12

DINNER IS WEIRD. IT'S NOT JUST THE FOOD, ALTHOUGH THAT IS definitely a bit weird—a ground-beef-heavy pasta thing invented by Shippy, which, he repeatedly tells us, is easy to make. I believe him. It's not *terrible*, just a bit odd: The texture of the meat is rubbery, and there's a strange aftertaste that makes me refill my water glass twice. I don't ask anyone how long the meat has been in GG's freezer, because I don't want to know.

What's even weirder is how everyone's acting. It starts when I get to the kitchen and the adults stop talking, like a scene from a Western. Nobody in the kitchen blows me away with a six-shooter, but there's a long beat of silence before Aunty Bec asks me, loudly, to set the table. (It's already set.) Dad, meanwhile, is leaning in to Aunty Vinka at one end of the table, talking intently and gesturing with his hands like he was born just south of Rome. While Shippy is doing the rounds, dolloping out huge servings of pasta almost against our collective will, Dad moves on to Aunty Bec. The whole thing couldn't be more suspicious if Dad had regrown the unfortunate mustache of the Pandemic Years. Nick's still in the hospital, by the way (told you).

My chair scrapes as I drag it closer to Dylan, who is moving lumps around his plate with one hand and holding a book open with the other. He yelps when I elbow him in the ribs, but I think he's faking it.

"What was that for?"

"The grown-ups are acting weird." I say this as quietly as I can, but the adults are so busy talking to each other in suspiciously vigorous whispers that they probably wouldn't notice if I screamed it across the table.

"Where have *you* been?"

"I think Dad took something from GG's room."

"What?"

"I have no idea. But remember I said there was a hidden drawer?"

"You said secret drawer."

"Same thing and who cares. I think he took something out of it."

"Did you ask him about it?"

"No."

"Why not?"

It's a fair question, and the answer, *because I think he'd lie*, feels like a betrayal of Dad. Instead, I pivot.

"There's something else."

"You killed GG? I knew it."

"I really want to go back and have a proper look for that missing box."

Dylan puts down his book (Ngaio Marsh's *A Man Lay*

Dead—a man's legs are on the cover and, call me the world's greatest teen detective, I don't think he's sleeping). "Why?"

"You've got to admit it's weird. She asks me to get this box down. Hours later she's murdered. Then the box disappears. What if the murderer stole the box?"

"What if she just put it under her bed, like a normal person?"

"Then I'll find it and we'll know."

Any answer Dylan might give disappears as Dad sits down on my other side, scraping his chair up to the table.

"What are you two whispering about?" Okay, so it's possible Dad is not quite as preoccupied as I thought. He forks a twirl of pasta into his mouth, then chews for a long time. When he speaks, it's around half a mouthful of tagliatelle. "What is this?"

"Just deconstructed Bolognese," Shippy says quickly. "It's a cinch to make, honestly. You just take some ground beef and brown it in a pan—"

Dad shifts in his chair, possibly preparing to leap at Shippy if Shippy's Recipe Corner goes for much longer. As he does, his T-shirt rides up and I see half a centimeter of paper protruding from the pocket of his jeans.

Before I can pause to ask myself some tough questions—like (a) What are you doing? and (b) Is this a good idea? and (c) Seriously, though, have you thought this through?—I snatch the paper and slide it clear of Dad's pocket.

"Whatha—" he says around a mouthful of (allegedly) deconstructed Bolognese. I'm exhilarated. This must be how

Hercule Poirot feels when he unmasks the murderer because of a chance remark made by a gardener about the tulip bulbs or something.

"Ruth, what are you doing?"

What I'm doing is trying to make sense of the paper in my hands. I see Gertie's name. A corporate firm I've never heard of. A dollar sign with a lot of . . .

"What is this?" I ask, holding the paper tight in one hand and crossing my arms so it's pressed against my body.

"Nothing important."

"You took this from GG's room."

It's not really a question but Dad nods anyway.

"Seeing Dylan ransacking the wardrobe made me think of the secret drawer and wonder if Gertie had kept anything there." He gives Dylan a jock nod he's not nearly blokey enough to pull off. "You almost had the right idea, mate." No mention of the fact that it was *my* nosiness and *my* disregard for parental authority that got us to GG's room in the first place. This must be how Hercule Poirot feels when he has to let the police take credit for the crimes he solves.

"It's some kind of life-insurance policy." I only just manage to make it not sound like a question.

"Can you give it back now?"

I do, but only because I think I get it.

"Life insurance?" Shippy repeats in a way that makes it clear this is news to him. "How much?"

Rob, who hasn't touched his own pasta, shifts uncomfortably in his seat but doesn't offer to leave the family to it. No judgment: I look out the window when we drive past car accidents too.

"Doesn't concern you, mate," Dad says. "It must have been taken out a long time ago, because the beneficiary is Gertie's son, who died years back. What was his name?"

"Henry?" Aunty Vinka asks, sounding vaguer than usual.

"I went to school with a Henry," Shippy offers, as helpful as ever. "He ended up in jail."

"He wasn't called Henry," Dad says, grumpy at the interruption. "His name was Martin McCulloch."

"Life insurance?" I prompt.

"Right," Dad says. "So if Gertie's son is the beneficiary and he's dead, she probably stopped paying the premiums a long time ago and it's a moot point. But if not, maybe there's a possibility the money goes into her estate?" He starts to fork up some more pasta, then changes his mind. "I'll have to take this to her lawyer. I've made an appointment for tomorrow anyway."

"Is her lawyer in Perth?" I ask.

"Margaret River. I'll go tomorrow and then I'll call the cops and see if we can head back to Perth. You've missed enough school as it is." (We're not going anywhere, in case you're wondering. This house is like that song about the hotel: You can never leave.)

"How much?" Shippy asks.

"I don't know if we should be discussing this," Aunty Vinka says, getting up to put on the kettle.

"Why not?"

"Isn't it a bit gauche?"

"I don't know what that means," Shippy says.

"Course you don't, mate," says Dad. "But you don't need to flap your hands either, Vinx. It's not a secret. Potentially it's worth about half a million dollars, but like I said . . ." Dad has to repeat his last three words to drown out Shippy's four-letter word. "Like I said, it's probably a moot point and we should all take a deep breath before Shippy starts sketching plans for a backyard pool."

I look sideways at Dylan, who's looking down at his plate, and I wonder if he's thinking the same things I am. I've always known that Dad would inherit a slice of the farm. But it's hard to get excited about inheriting part of a house that may or may not be sold or where you may or may not be forced to take all future family vacations until the end of time. Inheriting cash is so much more exciting. We could go on a trip to somewhere that isn't a three-hour drive from Perth. I might be allowed to buy a new phone that isn't just Dad's old one.

"Do you want more?" It takes me a moment to realize Shippy's talking about pasta, not money, and that at some point I finished everything in my bowl. I very much do not want more, but what I do want is a reason to stay at the table.

"Maybe a *bit* more."

He blobs in a huge spoonful, looking pleased. Only when I look down at the mound of gray meat and slightly congealed pasta do I realize the depth of my mistake. Looking up the table to where Aunty Vinka is eating plain pasta laced with olive oil and pepper is one of the few occasions I've ever thought longingly of veganism. Still, I sit there, listening to the grown-ups speculating about family law, a rare subject on which their knowledge is roughly comparable to my own (none of us has a clue), while also mentally sketching out every possible hiding spot in GG's room where she might have concealed a box. Why she would do such a thing, I have no idea, but I can't move on from the suspicion that the box is important and that, if I could just figure out what happened to it, I might know why GG died.

I'm right, but not for the reason I think.

13

AFTER DINNER WE WATCH A MOVIE: AN OLD ROM-COM ABOUT A woman obsessed with weddings and improbably unlucky in love. It's the only one of the DVDs everyone can (more or less) agree on, and it's charming in bits—and the bits when it's not provide welcome white noise for me to think. Dylan disappears to his room before the two romantic leads have even met each other, so I curl up next to Dad, pretending it's only to get access to the family block of chocolate being passed around. Friday night was movie night when Mum and Dad were still together, but nobody got that in the divorce and I miss the feeling.

When the movie's over and the two good-looking people on-screen have decided to be good-looking together permanently, I grab a book from the bookshelf—my cover story—and head to Dylan's room. *Room* is an oversell: It's more like a walk-in closet off Aunty Bec and Shippy's room, with a sliding door Grandad installed because there isn't enough room for a normal door. Harry Potter would really feel like he'd come home.

Dylan takes a long time to answer the door. A *really* long time considering the room is only just big enough for a bed. There's no space for a wardrobe or a chest of drawers—just a couple of shelves bracketed on the wall to hold a reading light and a stack of old *Women's Weekly* magazines. Dylan looks rumpled and suspicious when he finally slides the door open. I hold up the book, momentarily forgetting it's only my cover story, and he frowns.

"What's that for?"

"I've got a plan."

"Of course. Come in, Detective."

"If you're going to be like that about it—"

"Come in." Dylan stands back from the doorway and I sit, cross-legged, at the end of his bed because there's really nowhere else unless you have the upper-body strength to hang from the light fixture like a bat, which I don't. "So? What have you got?"

"The box."

"The box?"

"The one I told you about."

"You found it?"

"No. But I'm going to go look for it in GG's room."

"Now?"

"That's the idea."

Dylan looks less enthused than I'd hoped. It's not that I thought he'd whip out a flashlight and magnifying glass, but I expected slightly more than a slow blink.

"And in your mind our parents are doing what, exactly, while we're ransacking Gertie's room?"

"I never said *we*?"

Dylan blushes (ha). Just a little. Unfortunately, he recovers quickly. "Like I'm not coming with you."

"We'll wait until they go to bed."

"Okay." He nods. "I can't exactly sneak out of this room once Mum and Shippy are in for the night. But if I turn off the light and close the door, Mum probably won't even come to check on me."

"One request," I say quickly.

"Yeah?"

"Can we please do the thing where you put clothes under the covers so it looks like a person?"

"Seriously?"

"They always do it in the movies. It looks fun."

"Have I told you you're my favorite weirdo?"

"Not today."

We stuff a few clothes under the duvet to create a Dylan-like shape, just in case, then turn off the lights so it's pitch black in the room.

"You sleep like this?"

He shrugs. "It's okay."

It feels the way I imagine sleeping in a coffin would, but I don't say that and just scoot on out with Dylan. The real challenge is getting Dylan upstairs without running into the adults, but even this isn't as hard as you'd think: They're all still in the living room, arguing as the movie credits roll about whether the wedding industry is inherently patriarchal. (I'm not making this up—that's almost a direct quote from Aunty Vinka.) I get away with a "good night!" shouted through the door before I trot upstairs with Dylan.

"Do I hide under the bed or something?" he asks, crouching down to look underneath it. "Is that mouse poo?"

"I think you can just hide behind the door when Dad comes in." I point. "If he thinks I'm asleep he'll just stick his head in and go."

"Okay." Dylan flops onto my bed. "Tell me about the box while we wait. Then at least I'll know what I'm looking for."

"It's cardboard."

"A *cardboard* box, you say? I was assuming steel, but there you go."

I ignore him. "It's like one of those storage boxes IKEA sells." I make a motion with my arms that is supposed to be me turning a flat-pack bunch of cardboard into a convenient storage box, but Dylan looks at me like I'm having a seizure. "About this big." I move my hands apart. "And it had 'for M' or maybe 'to M' or something like that written in marker on one side of the box."

"What's in it?"

"I have no idea."

"Washing-machine receipts, maybe."

"Or, what about this: money. Or maybe not cash but, I don't know, gold bars? Jewelry?"

"Gold bars?"

"I'm not saying GG was a pirate—"

"It sounds a bit like you are."

"—but if she was taking out half-a-million-dollar life-insurance policies, maybe she had money we never knew about. Where did all that money go?"

"Paying the premiums. Life insurance is a scam."

"Dylan, has anyone ever told you you're really unhelpful?"

"Constantly. But you make me really believe it. Where do you want to look, anyway? We've already searched the wardrobe. What else is there? Dressing table? Under the bed? I don't suppose there's a convenient hatch to a hidden attic?"

"Not that I know of." The idea briefly excites me before I consider how unlikely it is that my grandad, who basically built this house, had the skill or enthusiasm to include a secret attic room and, even less plausibly, the self-restraint not to brag about it.

Dad's step on the stairs sends Dylan to his hiding spot and I click off the bedside light and pull the blanket over me, wishing I'd thought to take off my shoes first. I lie still as the door opens and don't breathe until it's closed again. The hand on my shoulder nearly forces out a scream until I see Dylan's face.

"Sorry," he whispers, so quiet I have to lip-read. "How long do we wait?" He points at the wall separating Dad's room from mine. I consider and hold up ten fingers. Dad's probably already out—I once saw him fall asleep while he was still brushing his teeth.

So we give it ten minutes before creeping out and up the stairs, going so slowly we're bordering on slo-mo. GG's bedroom door opens without the ominous creak I'm braced for.

"Should we turn on the light?" Dylan whispers. The only light in the room is coming from a hole in the cardboard covering the window. I start to answer, but a noise makes us both go rigid. We'd look ridiculous if there was anyone up to see us. (Is there anyone up to see us?)

The noise is, as the horror movies so rarely say, not coming from inside the house. I'm not as quiet as I should be in my hurry to get to the window and put my eye to the hole in the flattened box taped where a sheet of glass should be.

The garden is dark but there's a moon, and as my pupils do their thing, I can make out flower beds, the lemon tree, and . . . something moving? The longer I watch, the more I'm sure that the something moving very slowly across the grass is actually a *someone* and that the *shoo-shoo* noise that turned us into statues is the sound of their feet on the grass. I can't make out more than a human-shaped blob.

"There's someone there," I whisper.

This is the moment I should fly down the stairs and investigate. I want to. Mostly. There's a big part of me (we're talking head, torso, and three out of four of my limbs) that wants to do exactly that. If I'm serious about figuring out what happened to GG, I need to get out there right now to see who's taking an eleven p.m. stroll about the garden. The problem is there's a small part of me (my left arm, say) that is just straight-up scared of what—or, let's be real, who—I might find.

"I can't see anyone," Dylan whispers, bumping me out of the way to take my place.

"They're going around the house toward the front door," I say. "I'm going out there." I consider grabbing the sewing scissors out of GG's sewing basket, but realistically I'd probably trip down the stairs and impale myself on those tiny twin blades, and then everyone would think I was the Second Victim. Plus, Dad told me once that, statistically speaking, you're more likely to have a weapon used against you than have a chance to use it yourself. It's probably one of those made-up things parents say, like you'll explode if you eat a sandwich before going swimming, but I've never quite managed to scrub it from my mental hard drive.

"I'll come with you."

We're moving so fast on the stairs that I nearly go down the second flight headfirst when Dad's bedroom door swings open and he stands there, rubbing at his face.

"*Ruth?* You're up?"

"Uh, yeah." There doesn't seem much point in denying it.

Dylan collides with my back, knocking me down a stair and robbing me of any chance to pretend I'm going to the bathroom or getting a drink of water. I'm not entirely mad about it: How much easier to hand this problem to a grown-up?

"I saw someone outside in the garden," I say quickly, getting to the point.

"Outside the house?"

"Yeah."

"Are you sure?"

"Yeah." I don't mention that I saw them from GG's window.

I'm braced for Dad's skepticism, so I'm surprised when he takes me seriously.

"Okay. You two, go to Ruth's room. I'm going to have a look."

"I'll come."

"No, you won't."

Dad's fast down the stairs, even in the dark. We keep up but only just.

"Stay inside," he says to us once we're downstairs in the kitchen, before closing the front door, very firmly, in our faces. Dylan puts his hand on the door handle, but it's a question. I shake my head and we go into the living room instead, where a lump on the couch startles me before I remember it's where our newest guest is sleeping. Rob's snoring doesn't falter as Dylan and I lean against the window to follow the bob and weave of Dad's cell-phone light around the side of the house. This feels like a terrible idea, the moment in a scary movie when someone goes to investigate a weird sound in the basement or a strange light in the creepy-arse woods and it's impossible to have sympathy for their imminent butchering because they're too stupid to live.

Then the light disappears as Dad moves from the side of the house around toward the backyard where we saw the figure, and all I can do is stand with my cheek pressed flat against the glass. I can't see anything, which is bad, but I also can't hear anything, which is good because at least it means nobody is getting murdered. Not noisily, anyway.

Then a cloud shifts and there's enough light from the moon to see a figure walking close to the house, coming toward us.

I should have woken someone else in the house. I should have woken everyone in the house. I shouldn't have let Dad go outside. Mum is going to *kill* me.

Then the figure comes closer and I see that it's Dad, walking quickly but not dripping blood or sporting any obvious head wounds.

I meet him at the door. "Did you find them?"

Dad shakes his head. "I didn't see anyone. I walked all the way around and then back again."

"Oh."

"Don't look disappointed, Ruth. This is a good thing."

"But I saw someone. I really did."

"I'm not saying you didn't. I'm just saying I couldn't find anyone."

"Okay."

"Let's go back to bed. You too, Dylan. Do I even want to know why you two were prowling around the house at night?"

"I woke him up when I saw someone." I lie quickly and probably too easily to make me a good person.

"Wake *me* up next time" is all Dad says.

I want to ask if he believes me, but just asking the question makes it sound like I'm not sure, and I don't want Dad to think I got spooked by a shrub waving in the breeze. Also, do I want to know the answer? Dad insists on escorting me back to my room, so there's no chance to debrief with Dylan before he slopes off back to his.

Back in my bedroom I crawl under the blanket, my heart still beating too fast to make sleep possible. My brain is asking my eyes if they're absolutely sure they saw what they saw when I hear the sound of a key being inserted into the keyhole of my door and then the click of it locking me in for the night. It's both reassuring and scary to consider that Dad might have believed me more than I thought.

14

SOMEONE IS BANGING ON MY DOOR. MY FIRST CONSCIOUS thought is that someone else has died. This is not a crazy idea—GG is not going to be the last victim of this family getaway gone wrong—but when I finally get out of bed and make it to the (now-unlocked) door, I can tell from Dylan's face that nobody has died. Or, if this is Dylan's *someone has died* face, then he's probably the murderer, because he's *excited*.

"How long have you been out here?" I act like I'm rubbing at the sleep in my eyes, but really I'm trying to avoid breathing in his direction.

"Downstairs." He's a little out of breath and still in his pj's.

"Is everyone okay?" I ask anyway, because, I don't know, maybe Dylan *is* a murderer?

"It's Sasha."

My brain must be enjoying a power nap after a night crunching the numbers, because it takes me a moment to even remember who Sasha is. "The neighbor?"

"Yeah."

"He did it?"

"What?"

"Sasha killed GG?"

"No, you idiot: He's here and he has news." Dylan is hustling me down the stairs a little faster than I'd like. It would be a real bummer to slip and break my neck before I even get to find out what the news is.

"Slow down."

"Hurry up."

We make it to the table, alive, to find Sasha standing with Aunty Bec while Dad pours coffee into a row of waiting mugs. Sasha looks a little startled by the arrival of two semi-breathless teenagers, but recovers quickly.

"Hi. It's Ruth, right? And David?"

"That's right." I smile, sitting down.

"It's Dylan," Aunty Bec says.

"Sasha's got news," Dad says to me. "But maybe you know that already."

"What's happened?"

"It's the police."

"Have they arrested someone?" I do a quick head count. No Aunty Vinka and no Shippy. If I had to pick one as a murderer, it wouldn't be the hippie who puts out bowls of water for the birds in her garden every summer.

"Nobody's been arrested and this isn't official," Sasha says quickly. "I've got a friend on the force who told me that some of the jewelry taken from Gertie's room has turned up in Perth at a pawnshop."

There's a moment where I wonder what GG's jewelry is doing in a sex shop before my brain wakes up for good. (Also, why did nobody tell me GG's jewelry was stolen? It's the curse of the amateur detective to be kept in the dark, but it's more fun in books, not so much in real life.)

"What does that mean?" Aunty Bec asks.

"It means the Perth cops are investigating too."

"That's good news, right?"

"It's a lead," Dad says, sounding like an extra from a police procedural.

"At least we know the cops are doing something," Aunty Bec says.

"I thought I'd come and tell you myself," Sasha says. "Have the local police been in touch with any updates?"

"Not really," Dad says. "All they've said is that the investigation is ongoing and they don't think we're in any danger here in the house. But I've got to call Detective Peterson today anyway to see if Ruth and I can head back to Perth."

The grown-ups chat a bit about the Case So Far and a little bit about What This All Means, and everyone seems more relaxed than they have since we all learned that a typewriter can be a deadly weapon. It takes me a few minutes of listening to this before I understand why: If the person who killed GG and stole her jewelry is off flogging it for cash in Perth, it can't have been any of us, since we've all been stuck in this house.

There's a huge yawn from the doorway, and Rob wanders in from the living room, wearing boxers and a T-shirt, a sartorial misstep he looks like he regrets when he sees us gathered there. He gives a startled gasp, then makes absolutely no effort to retreat in search of, I don't know, some pants.

"Oh man," he says, staring at Sasha like he's never seen a *Farmer Wants a Wife* contestant in the flesh. The horror appears to be mutual: Sasha is staring at Rob like he's never seen a middle-aged man's upper thigh before (and maybe he hasn't?). Rob pulls at the bottom of his T-shirt like it might turn into a pair of pants, given sufficient encouragement.

"What's this?" Rob asks. Then, possibly realizing how this sounds, he goes on: "Sorry, I didn't realize we had company." He releases his T-shirt and extends a hand. "Name's Rob."

Sasha looks at Rob's hand like he's still hoping pants are an option. Only when it's clear that's not going to happen does he grip the offered hand.

"Sasha."

"Sasha's from the farm next door," Dad says. "He's brought some news about Gertie."

"Nothing official." Sasha repeats the party line, looking even less comfortable than before. "Sorry, are you . . . a member of the family too?"

Rob shakes his head. "Nah, I'm just a blow-in. What's the big news?"

"Some of the jewelry stolen from the house during the break-in has turned up in Perth," Dad summarizes helpfully. "Rob's staying with us for . . . a bit," he adds to Sasha.

Rob absorbs this information as much as someone still half asleep can. "So, Sasha, you're on the farm next door, are you?"

"That's right."

"You must be doing well for yourself."

"Sure. How do you fit in, Rob?"

"We really appreciate you keeping us in the loop," Aunty Bec says before anyone has to try to answer that one, flashing Sasha a smile.

"I wasn't sure if it was too early to drop in on city people," Sasha says. "But I've got a busy day and I thought you'd like to know. I won't hold you up."

"Hey, mate, have you got a sec?" Rob asks, and Sasha gives him an alarmed look. Possibly he imagines this is a free-love arrangement (he really does seem concerned about the pants situation) and Rob's about to proposition him for some kind of a sevensome, but all he says is: "Yeah?"

"That your truck out there?"

"Yeah."

"Okay if I take a quick look? I'm in the market."

Sasha doesn't seem to find this request as weird as I do (in fairness it's only about the tenth weirdest thing going on in this house), because he just shrugs and the two of them walk out together. Rob does not bother to put on pants.

"Well, that lets us off the hook," Dad says when the door shuts. "Most of us, anyway."

"What do you mean?"

"Only one of us was out of this house long enough to make the drive to Perth and back." Dad takes a slurp of his coffee, almost certainly to be dramatic. "Where is Shippy, anyway?"

"Screw you, Andy," Aunty Bec says, but that's as far as things are allowed to escalate because Aunty Vinka's car appears outside. We watch her stop to chat with Sasha and Rob in the driveway for a bit; then she and Rob come inside. Both of them look worried.

"Is there a phone charger around here?" Rob asks, looking at the phone in his hand.

"No reception," I say automatically. "But, yeah, there's one by the microwave. You can unplug my phone if you want."

"Where's Nick?" Dad asks Aunty Vinka. "Isn't he supposed to be—"

"He's still in the hospital."

"More tests?"

"Not exactly."

"Vinx?" Dad says.

"Nick's . . . look, it turns out he's got one of those hospital superbugs," Aunty Vinka says, getting the words out so quickly they all run together.

"What?" Dad, rather unfortunately, starts to laugh. "Are you kidding?"

"I am not."

"So he's not coming home?"

"They're keeping him in for a bit longer." Aunty Vinka sits down at the kitchen table, so forcefully her earrings and bracelets jangle. "I can't believe this. I'm never getting out of this town."

"Coffee?" Dad asks, maybe feeling bad about laughing. (It'd be a first.) "Or, sorry, an herbal tea?"

"Go on," Aunty Vinka says, "make it a coffee."

"It must be serious."

"He's going to come out of that hospital worse than when he went in."

"Is there anything we can do to help?"

"You could make it a strong one. What's going on with the hot neighbor, anyway? He said something about porn, but I didn't really take it in."

"The cops have found some of Gertie's jewelry up in Perth," Dad says, chucking the old coffee grounds into the compost bin.

Aunty Vinka gets it right away. "Finally, some good news."

"Speaking of Perth," Dad goes on, "I wanted to stay until Nick was out of the hospital, but that feels like a losing battle, so Ruth and I should probably head back today—*if* the cops say it's okay. The boss left some pretty choice voicemails on my phone."

Dad is a journalist, but not the cool kind who expose political scandals or interview celebrities. He mostly covers local government, although it's hard to tell because I fall into a light coma every time he tries to bring it up. It's that exciting.

"That's fine."

"I'm going into Margaret River this morning to talk to Gertie's lawyer." He gestures to a pile of papers arranged haphazardly on the kitchen counter next to where Rob is still messing around with his phone. "If we get the all clear we'll hit the road this afternoon." Dad looks at me and I nod.

This is good news (mostly) and I'm (mostly) happy to hear it. There's only a small part of me (tiny) thinking about how my window for working out what really happened to GG is closing faster than my laptop browser window when Dad comes into my bedroom. Sure, there's nothing to stop me from working on what I've started to think of as the Case back in Perth, but it's not the same. I know that once I have streaming and the internet and friends back in my life, even something as serious as the Case of the Murdered GG will slip away in favor of more solvable mysteries like Can I Pull Off Blunt Bangs? (I'll solve this one for you right now: no.)

Shippy comes into the kitchen just as Dad is pouring out fresh coffee.

"Thanks."

"It's not for you, mate."

Rob, who is now settled at the kitchen table, looks up. "Ship-man, I thought you'd died," he says, apparently not realizing this might be in bad taste. "Enjoy the sleep-in?" Shippy just grunts. "I've got to run into town for a bit later. You got any plans to check out the water?"

Shippy looks across at Aunty Bec, but only for a moment. "Sure."

Aunty Bec gets those two lines between her eyes that Mum gets when I'm doing something she disapproves of. "You're going surfing?"

"Maybe I could at least check out the swell?" Shippy says hopefully.

Aunty Bec looks like she's trying to communicate something with her eyes, possibly *Have you forgotten how well it worked out last time you went surfing?* But all she says is: "Sure."

Dylan disappears to the living room. A moment later the TV clicks on, and I make myself some toast and follow him.

"What are you looking for?"

"*Death on the Nile*," he says, stopping his clicking when he sees Gal Gadot's face on the screen.

"It's pretty good, except for this stupid backstory—"

"No spoilers." Dylan holds up a hand.

"The book is, like, fifty years old."

"So's your boyfriend, Sasha."

I flop onto the other half of the couch, which creaks a bit more than is flattering. It doesn't take me long to get pulled into the familiar story.

When it's time for an ad (an ad! How did our parents ever live this way?), I decide to bring up the thing I've been thinking about all morning. I sit up on the couch and turn to face Dylan.

"What?"

"I've got a favor to ask."

"You're eloping with Sasha and you need a ring. Sorry, but I don't really do jewelry."

"Do you want to hear or not?"

"Not about your wedding night."

"Gross."

"You're the one who has a crush on an old man."

"I need your help to search GG's room again." That shuts him up (but not for long).

"When?" he says after a long beat.

"This morning. Dad's going into Margaret River. Shippy's going to the beach. The house will be quiet. If I'm going back to Perth later this afternoon, then I want to look for that box one more time."

"You really think it's important?"

"It's the only lead we have, isn't it?"

"Are teenagers supposed to have *leads*?" I don't respond to this provocation, just give him the eyebrow treatment until he cracks. "And my role would be?"

"Lookout. You can make sure none of the grown-ups come upstairs, or warn me if they do."

"What's my warning, then—hoot like an owl or just scream?"

At the sound of footsteps we both roll back to face the TV.

"Whatcha watching?" Dad asks, hanging over the back of the couch.

"*Death on the Nile*. There's an Agatha Christie marathon on ABC."

"Is this the one where they're all in on it?"

"That's the one on a train. This is the one on a boat."

He watches for a few seconds. "The old one's better," he says, and I just shake my head because, to my dad, the old one is always better. I think he genuinely believes that music and film peaked creatively in 1999.

I watch people murder and get murdered on-screen as my family departs around me. Shippy and Rob go first in Aunty Vinka's car, accompanied by Aunty Bec, who insists she wants some beach air but is probably more invested in making sure Shippy returns. Aunty Vinka crams a floppy hat on her head and sets off for a walk. And then finally Dad leaves for his meeting with GG's lawyer in Margaret River—though only after checking with me (three times) that I don't want to go.

"Keep the door locked," he says. "Aunty Vinka said she won't be long."

Dylan and I are alone.

"They've all gone out. Surely I can come upstairs too," he says.

"Lookout is a crucial role."

"So you be lookout and I'll take box duty."

"Seriously, Aunty Vinka's only gone for a walk; she could be back at any time. Dad could forget his phone and come back for it—he can't navigate further than the driveway without that thing. I *need* you, Dylan."

Dylan rolls his eyes, but the movie is just getting good, so I don't think he's that annoyed.

"Fine. Just make sure you tell me what you find."

"Obviously," I say. And, when I say it, I have no idea that I'm lying.

15

I KNOCK LIGHTLY ON GG'S DOOR (WHO DO I EXPECT TO ANSWER?) before swinging it wide open.

My chest feels tight with anxiety: This might be my only opportunity to be here without people bursting in to ask perfectly valid questions like *Why are you in GG's bedroom?* and *What are you looking for?* and *Are you insane?*

I'm regretting not bringing Dylan with me. It would feel like an adventure with him cracking jokes. Solo, it's harder to forget GG died here. I need the lights on.

The box isn't back on top of the wardrobe or in it. It's not behind the curtains or under the dresser.

When I crouch to look under the bed, I can see several boxes, all pushed hard against the wall where my stubby arms can't reach them. I can't tell if any of them are the box I want. Why GG would ask me to fetch her a box, only to almost immediately stash it in an inconvenient location, where presumably she would also struggle to reach it, I can't say. Then again,

GG did plenty of weird things, up to and including getting killed with an antique typewriter, so it wouldn't be the strangest thing she's ever done.

From downstairs there's the sound of a plate smashing and a yelp. Dylan strikes again. Maybe excluding him from this excursion wasn't such a bad thing—he'd probably trip over and smash GG's bedside lamp, leaving me to explain to the cops why we were rampaging through what may or may not still be a crime scene, looking for a cardboard box that probably just contains fifty years' worth of recipes GG never got to cook because all Grandad really liked was steak sandwiches.

Lying flat on my stomach, ignoring the pain in my shoulder (which thinks I'm ninety-four, not fourteen), I commando-crawl under the bed, shivering at each puff of dust that goes up my nose. It's streaming by the time I reach the boxes, and I see right away that none are the one I'm looking for. Still, I drag them toward me, just in case they're chock-full of clues and not, say, receipts for appliances that are currently failing to decay in a landfill.

I'm just about to wriggle out from under the bed with my (pretty lame) booty when I hear it: footsteps outside the door and voices, low but familiar.

". . . now?"

"We might . . . home tomorrow. I don't think poking around here at night is a good look, do you?"

"Dylan's downstairs."

"Just be quick."

There's a moment when I could alert them to my presence.

Things might have played out differently if I had. Instead I instinctively curl into the fetal position, my body directed by the ancient bit of my lizard brain that believes in the need to protect my vital organs. Never mind that I'm not hiding from saber-tooth tigers (did humans even coexist with saber-tooth tigers, or have the *Ice Age* movies lied to me?), my body has assessed the two people in GG's room as a threat. Who am I to say it's wrong?

"How long has this light been on?"

"Focus. Where did you say it was?"

"She put it in one of the shoeboxes with a bunch of old receipts."

"Why?"

"She said nobody would ever look there."

"Because it's a mental thing to do. You're sure the kids didn't find it?"

"They would have said something. But I've got no idea where she put it."

There are the sounds of GG's belongings being moved about, of drawers running on their tracks, and I wait for their conversation to betray what they're looking for. Lying as quietly as possible, not sneezing at the dust tickling my nose hairs, is all I can do.

"No, that's not . . . *Yes!*"

"Have you got it?"

"No, I found Gertie's old button collection. Yes, I've got it."

"Let's get out of here."

"Okay. Um, what do we do with it?"

"Put it in your pocket."

"I mean long-term. Do we throw it in the bin?"

"Would the police check the bins?"

"Light a fire."

"This time of year?"

"What have you got, then?"

"We'll get rid of it away from the house. Take it into town tomorrow or something." There's the sound of the wardrobe doors being closed, a little roughly. "I can't believe you got me into this."

"I didn't *get you into* anything."

"She was a sweet lady, that's all I mean. I feel bad."

"Hurry up, I think I hear something."

Footsteps, some shuffling, and the bedroom door opens and closes.

"Was the door closed when we came in?" one of them asks, but I don't hear the reply, possibly because my heart is busy loudly trying to remove itself to a location somewhere outside my body.

I stay under the bed for as long as I can, until my legs have gone past prickly to pins and needles and landed on numb. Then I crawl out, dragging the boxes behind me. I pull the lids off, more for something to do than because I'm excited by the possibilities. One of them is full of old CDs, stacked three deep. Another is full of *Women's Weekly* magazines, each edition dog-eared and with slips of paper protruding from relevant pages, so maybe I wasn't way off with the recipe prediction. The third has one of those stretchy exercise bands and a pair of hand weights that look like they've done ten reps, tops. I repack the boxes and push them back under the bed. There's no point in showing any of this to Dylan.

Worse, Dylan is now the last person I can talk to about what's just happened. Until now he's been the Watson to my Holmes: the sidekick with whom I can discuss my thoughts (mostly) and kick around theories (definitely). The conversation I've just overheard in GG's bedroom has utterly wrecked that dynamic, however. How, exactly, am I supposed to tell him that I just heard his mother and her boyfriend steal something out of GG's wardrobe? And, even if I could overcome that particular obstacle, how, please tell me, am I supposed to bring the conversation around to the possibility that they had something to do with her death?

16

I TELL NOBODY WHAT I OVERHEARD. I REALIZE HOW DUMB THAT must sound to someone reading this from the safety of the couch, or their bed, or maybe on a bus, trying to tune out the guy listening to music without his earphones (why, my guy, why?). As an enthusiastic reader of crime stories, I'm aware that when the local village busybody finds a crucial clue to explain who it is who bumped off their neighbor or the bloody vicar (there's always a vicar in these things, and I still don't really understand if they're the same as priests), they invariably decide it's a great idea to keep what they know to themselves. Sometimes it's because they want to blackmail the murderer or sometimes it's because they can't believe the murderer would have hurt anyone. Either way, it never ends well. Most of the time they become Body Number Two—and while that's often the murder that helps the detective solve the first crime, that's not much consolation to Body Number Two. (There *is* about to be a Body Number Two in *this* story, in case you're wondering, but it's not me. How would I even be writing this if I'd been bumped off along the way?)

My first idea is to tell Dad. The child's solution to every problem. Not only will he know what to do, but I know what he *will* do, which is call the police. He might even insist that we drive to the station together. The problem will officially be in the hands of grown-ups. Dylan will be devastated and feel betrayed and my family dynamics will be permanently shredded, but none of it will be my fault, exactly, and nobody looking at the available evidence could argue that I haven't Done the Right Thing.

But! As I ponder my next move, it occurs to me (and maybe it's occurred to you too) that I have nothing in the way of proof. Clearly, Aunty Bec and Shippy are up to something shifty. Clearly, they also took something from GG's room, maybe something that incriminates them. But without that something, there's nothing to stop them from denying they were ever in GG's bedroom, suggesting I'm a crazy person, and, oh, I don't know, murdering me and making it look like an accident. Worst-case scenario, obviously. Dylan might believe me (he knew I was in GG's bedroom, after all, and he must have seen his mum and Shippy go up the stairs after me), but I'm not confident the word of two teenagers counts for a great deal with the Dunsborough police. Or in court.

Dylan asks me about the box the moment we're alone together back downstairs, of course. But all I tell him is that I didn't find anything. He's so chuffed to relate how he smashed a plate to let me know Aunty Bec and Shippy were back early that I don't have it in me to admit his warning went over my head.

"Shippy decided not to surf," he says. "What were they even doing upstairs? They didn't go into Gertie's room, did they?"

"They didn't see me" is as close to an explanation as I offer. Then I just act interested in the movie.

I spend the afternoon trying to put together the pieces I've got: the missing box, Aunty Bec and Shippy's sketchiness, GG's life-insurance policy, and someone sneaking around outside. I can't find my phone (is it possible this house is a Bermuda Triangle kind of a deal, having made first GG's box and now my phone disappear?) and so have to resort to making notes with pen and paper, which makes me feel a bit like I'm back at school. Then something happens to disrupt my puzzling. Actually, it would be more accurate to say that *nothing* happens, but maybe that's too confusing? The thing that both does and doesn't happen, if you see what I mean, is that Shippy's new best friend, Rob, fails to return from the beach.

It takes a while for anyone to notice. Does that say something about Rob? Maybe. But, also, the house is big and everyone's doing their own thing and it's not until Dad comes back in the afternoon and asks where Rob is that everyone seems to realize, at the exact same moment, that they have no bloody idea.

"Is he not back?" Aunty Vinka frowns.

Shippy just opens his mouth and shouts: *"Rob?"* There's no reply.

"He's not in the *house*, Shippy."

"He must be still surfing, then."

"I thought *you* were surfing," Dad says to Shippy.

"Decided not to," Shippy says, with a glance at Aunty Bec that probably only looks suspicious as hell to me.

"Rob, uh, wanted to stay at the beach for a bit, but I thought he'd be back by now." Aunty Bec sounds concerned, maybe even guilty for having left Rob behind. Or is that just because I know she has something to feel guilty about?

Shippy pulls out his phone to look at the time. "He might still be surfing."

"How exactly was he expecting to get back here without a car, or dare I hope that our time with Rob has come to a close?" Dad asks.

"He said he could get a lift back here with a friend." Shippy is leaning against the door of the kitchen and studying his phone, like it might provide him with anything other than the time and an update on how long an iPhone battery can last when you use the phone for absolutely nothing at all (actually, ages).

"You just left him at the beach?" Dad says. I look for Dylan to see what he thinks, but, like Rob, he's missing. Unlike Rob, I'm pretty sure he's not *missing* missing and is, rather, hanging out in his tiny box of a bedroom.

Shippy shrugs. "He's a self-sufficient guy."

"He's couch surfing at, what, forty?" Dad again.

"He's a free spirit."

Dad mumbles something that sounds like "a freeloading spirit" (which would be an aggressively on-brand Dad joke), but I can't be sure.

"Have you packed your bag, Ruth?" Dad asks me.

"Did the police say we could go back to Perth?"

"Sure. They have all my details."

"Not yet. What time are we going?" I both do and don't want to get out of here. Sharing the house with Aunty Bec and Shippy is making my skin itchy.

"I don't know," he says, looking at the kitchen clock. "It took longer than I thought at the lawyer's: You can really tell these guys are used to getting paid by the hour. Maybe we should wait until after dinner—more time for you to pack, and maybe Rob will have turned up by then so we can exchange our tearful farewells."

Rob hasn't turned up by dinner.

The meal is intensely awkward for reasons that have nothing to do with Rob. Maybe that's not fair—it's intensely awkward for me personally, but it's entirely possible I'm projecting my discomfort onto the rest of the family and everyone else is having a ball. In my desperation not to sit too close to Aunty Bec or Shippy, I wedge myself between Aunty Vinka and Dad, which means I'm subjected to a lot of sibling banter, mostly around Aunty Vinka's new business idea, which involves curating "artisanal soap" to be sent to subscribers once a week. Dad keeps trying to point out that nobody uses a bar of soap every week, but he's lacking some of his usual appetite to go in for the kill.

Aunty Bec is trying to talk to Dylan about school, but he's reverted to monosyllabic grunts, so she's not making much progress.

While pretending to be fascinated by the contents of my stir-fry (it's harder than you'd think to look really, really focused on a piece of bell pepper), I spend most of the meal mentally compiling a list of reasons Aunty Bec and Shippy might have had to bump off GG.

1. Money. As in: Aunty Bec will inherit now, instead of waiting for GG to die of natural causes.

That's it. That's the only motive I've got.

There could be other stuff, of course. There always is in a proper mystery. Bec mentioned having visited GG by herself recently, so maybe GG saw her do something bad (an affair? A hit-and-run?) and was blackmailing her? Or maybe Shippy tried to steal something (jewelry? Whatever was in that box? An unexpectedly valuable stamp collection GG never mentioned for some reason?) and GG caught him and they got into a fight and he grabbed the typewriter and . . . ? But nothing feels convincing.

The window for me to tell the family what I overheard up in GG's room is shrinking. Dinner is over and the clearing-up has begun. In another ten minutes Dad will be loading our bags into the car—assuming I ever find my phone, which is still very much MIA—and I still won't have told anyone what happened or didn't happen. I just wish I knew for sure. Can I live with the uncertainty of spending holiday celebrations with two maybe murderers for another ten years? And follow-up question: Would that be better or worse than opening Christmas presents with two people I'd wrongly accused of murder?

Dad gets up to clear the plates, and I stand and push my

chair back from the table. Nobody looks at me because they don't realize that I'm about to make a speech. Or is it an announcement? A revelation? I have to say something. Don't I?

"Everyone," I say, but my voice is slow to catch up, so it's less pronouncement than gasp. Worse, my single gasped word is entirely silenced by the slam of a car door. And then another.

"Rob," Shippy says, like he never doubted it.

"Rob," Dad says, almost disappointed.

"Rob," I say, relieved.

There's a knock at the door.

Dad answers, revealing not Rob but two uniformed police officers. One of them is Detective Peterson, who interviewed us before, and the other is a younger man, whose face tells a story. (That story is a short one called "I Think You Should Sit Down We Have Bad News.")

"Can we come in, sir?"

17

ROB IS NOT DEAD. BUT HE MIGHT STILL DIE. IMAGINE IF THE COPS had said it just like that. Instead it takes them forever to make the jump from "involved in a hit-and-run" to "critical condition" and "intensive care." Mostly they're intent on trying to figure out how well we know Rob (barely), where we've all been today (all over the place), and whether any of us might have had a reason to run him down in a car (don't ask me, yet).

It's a minor miracle (think Jesus's face appearing on your toast, not a proper one) that I'm allowed to stay in the room with the cops at all. If Dad was thinking clearly, he would have sent me upstairs. Instead he's too busy asking questions to notice as Dylan and I slip onto the corner couch, taking up as little room as possible by squashing our hips together.

Detective Peterson finally gets around to telling us that Rob's been in a serious "accident" (her word, not mine) and is in the hospital, and Dylan squeezes my leg and mouths *second body.* Rob's not the second body, by the way. I wasn't being cute, promising a body and delivering a coma patient—for now, at least, Rob is very much alive.

Shippy immediately embarrasses himself by saying, "No, he's just surfing," as if the cops are confused and the half-dead person in the hospital is merely in the process of catching a wave. Detective Peterson gives him a *honey, no* kind of a look, and Aunty Bec pats Shippy's leg, which is quite nice of her, because if my (nonexistent) boyfriend was that thick in public, I'd be forced to pretend we'd never met.

Rob is not surfing. Rob was hit by a car just outside Dunsborough earlier today by someone who failed to stop. The cops seem to think it happened in the afternoon, but he wasn't found until the evening when a passing driver stopped to check the pouch of what they thought was a dead kangaroo.

I listen in silence and ask a question only when it seems like nobody else is going to ask the obvious thing.

"How did you know to come here?"

Everyone looks at me.

"Robert had a piece of paper with this address in his wallet," Detective Peterson says, talking to me and not Dad, which makes me like her. "Good question," she adds, which makes me like her even more.

"That's weird," I say, probably pushing it.

"I was going to ask if you wrote down the address for Robert when you left him at the beach, Matthew?" I look around to figure out who she's talking to before I realize it's Shippy, who's shaking his head before the question is finished. I guess I knew

Shippy couldn't be his first name, but how did I never know it was *Matthew*?

"Yeah, nah, he knew how to get back here."

"Did he say how he was going to make it back?"

"He said he'd grab a lift with a friend."

"Did he give you the friend's name?"

"I dunno that he meant anyone in particular. He knows a lot of people."

"Did he seem himself when you left him on the beach?"

"Sure, but I barely know him."

"He didn't mention anything odd to you? Being stressed? Having somewhere to be?"

"No." But Shippy makes a face. "He was a bit skint, maybe."

"He was having money troubles?"

"Just an impression I got. Like, he was kind of obsessed with how big this place was and how much it was worth. It was a bit off."

"What does he do for a living?"

"I think he said he's a joiner, but he didn't seem to be working at the moment."

"Right." The detective writes that down, and I wonder if she, like me, is trying to remember what a joiner does. (It's got to be something to do with . . . carpentry, right?)

When it's time for our alibis (the cops never actually say this, but it's obvious what they're after), I tell the truth. Mostly. My only lie is of omission. I tell the police I was home all afternoon. True. I tell them I watched a movie with Dylan. Also true. I do not volunteer any details about my foray to GG's room, but if they'd asked me specifically "did you happen to go into your late step-grandmother's room and overhear a potentially incriminating conversation, the implications of which you're still grappling with?" I wouldn't have lied. At least, I don't think I would have lied.

Everyone else gives their answers: Aunty Vinka was out walking and then in her room, supposedly working on her artisanal-soap business plan but probably just napping; Dad was in Margaret River with GG's lawyer; Aunty Bec was with Shippy, first at the beach and later back at the house. They make it sound like dropping Rob off at the beach and coming back to the house was always the plan, which maybe it was? Dylan was here. I can vouch for him, at least: He never left the house.

I'm not the only one who notices the whole *where were you the night of* vibe.

"This *is* just an accident, right?" Dad asks. "It doesn't have anything to do with Gertie's death?"

"We're not ruling anything out at this stage."

"Okay." Dad seems to find that as reassuring as I do. "Were there any witnesses?"

"We will be putting out an appeal for anyone to come forward." That's not a no.

"What was Rob even doing on the road? Was he walking home?" Dad prods.

"We're not ruling anything out."

"Right."

"Did Robert know your stepmother, Gertie?"

"No," Aunty Vinka says right away. Then she corrects herself. "Not that I know of. She died before we even met Rob. I guess it's possible they might know each other, but it's hard to imagine them being friends."

"Rob didn't know her," Shippy says.

"How do you know?"

"He asked me about those." Shippy points to the living-room photo wall. I'm there on the beach as a three-year-old, in my school uniform at eight, and as a tween in a family portrait taken for Dad's birthday. Dad and Aunty Vinka are well represented, and there are a few photos of distant relatives I've never met whose names I could possibly recall with a gun to my head. Aunty Bec hasn't made it onto the wall, and now, I suppose, nobody will bother. Grandma is there with six-year-old Dad on her knee, hung above a smaller photo of a young GG with her late husband and son, and a larger one of her that must have been taken in the last five years. "He would have said if he recognized Gertie."

"What do you mean he was asking about them?" Dad asks.

"He was just, you know, asking who was who: I pointed out Gertie and he didn't say anything. Why would he do that if he knew her?"

The still-unnamed policeman is writing this all down in his notepad. I have no idea what the various insignia on his uniform mean, but if he's the one transcribing and Detective Peterson is asking the questions, she's probably his boss.

When it seems like things are wrapping up, Dad says: "My daughter and I were planning to head back to Perth tonight. Is that still okay? She's got school and I'm missing work."

Detective Peterson looks at him thoughtfully. I wonder if she finds his desire to get out of town suspicious.

"I've got to get back for work too," Aunty Bec adds.

"You can't go back to Perth now," Aunty Vinka says, sounding genuinely appalled. "Rob's in the ICU. He might die. We'll need to talk to his family."

"Hey, at least Nick will have someone to talk to while he's recuperating," Dad says, unable to resist a gag even with the cops right there.

"He probably doesn't even have a family," Shippy says.

"What are you talking about? He might have parents who'll want to talk to us."

"I just met the guy. What am I going to say to them?"

Detective Peterson stands up and the policeman does the same. "It would be preferable for you to stay in town," she says to Dad, "at least for another day. We're also going to need to take a look at your cars. Is that going to be a problem? I assume that's them out in the driveway?"

Dad, so tough when it comes to being cynical about power and authority when he's working or trying to give me an unsought life lesson, crumbles in the face of this petite detective, with her too-sharp green eyes and biceps that suggest she could take him if it came to a fight.

"Whatever you need," he says.

Everyone makes a big show of being polite as the cops ask a few more questions and agree on a time for the grown-ups to drop in to the station to make a formal statement tomorrow, although it's obvious we're all desperate to be alone to discuss What This Means.

"Well," Dad says, flopping back onto the couch, with a view of the two cops and their flashlights as they start to examine his car. "This has turned into the least relaxing vacation of my life. Worse than that time we got Bali belly with Mum."

I don't particularly want to think about that trip, which was our last as a family before Mum and Dad sat me down to say that, while this had nothing to do with me, and they would always be my parents, blah blah, separate homes, blah blah, always love each other, blah blah, not your fault. Yes, wanting your parents to get back together is lamer than that Lindsay Lohan movie about wanting your parents to get back together, but they just never seemed that unhappy.

Instead of remembering the Balinese villa with our own pool, I think about how weird it is that, an hour ago, I was psyching myself up to expose Aunty Bec and Shippy as . . . something, and now I have no idea what to do with this extra plot twist of Rob's near-death experience.

The grown-ups were all out of the house for at least some of the afternoon, meaning any one of them could have potentially detoured to run Rob down on the side of the road—assuming Aunty Vinka had access to a car we don't know about, which I'll concede is a bit of a stretch. But none of them have a reason to hurt Rob, not unless they're nursing a secret backstory they've kept under wraps or—an unwanted thought intrudes—unless Rob knew something about GG's death and his arrival at the farmhouse wasn't a coincidence after all. Could Rob have come here to confront, even blackmail, someone in my family? If so, who?

I need my phone to write these theories down, but I still haven't seen it since breakfast, which is no longer just bumming me out but officially freaking me out. I've searched my room, my bag, and the living room and checked every pocket of every item of clothing I have here. Worse, Dad refuses to be sympathetic, telling me I could do with reducing my screen time, like he isn't attached to his own phone under normal circumstances. I miss its weight in my hand, even if it is essentially just a very expensive clock most of the time right now. My mind is a mess. I need more time to think things through, but I'm scared someone else is going to get hurt if I can't work out what's happening. I need an accomplice, even if the only person I can ask is the one person I shouldn't.

I nudge Dylan with my elbow, and when he looks sideways, I nod toward the door.

Kitchen, I mouth.

18

"SO," DYLAN SAYS ONCE THE KETTLE IS BOILING LOUDLY ENOUGH to muffle our conversation at least a little bit, if we squash together beside the fridge. "What the hell?"

"I know."

"Are we agreed it can't be a coincidence that someone tried to kill Rob?"

Give Dylan all the points for enthusiasm: He's jumped right in, without either of us having to pretend we're more concerned about Rob than intrigued by the mystery around him. I am not a psychopath (I mean, probably: Those internet tests did seem somewhat legit), but it's hard to get that worked up about a guy I just met, whose only connection to me was a fledgling friendship with Shippy.

"Coincidences do happen, but, yeah, it's weird." In the heat of my desire for someone to confide in, I've neglected to consider how to work my way from *Rob's accident might have been related to GG's death* to *Say, do you think your mum had anything to do with it?*

"Shippy says Rob definitely didn't seem to know GG," I say, instead of what's in my head.

Only as I say this does it occur to me that Shippy might have his own reasons to pretend Rob didn't know GG.

Dylan sets out two cups beside the boiling kettle. "Sure, but the thing about Shippy is: He's an idiot."

My laugh comes out like a honk. All this nervous energy has got to go somewhere.

"Did you know Shippy's name is Matthew?"

"Yeah, of course. What's that got to do with anything?"

"Matthew. *M.*" I wait for Dylan to get there, then lose patience and just drag him all the way up to my point. "The letter on the missing box: 'for *M.*'"

Dylan doesn't look as impressed with this as I'd hoped. "If the box was for Shippy, why wouldn't Gertie just give it to him, though? We were here together all weekend."

"I guess," I say, grumpy.

"Don't you think it's a bit suspicious that Rob was asking about everyone in the photos?"

"Not really."

"It's a weird thing to do."

"It's polite chitchat."

Dylan is going through the cupboards looking for tea bags. "I thought maybe he asked about the photos because he *recognized* Gertie or thought that he did."

"Okay . . . ," I say, not hating this.

"Maybe when he saw that photo, he realized he knew something about her death."

"Something that almost got him killed."

"You've gone full Benoit Blanc, and I'm into it."

"Shut up." But I'm pleased. I love those movies.

"You know what I think we should do?"

"Murder Shippy in his sleep and blame it on the killer?"

"Go into town and try to talk to some people who knew Gertie. You know, sniff around."

"You're not a beagle, Dylan."

"I was thinking more like one of those pigs that can sniff out truffles."

"They always look so pleased with themselves."

"The pigs?"

"Yeah."

Dylan laughs. "Okay. What do you think?"

"About the pigs?"

"About going into town."

"Maybe. We'd have to come up with a story for our parents, though."

Dylan finally locates the tea bags and makes the tea. I can tell it's too weak without tasting it, because he didn't leave the bag in long enough, but I don't say so.

"There's something else," I say, keeping my voice low now that we no longer have the cover of water molecules boiling themselves into a frenzy.

"What?"

"I need to do something, and I think I need you to help me."

"Anything for you, Watson."

"I—wait just a minute. If anyone's Holmes, it's me."

"What about: You're Enola and I'm Sherlock."

"Hard no."

"Enola's cool."

"We're getting off track. I need a favor."

"What is it, Sherlock?" Dylan takes a gulp of his tea. "Did that feel better? Or did it feel wrong, and you realized in your heart you're more of an Enola?"

"Dylan."

"You're smiling."

"I am not," I lie. "This is serious."

"It sounds it."

"Can you get the grown-ups out of the house tonight? Just for like twenty minutes."

Dylan gets serious. "Tonight?"

"Only for twenty minutes."

"Why?"

"I have something I need to, uh, follow up."

"What is it?"

"I can't tell you. But I need to search the house." Technically, I only need to search one room, but I can't tell him that I suspect his mum and Shippy stole something from GG, which is now concealed in their bedroom.

"Didn't you *just* call this a partnership, and now you're doing the thing all detectives do in books where they leave the sidekick in the dark until the last ten pages?"

"I'm not hiding anything big," I lie some more. "I just can't tell you right now. But I will."

"Is this about the missing box? Do you know where it is?"

What's one more lie between (half) cousins, really? "Maybe."

"So where—"

Aunty Vinka comes into the kitchen and stops when she sees the pair of us talking with what she clearly deems to be a suspicious amount of intensity. I lift my tea in her direction. "We just boiled the kettle if you want a cup."

"What are you two doing in here?"

"Making tea."

"Uh-huh."

"And talking about Rob." I assume an expression that (I hope) suggests that the sudden near death of a man I knew significantly less well than our mailman has left me sad and confused, rather than suspicious and plotting.

"It was such a shock," Dylan adds, possibly overegging it.

"We're all still trying to process it," Aunty Vinka says, her voice going as soft as one of the gauzy pink curtains she has everywhere in her house. (Between that and the amount of incense she goes through, her home is a total fire hazard.) "Tell me how you're both feeling."

"It seems surreal," I say, and, for a change, I'm not even lying. "He was here this morning—without pants, which was weird but also not the point—and now he might die."

Aunty Vinka has bought it, and I should feel more guilty than I do. (Maybe the tests were wrong and I *am* a psychopath. Although, would a psychopath spend this much time worrying about being a psychopath?)

"I have some great meditation exercises if you're interested."

"I was wondering," Dylan says quickly, "do you think we could do something as a family to get out of the house tonight? Maybe go for a walk down to the dam or something?"

"The dam?" Aunty Vinka looks as surprised as she should. "What for?"

"I just want to clear my head," Dylan says. "I thought maybe everyone could do with some fresh air?"

It's not, frankly, the most believable excuse I've ever heard. A fifteen-year-old boy suggesting a post-dinner walk with his extended family does not come off quite as naturally as Dylan seems to believe. But Aunty Vinka loves to think the best of people, and it's obvious that she wants to take him at face value and not ask some relevant questions like *What? The? Hell?*

"That's a great idea, Dylan. What do you think, Ruth?"

"Sounds good." (There's no way I'm going on that walk, obviously.)

Surprisingly, everyone goes for it—even Shippy, who seems more baffled than flattered when Dylan makes it clear he wants him to come too. They're all changing into sensible walking shoes and searching for flashlights when I make my move, sidling up to Dad, who's sitting on the bottom of the stairs with his feet resting on the base of the lamp to more easily lace up his sneakers. That task is proving more difficult than you'd think because he's got Band-Aids on two of his fingers.

"What happened?" I ask.

"Oh. Knife slipped when I was chopping up fruit," he says vaguely, but his eyes are on the dusty floorboards. "We really need to get out the vacuum. I think dirt works differently in the country: This floor was spotless the day we were supposed to leave, you know."

I ignore Dad's looming treatise on country dirt and get right to it.

"Dad, do you mind if I skip the walk and stay home?"

"Why?"

"I've got cramps." I touch my stomach suggestively, confident that Dad has not been keeping notes on my menstrual cycle.

"Exercise is good for period cramps," he says, and, damn it, why can't I have a dad who starts hyperventilating when he hears the word *period* like our PE teacher at school who lets me sit out cross-country twice a month because he's never bothered to keep track.

"I just want to take some Panadol and have a hot bath."

"Okay," he says, and I try to smile wanly. (Period pains: getting young women out of social commitments since, well, forever, I assume.) "I'll stay with you." Ah, crap.

"No, you go. Honestly, I'd like to have the house to myself for a bit."

I once read an article about how to spot a liar that said you should never trust anyone who uses the word *honestly*. Dad, perhaps, never read that one. Or maybe he's just foolish enough to trust the word of his beloved only child because all he says is: "Are you sure?"

"I'm sure."

"We won't be long."

"Take your time," I say, trying not to sound like I'm begging.

Shoes laced, he stands. "You're not up to anything, right?" he asks, which I guess I can't really be mad about.

"What would I be up to?"

"If I knew that, I wouldn't be asking."

"Dad, I have period cramps. That's it."

"Okay. I believe you."

"Thank you."

"I'll lock GG's room just in case." He clearly doesn't know that *I* know there's no lock on GG's door.

"Knock yourself out."

The bath is running and I'm lighting a candle I found in the cupboard (it's the little details that make a good lie) when Dylan finds me in the bathroom.

"Job done."

"A *family walk*? It's a bit too wholesome to be believable, isn't it?"

"Mum and I go for walks at home all the time," he says defensively.

"Sorry. I'm just on edge." I set the now-lit candle beside the bath and admire my handiwork.

"Are you seriously not going to tell me where you think the box is?"

"I'll explain after."

"Come *on*. I'm your co-conspirator. The Ken to your Barbie."

"Have you even seen that movie?"

"Just tell me."

"There's no time."

As if to underline my point, someone knocks on the door. "I'm in here!" Dylan and I chorus together. Then we catch each other's eyes and crack up, releasing tension in our giddy, hiccupping laughter.

"Is it bad that I'm kind of enjoying this?" Dylan asks.

"Which part?"

"The scheming. What do you think could be in the box? I hope it's a pile of money and we'll all be rich."

"You think it's money?"

"Maybe."

"Why?"

"Why not? Stop trying to burst my bubble."

"What would you even do with untold riches?"

"Travel the world? Buy a car? Pay for college so I don't wind up with a massive debt?" He nods at the door. "We'd better get out there before they think we're being inappropriate in here."

I ignore the blush creeping up my neck and ears. "We're basically cousins now—don't be gross."

Dylan makes a face I don't understand. I've never been sure if Dylan knew how badly Ali and I were crushing on him back in the day, although the summer Ali turned up in a white bikini on our family outing should have been a clue. (Not a super-practical choice if you want to get wet, the white bikini.)

"Half cousins, surely" is all he says.

Everyone (eventually) departs on the wholesome family walk. I still can't find my phone, which is starting to feel like I've misplaced a limb, so I set a twenty-minute timer on the microwave instead.

The door to Aunty Bec and Shippy's bedroom is shut, but there's no lock to be locked. Inside it's messy: two open suitcases on the floor, as well as clothes on the bed and the carpet. There's a musty smell in the room, which might be unwashed sheets or unwashed Shippy or both. The room isn't huge, but the number of hiding places feels, in the moment, infinite: There's the bed, the closet, the chest of drawers, and the suitcases. Twenty minutes feels optimistic.

I start with the closet, which is full of old linens, Grandad's clothes, and an assortment of hats, shoes, and rain jackets. Nothing looks obviously disturbed, but I lift up sheets and towels anyway and dig my hand into each pair of shoes in turn. I check under the bed, under the blankets, in the pillowcases, under the mattress. I go through the chest of drawers, which is filled with towels. It's a whole lot of nothing.

The bedside table is similarly easily dispatched, given it's only big enough for a couple of old Inspector Morse novels and some out-of-date medication for athlete's foot. Gross.

I'm halfway through Shippy's bag, scared of what insights into his personal life I might find, when I hear a noise from the other room. I look at the clock on the bedside table. I'm pretty sure I've still got a good eight minutes to go, but that's assuming Dylan (a) remembers the plan and (b) finds a way to stick to the plan, neither of which is guaranteed.

Cracking the bedroom door to hear better, I listen for the telltale sound of the front door, voices, or a pair of shoes being kicked off. But all I hear is the sound of . . . oh! No no no no no!

I run down the hallway, catching my hip on the bathroom door in my urgency. The floor is wet, water pouring over the lip of the bath too fast for the tiny drain on the floor to keep up. Dumb, dumb, dumb! I turn off the bath and pull out the plug, sloshing more water onto the floor in the process and completely wetting one arm of my terry robe. Brilliant. There are towels under the sink (so many towels in this house for the one person who lived here) and I throw them onto the floor to soak up the damage, which isn't quite as bad as I feared. It's *wet*, but the water seems to be contained to the bathroom, not the corridor outside. If the towels and the drains do their work, it should be presentable by the time everyone gets back in . . . I race into the kitchen to check the timer . . . five minutes. Yikes!

Aunty Bec's bag has a lot of clothes but nothing of note, unless you take an interest in her collection of cute dresses and sweaters, which under other circumstances I might.

Three minutes. I sit on the edge of the bed and scan the room, trying not to panic. The search has been, by any reasonable definition, a failure. If Aunty Bec or Shippy hasn't yet destroyed whatever they took from GG's room, they probably took it with them on the walk. Maybe they even suspected the real reason I wanted to stay behind and are getting rid of whatever it is, possibly while maniacally laughing just to really make the point, while I sit here like an idiot.

Two minutes. I make a half-hearted effort to put the suitcases back the way they were before, although I seriously doubt Shippy is going to remember which shirt was scrunched up in a ball in which corner of the case.

One minute. I'm halfway out the door when my foot catches on a pair of sneakers and I trip, grabbing the doorknob to right myself and cracking my head on the door as I do. Bloody hell, I'm having a night. My hand comes away clean when I hold it against my head, so at least I don't have a gaping head wound

I'll need to explain. Head aching, I pick up the errant sneaker and return it to its mate. The movement dislodges something tucked into the toe of one of the sneakers and a folded piece of paper springs out. It has the look of something that's been folded and unfolded more than once.

The moment I open it, I know that this is what I've been looking for, even if I don't understand right away what it is. Okay, I'm not an idiot, because I know what it is: It's a letter. I just don't understand what it means. Not at first.

The letter is addressed to GG and dated last month. It's from a company called Sure Solutions, which means nothing to me, although the return address shows that it's based in Melbourne. The letter references test results on a sample, but what the sample is or what the test results are I can't tell right away. I take a deep breath to slow my thumping heart and try to read through it more slowly. There's a bunch of numbers, some talk of probabilities, and, *oh crap*, this can't seriously mean that . . .

"What the hell?"

I look up from the spot where I'm kneeling on the floor, letter in my hand, looking as guilty as a puppy sitting next to a puddle. Shippy, wearing an LCD Soundsystem T-shirt and a face full of rage, is standing in the doorway.

19

"I THOUGHT YOU WERE DOWN AT THE DAM."

This is, you don't have to tell me, not a great line. It's not a denial. It's not an excuse. It's straight-up self-incrimination, and I really thought I'd be better than this in a crisis. I'm disappointed in myself.

"I'm back." His face, which normally tends toward blandly benign, is crinkled into an expression that might be anger. It might even be rage. "What are you doing in my room?"

I could point out that this really isn't *his* room and it's really not even *Aunty Bec's* room and if it's anyone's room but GG's it's closer to being my *dad's* room than his, which makes it closer to being *my* room than Shippy's, but of course I don't say any of that because there's still a chance I can just walk away from this.

"Sorry, I was just looking for, uh, a tampon."

This is more like it. Obviously, it makes no sense at all that I'd be looking for a tampon in Aunty Bec's shoe, but I'm operating, for the second time tonight, on the instinct that anything to do with periods makes dudes like Shippy profoundly uncomfortable. I may have failed with Dad, but Shippy seems like a guy who could be brought undone by the phrase "heavy flow."

Except Shippy is either more enlightened about menstruation than I thought (unlikely) or he doesn't believe a word I've said (more likely) because he doesn't seem remotely bothered. Instead he chooses this moment to notice the letter in my hands. His eyes go to Aunty Bec's running shoes, and I know I am more screwed than Ali that time her mum discovered her secret TikTok account. (It was actually super wholesome, dedicated to where to find the best banh mi in Perth, but do you think her mum wanted to hear that?)

"Where did you get that?"

He knows the answer, so I don't bother saying anything. I just stand up and shuffle backward as he comes further into the room, shrinking it instantly. The door is still open, but he's between me and it, and there's a vein in his neck that's suddenly as thick and dangerous as a snake.

"Give it to me." This is not a *pass the salt* or *make us a cup of tea* kind of a request. This is a demand.

Over Shippy's shoulder I can see the empty hallway. Did Shippy come back alone? I desperately want my dad, but I'd settle for Aunty Bec, who, even if she did have something to do with GG's death, surely wouldn't let Shippy actually hurt me. Not like this, anyway. Probably not. Would she?

I try to do something brave, the kind of thing a real girl

detective in a book might do, safe in the knowledge that she's the hero of the story and will definitely survive until the end. (I do *not*, in case it's unclear, possess the same certainty at this stage in the proceedings, but I have to do something.)

"Where did *you* get the letter?"

"None of your business. Hand it over."

"It's not addressed to you."

"It's not addressed to you, either." He has a point.

"You took it from GG's room." That's the sentence that means I can no longer pretend this is an innocent mix-up or a chance encounter. But, really, Shippy's heart-attack face does not give the impression of a man who is willing to give me the benefit of the doubt. The fact that he's here at all suggests he came back on purpose because he was worried about what I might be up to.

"What do you mean?"

"You took it from GG's room."

"No, I didn't."

"I was there."

"No, you weren't." An admission, not that he notices.

"I was under the bed." It's not really possible to say this without sounding like a creep or a weirdo, but I refuse to feel guilty about what was ninety-five percent an innocent coincidence. He takes a few beats to digest this, looking like he's trying to decide whether to deny it and go defensive or get even angrier.

"You were spying on us?" Option B, then.

"Not on purpose."

"Are you seriously going to make me take the letter off

you?" he asks, and his red cheeks are a little more purple than they were before. A spontaneous heart attack still seems like too much to hope for.

"I guess so," I say, trying to sound as tough as John Wayne when he's just come across the baddies, even though I have neither a gun nor a horse to carry me away. (Those old Westerns may be kind of problematic, but they're good at teaching people how to pretend to be brave.)

Shippy takes another step into the room. "Give me the bloody letter, Ruth."

Language, I think but do not say.

I take a step back like a good dance partner might, conscious that I'm getting closer to the wall. If I can get out of this room and out of the house, I think I can outrun Shippy. But there's an *if* in that sentence.

Also, if I do run—*flee* really is the word—I will have set something in motion that can't be stopped. If I run and if Shippy catches me . . . what then?

"What happened to GG?" I ask, stalling. My brain decides now is the perfect opportunity to remind me that Shippy was the only one out of the house long enough to have taken GG's jewelry to Perth. The moment Sasha told us about that jewelry should have been the giveaway: Shippy could easily have made up the whole story about the flat tire and driven to Perth and back. Okay, maybe not *easily*, but he could have done it. Then there's Rob's "accident." Again, too late, it seems obvious that, if anyone tried to kill Rob, Shippy would have to be the prime suspect. He *invited* Rob here in the first place, and if Rob somehow had a suspicion about GG's death, then Shippy—the guy who helped him out by offering him a place to sleep—is the only one of us who might warrant a conversation first instead of going straight to the cops. Maybe Aunty Bec wasn't with him the whole time they were out of the house, like I assumed. If she stopped off at the shops or to get a coffee, it would have been so easy for Shippy and Rob to leave the beach together, for Shippy to come up with a reason for Rob to get out of the car, for Shippy to turn the car around, and . . .

"What are you talking about?" My mind has been free-wheeling to such an extent I can barely remember what I asked Shippy. Luckily, he's quick to remind me. "I don't know anything more about Gertie's death than you do."

This might still be okay, I tell my heart in an effort to slow it down. This isn't yet unsalvageable. I take another step back, even though Shippy hasn't moved. I'm standing beside the bed, and I wonder if I'm fast enough to spring onto the mattress, roll across it, and get up and out the door before Shippy makes it across the room. Unlikely.

"So, what about this letter?" I wave it, still mostly just playing for time, while the part of my brain that isn't frozen with fear comes up with a better plan.

"Give me that."

"Or what?" I ask the question before I realize just how much I don't want to hear the answer.

"Or I'll give you—" he starts to say, but stops when we both hear the same thing: the sound of the front door opening and muffled voices—voices!—from the other room. Abandoning all pretense that, hey, this is just a comical misunderstanding we can definitely joke about later, I shout *"Daaaaaaaad!"* as loudly as I can, which is pretty loud. My throat hurts when I'm done.

My dad is not, as I think I've made clear, a heroic sort. He's more about cracking gags and making snide comments than he is about running into burning buildings. He got robbed on the street once and cheerfully handed over his wallet and phone to the guy robbing him because, as he told me later, who wants to get stabbed over an iPhone 7 with a cracked screen? But when I see him running down the hallway toward me a beat later, he looks as badass as Tom Cruise ever has in any of those dumb movies where he zip-lines off a building or rides his motorbike off a mountain.

"Dad," I say again.

Shippy's vibe changes when Dad makes it to the doorway. Like a window blind has been snapped into place, his regular expression of relaxed indifference is back on, and, while I can still see the rage now that I know what I'm looking for, he looks, more or less, like the Shippy I've always known.

"Ruthie? What's wrong?" Dad pushes past Shippy and comes over to where I'm standing, back flat against the wall, although I wasn't aware of taking that last step. There are more footsteps from the other room, and Aunty Vinka and Dylan appear in the doorway too. Finally I feel myself relax enough to sit down on the bed and open the hand crushed around the letter. (My nails have left half-moon creases on my hand.) "What happened?" Dad asks me; when I just shake my head, he repeats the question to Shippy in a totally different tone of voice that tells me his mind has gone to the obvious Bad Touching place.

"What's happening?" Aunty Vinka asks, looking between Shippy and me like one of us is going to explain.

"Sorry," Dylan pants, a little out of breath, and we're lucky nobody seems to notice his non sequitur and think to ask who he's apologizing to and for what.

"Nothing happened," Shippy says, and he's obviously trying to clear the air, but this is a guilty-as-hell thing to say.

"I'm okay," I say.

Aunty Bec arrives then, her eyes going from Dad's expression to Shippy's obvious discomfort to me, now shivering on the bed. (It's the adrenaline wearing off, I suppose, but it feels pathetic.) Nothing *happened. Nothing* happened.

"What's going on?"

"Nothing happened," Shippy says again, echoing my thoughts while managing to sound incredibly defensive. "I came in here and Ruth was going through my things."

"That's not true." I'm not lying (a pleasant change for me). Yes, technically, I absolutely went through Shippy's things. But he's lying when he said he saw me do it: He's only deducing (correctly) that I went through his stuff in order to find the letter. "I was looking for . . ." I don't know how to end that sentence, so I start a new one: "I found this letter. It's addressed to GG. I think they know something about GG's death."

"Who's *they*?" Dad says, just as Shippy says, "That's bull."

I pass Dad the letter, only letting it go reluctantly, and he smooths it out on the bed.

"I don't know what she's talking about," Shippy says. For the first time since he got here, I look at Dylan and there's a question there, but I can't tell what it is, so I just shake my head, meaning *not now*. Then I look away, because it's going to be easier to say what I have to say without looking at him.

"They took this letter from GG's room," I say, eager to get my story out before Shippy has a chance to tell his.

"Who's *they*?" Dad says again.

"Shippy and Aunty Bec. In GG's room, uh, they found something—I think it was this letter."

"Ruth?" That's Dylan, but I don't look at him. I can't.

"What the—" It's Aunty Vinka, who almost never swears in front of me, even that time Dad nearly severed his thumb with the electric carving knife. (Don't ever use an electric carving knife.)

"What's going on?" Aunty Bec asks like she doesn't know. "What are you saying, Ruth?"

I think about the conversation I heard, trying to get the words right. "I was in GG's room before and I heard Shippy and Aunty Bec talking. And Aunty Bec said something about Shippy making her do something to a sweet old lady." I can't get the sentence *they might have killed her* out while Dylan is looking at me with his saucer-plate eyes. "And they took this letter. I'm not totally sure what it is, but I know *he* wants it." I nod at Shippy.

"We weren't talking about Gertie's death," Aunty Bec says.

"*Bec!*" It's Shippy, looking furious or hurt or a combination of the two.

"It's over," Aunty Bec says, and she sounds tired. "There's no point."

"What were you talking about, then?" I ask.

"We were looking for that letter. We thought that if the cops found it, well, it wouldn't look good for us."

"You are *kidding me*," Dad says loudly, hitting the letter with his open hand, and I know that he's figured it out too.

"What's it say?" Aunty Vinka asks, and Dad passes it to her, looking dazed.

"That's about you?" Dad asks Aunty Bec. She doesn't say yes but she doesn't deny it either, which apparently is all the confirmation Dad needs.

"Is anyone going to tell me what's going on?" Dylan asks, and he might be asking me, but I can't say a thing.

"It's bloody . . . it's *unbelievable* is what it is," Dad says. "You absolute . . . We've got to call the cops. Who has a phone?"

"There's no reception, Andy," Aunty Vinka says very gently, not looking up from the letter. Dad is too angry to look embarrassed.

"We didn't *hurt* anyone," Aunty Bec says.

"Can I see the letter?" Dylan asks, ignored by everyone.

"Debatable," Dad says. "If this isn't a motive for murder, then I've never seen an episode of *Columbo*."

"What's in the letter?" Dylan asks.

"What's *Columbo*?" Shippy asks.

"This can't have been Bec's idea," Aunty Vinka says, mostly to herself, turning the letter over just in case there's an explanation for all of this on the back. (There isn't.)

"Where did you find it?" Dad asks me.

"In Aunty Bec's shoe, but they took it from GG's wardrobe."

"Can *someone* tell me *what's in the letter!*" Dylan sounds ready to explode.

"It's the results of a DNA test," Dad says, possibly because he, like me, fears that Dylan is at risk of winding up splattered around the walls in tiny pieces.

"What does that mean?"

"It means that Shippy and Bec—sorry, Dylan, your mum—are liars."

"What?"

"Bec is *not* our half sister. She was *not* Dad's secret love child, and she is definitely *not* entitled to a share of Dad's—or Gertie's—fortune."

20

IF I COULD, I'D SKIP OVER THE WHOLE NEXT SCENE AND JUST GIVE you the bullet points. It's not that what happens isn't important. (It is.) It's not that it doesn't contain clues to the truth about why GG died. (It does.) It's just that, while this family-drama stuff might read on the page like a helpful information dump, when you live through it and then have to *relive* it, it's kind of a bummer.

We gather in the kitchen because there's too many of us to fit comfortably in Bec (hold the Aunty) and Shippy's bedroom. Nobody seems sure how to act. Is this a confrontation? An intervention? A seriously awkward extended-family get together, not entirely dissimilar to that Christmas lunch when Aunty Vinka's then-boyfriend got drunk and passed out in the bathroom? Aunty Vinka is (massive surprise) making tea from some of her stinky herbal concoctions, while Dad keeps staring at the letter as though the numbers and letters might rearrange themselves to reveal something new.

Dylan won't meet my eyes, but that might be because I'm not trying too hard. Still, every time I sneak a look, he's staring straight at the kitchen cupboards, and they can't possibly be that interesting. It's hard to say whether he's (a) furious with me for ratting out his mum and her shifty boyfriend (likely) or (b) furious at them for, well, being the worst (also likely) or (c) a combination of the two (ding, ding, ding) with a sprinkling of justifiable rage that I didn't say anything earlier. Now is not the moment to ask the only question I really want to ask him: *Did you know?*

"So," Dad says, taking charge because of a lack of reasonable alternative candidates. He's put his chair so close to mine he keeps accidentally banging my ribs with his elbow, but I don't mind. "Which of you wants to tell us what's been going on before we call the cops?"

"There's no—"

"*I will go to the paddock!*"

"Okay, okay."

Aunty Vinka puts a mug of something unidentifiable in front of me, and although it does smell disturbingly like my schoolbag on a Friday afternoon, I take it gratefully because pretending to drink it gives me something to do.

"I'm sorry," Bec says, but it's clearly the kind of sorry-not-sorry apology celebrities make after posting something racist/sexist/transphobic on Instagram, because the next words out of her mouth are "but this is ridiculous."

"What do you expect, Bec? You've been pretending to be my *sister*. That's something a soap-opera character or a crazy person does. Since you're not on a soap opera, I can only imagine that you're a crazy person." I can tell Dad is the kind of furious he usually only gets around election time by the fact that he's using the word *crazy* as an insult—something he always tells me off for doing. The one time I said "this is mental" about an economics assignment, he gave me a ten-minute lecture on mental-health stigma that made me late for tennis practice.

"This isn't about you, Andy."

"Of course it is."

"What do you want from me? I've already said sorry."

"How about you start with why you did it, and we'll decide whether to call the cops."

There's a long pause, during which Bec presumably weighs her options and finds bugger all in the way of graceful exit strategies.

"What do you want to know?"

"Why?"

"It was an impulse. It wasn't planned."

"An impulse to deceive your oldest friends," Aunty Vinka says, and, unlike Dad, she seems to have landed on hurt rather than rage. Perhaps the hurt will come later for Dad, the way I sometimes get super furious when I stub my toe, before the pain really has time to kick in.

"An impulse to make money," Dad says.

"An impulse to *belong*," Bec says. "I don't have any family now Mum's dead."

"You were *already* part of our family," Aunty Vinka says. "You have Christmas with us almost every year."

"It's not the same." Bec looks around, maybe to see how we're taking it. "I'm not even included in the Secret Santa." She says the second bit quietly.

"So this is about wanting to add to your supply of scented candles?" Dad says (and I feel betrayed because I gave him a candle last year).

"Once your dad died and you found that letter, we all knew he had a kid out there somewhere that he'd never met. One night I was thinking about how my life would be different if it was me, and then I thought, *Why not?*"

"Wow," Dad says.

"That kid is never going to be found—they could be anywhere in the world. I'm adopted, and my mum was best friends with your mum. It's not completely impossible to imagine she adopted the child of her best friend's husband and just . . . never told anyone."

"Not impossible, but it didn't actually happen," Dad clarifies, and, man, he is *piiiiissed*.

"I did think that was a pretty cold-blooded thing for your mum to do," Aunty Vinka says thoughtfully. "Not really like her at all. Much more of a Virgo vibe."

"I didn't think it would hurt anyone. My parents are dead. I'm an only child. You wanted to believe me. Don't pretend you weren't happy when you found out it was me."

"It *wasn't* you," Dad says.

"Not technically."

"Not even a little bit. The DNA test you showed us, I suppose that was faked?"

"Yeah."

"How do you fake a DNA test?" Aunty Vinka asks.

Dad and I answer her at the same time: "The internet."

"I'm *sorry*, okay? In a weird way I thought it would make everyone happy. It seemed like the definition of a victimless crime." Bec looks momentarily so glum, so *actually* sorry, that Aunty Vinka reaches across the table and touches her shoulder. She is way too nice, but then she wasn't in GG's bedroom to hear Bec and Shippy going through her stuff. She wasn't in their bedroom when Shippy came home, and she didn't see the way that he looked at me.

Dad isn't buying it. "And the small matter of your inheritance was of no consequence, obviously," he says. "I'm sure you planned to renounce your share of Dad's estate at any moment."

"Is this about me lying or is this about money, Andy?"

"Let's say both. I am curious, though: When did you realize you had to bump off Gertie to get your hands on the money sooner rather than later?" *Way to raise the stakes, Dad.*

"Don't be ridiculous," Bec says. She sounds shocked, but surely she knew this was coming.

"So it's pure coincidence that the one woman who knew you were a fraud, who knew that you'd lied about being her late husband's love child, and who stood between you and a garbage truck full of money, happened to be killed when you were staying in her house?" The sarcasm in Dad's voice is thicker than *War and Peace*.

Teenagers are supposed to disagree with everything their parents say, and usually I do my best, but Dad has a point.

"You think I could *kill* someone?" Bec asks, sounding incredulous. "Honestly?" She looks at Aunty Vinka. "You too?"

Aunty Vinka doesn't say anything, but Dad makes a disgusted sound deep in his throat. Disgusted and a bit disgusting, like there's a lump of phlegm down there he's thinking about hacking up. Rank. "If you can lie about being my sister, you can lie about anything. I think we should call the police."

Shippy decides to enter the chat.

"I don't think that's necessary, mate. What would you even tell them?"

"The truth. They should know that you've been lying to us all and that Gertie found out about it."

"That's only relevant if you think Bec killed Gertie."

"Maybe she did!"

"You can't honestly think that."

"You're using the word *honestly*? To me? Right now?"

"I get that you're angry." Bec's voice has gone a bit conciliatory, which I could tell her is the wrong way to handle Dad. It didn't work when I spilled Coke on his laptop, and it's not going to work now. Dad catches my eye and I see the moment when he remembers I'm hearing every word of this, which is probably enough trauma to keep any future therapist in vacation homes. Plural.

"I'm not angry. I'm *furious*," Dad says. "And, Ruth, I know this all came to light because of you, but I really think you should get upstairs right now."

I look to the court of appeal.

"I suppose she has already heard everything," Aunty Vinka says, but reluctantly. Somehow she and Dad have reversed roles since that first family meeting when we talked about GG's death and she was the one who wanted to send me away. How can that have been only days ago?

"She hasn't heard me bloody murder Bec."

"Try not to say that in front of the police," Aunty Vinka suggests.

Until now I've stayed quiet in the hope of being overlooked. But if Dad is going to kick me out anyway, there's very little downside to saying my bit.

"I heard you in GG's room, remember?" I say this to Bec, because I can't look at Shippy now and maybe I'll never have to again.

"The night she died, you mean?" Bec says. "Yeah, I spoke to GG that night—I already told the police that."

That wasn't what I meant, but now I'm briefly distracted as I try to figure out where that piece of the jigsaw goes. Could Bec have been the person I heard in GG's room while I was going to the bathroom? Definitely. It doesn't mean she didn't kill her, though. And if that was her talking to GG, then where was Dad?

"Not then," I say. "I heard you and Shippy talking in GG's room this morning." I keep my eyes on Bec, ignoring Dylan and Dad, both of whom have gone as tense as an antelope on the Serengeti that's just spotted the tuft of a lion's tail. "You said Shippy had made you do something to GG and you felt bad about it." I'm not sure I've got the words quite right, but it's close enough. You could flick back a few pages and see for yourself, but, trust me, the case doesn't turn on the exact words I heard or didn't hear. It's going to turn on . . . no, no, just kidding, you'll find out soon enough.

"It sounded like you had done something. To GG." I drop my eyes at the last bit because accusing someone of murder is harder than you'd think, and I've always liked Bec. That feeling clearly isn't mutual right now, because Bec gives me a look that somehow conveys deep personal betrayal. Unlike Shippy, she still doesn't give off *capable of murder* vibes. But how many serial killers would last long enough to keep upping the body count if they walked around looking extremely guilty every day of their lives? Jack the Ripper would probably just have been known as Jack the Guy Who Killed That One Sex Worker Before He Got Caught.

"What else did they say?" Dad asks.

"They were looking for the letter and Bec said something about GG being a poor old lady, or maybe it was a nice old lady."

"It's not like that," Bec says. "I was talking about *this*—the DNA stuff. I felt like Shippy had pushed me into it."

"*That's* nice," Shippy says, shaking his head so a couple of his curls fall into his face and stick to his forehead. I don't understand how someone who goes in the ocean every other day can still have dirty hair. Shampoo scientists should be studying this guy.

"*I* said it as a joke. It was you who said we should do it for real."

"Come off it, Bec."

"Guys, save the domestic for when you're in a police cell," Dad says.

"We did not bloody murder anyone!" Bec nearly shouts. She stands up, seems to realize there's nowhere to go, and sits down again, which is embarrassing for her. "Yes, I did a pretty bad thing and, yes, I lied to you all, but I would never hurt anyone and I can't believe you can imagine I would ever have hurt Gertie."

There's a silence that's probably supposed to make us all feel ashamed, but I just use the opportunity to work through some questions in my head.

"When did GG find out the truth?" I ask.

Bec looks like she's going to tell me to get stuffed, but maybe she remembers she's trying to win us over here. It's like when a substitute teacher at school has to deal with a heckler for the first time and they're clearly *so mad* but they have to laugh it off or risk losing the class.

"Gertie said that she got the results a few weeks ago, but she only told me about it on this trip. Shippy and Dylan and I drove down with Vinka and Nick, and that first day Gertie asked to talk to me. She said she knew I wasn't, uh, related and that she'd had a DNA test done."

"How?"

"She'd taken one of my hairs on another visit." Bec looks... what? Impressed? I sure am—I would never have imagined that GG had it in her. "Pretty stealthy, really."

"What made her suspicious enough to go full Angela Lansbury?" Dad asks, and I don't point out that DNA doesn't feature highly in *Murder, She Wrote*, which is a seriously old murder-mystery show that ran forever ago but holds up pretty well if you course-correct for all the casual sexism. (If you're interested, someone uploaded a whole bunch of full episodes to YouTube, and I'm not saying it *wasn't* me.)

Bec chews on her bottom lip like it's a stick of gum. "Are you sure you want to do this now?"

"I'm sure."

"She told me she was going through your dad's papers and she found some more details about the baby that was put up for adoption, which made her think it couldn't have been me."

"*What?*" Dad says.

"There's more than that letter?" Aunty Vinka says.

This—can you tell?—is a legit bombshell. The whole love-child deal only came out in the letter Grandad left behind, complete with a whole *to be opened only in the event of my death* thing. He wasn't scared of snakes, but he was not a brave man, my grandad.

"I don't know whether your dad meant to leave the papers for you with the letter or not," Bec says, anticipating everyone's next question. "Gertie wasn't sure what to do with them, so she gave them to me. She said she didn't want to cause a rift. She said that she would keep my secret if I wanted her to. She said we'd still get an even share in the will."

"What?" Aunty Vinka asks, just as Dad says, "Bull."

"It's true."

"Did she know where the baby is now?" I ask. "I mean, obviously it's not a baby anymore."

"No. The baby really was adopted out, though. I'm not sure why—I think the mum was pretty young." We all take a minute to be disgusted by my late grandad (how young "pretty young" is I both do and do not want to know) before Bec keeps talking. "All I remember is that the baby was called Nicky by the adopted parents and I think they were living here in the southwest, at least for a bit. Green eyes, that was the big one." We all take a moment to look at Bec's brown eyes.

"Can I say something?" Aunty Vinka asks, immediately answering her own question when she goes on. "There's something I want to say." She comes up behind Bec, and I see non-Aunty Bec flinch as actual-Aunty Vinka's free hand lands on her shoulder. "I forgive you." In a rose-pink caftan thing, with her hair wild around her face, Aunty Vinka looks like a hippie from the sixties or someone who pickles her own vegetables and crochets blankets. (Actually, she definitely *does* do both of those things, although the scarf she once crocheted for me was so bad that Mum let me take it to the secondhand shop, and even the lady behind the counter was all "really?" when I handed it over.) "I forgive you," she repeats. Her eyes are half closed, so she probably doesn't see Dad's eye roll.

"Um," Bec says, looking like she's waiting for a *but*.

Aunty Vinka takes a step back and opens her arms. There's a moment when it seems like Bec won't get up, either because she's not the hugging type (she's really not) or because this is all super cringe (it really is), but then she stands up and allows herself to be hugged without giving much back. I look at Dylan in the hope of exchanging *she is too much* looks, but he's now staring at the table like it has insulted his girlfriend (and everyone knows I'm the only one who's been doing that lately).

Aunty Vinka is still talking. "You made a really bad decision and lied to us. But I still love you. You might not be my sister, but you're still family."

She's absolutely not.

"Thank you," Bec says after a slightly-too-long pause. "I appreciate that."

"The thing is," Aunty Vinka says, releasing Bec, "if there's anything else that you want to tell us, now is the time. This is a safe space." This feels like a stretch, given two residents of this *space* have been recently hospitalized and another is dead.

Bec looks unsurprised. This, presumably, is that *but* she was waiting for. "What do you mean?"

Aunty Vinka looks at her toes, which are painted rose pink to match the caftan. "Like with Gertie," she says, and Bec's jaw clenches shut.

"Are you serious?"

"I'm not accusing you of anything. I'm just asking."

"I cannot believe this."

"The police are going to ask." Aunty Vinka is such a spider-under-glass-trapping, oat-milk-drinking, gluten-fearing hippie that I forget sometimes she's also Dad's sister. You don't spend twenty years under one roof without rubbing off on each other, I guess.

Bec pushes her chair into the table, a move that's unnecessary but probably feels pretty good. "Call the police if you want. I have nothing to hide."

"What about fraud?" Dad says. "The police might be interested in that."

Bec makes a noise that's as close to *pfft* as I've ever heard in real life. "The Dunsborough cops aren't going to care whether

I lied about my parents. They want to solve a murder, and the sooner they figure out I had nothing to do with that, the better. Come on." The last two words are delivered to the tops of Shippy's and Dylan's heads.

Seeing Dad's face, she adds, "I'm not making a run for it: I'm going into the bloody garden for one of Shippy's secret bloody cigarettes, and don't even try to tell me you don't have any, Shippy, because I don't want to hear it.

"Dylan?" Bec is looking at her son, who hasn't moved. "Will you come outside?"

He stands up but shakes his head. "You are unbelievable."

"Dylan," she says quietly, "we can talk in the garden."

But Dylan goes the other way: out of the kitchen and toward his bedroom. We all hear the sliding door bang shut, and the only shock here is that we don't also hear the door fall off its tracks and add to the death count.

It's a relief when Bec and Shippy disappear to the garden.

"Are you sure they're okay out there?" Aunty Vinka asks.

"They're not going anywhere without Dylan. Anyway, they don't have a car." Dad turns to me. "Are you okay, Ruthie?"

"I'm okay."

"I'm sorry you had to see all that. I should have sent you upstairs."

"Stop trying to send me upstairs."

"Ruth, you're a kid."

"I'm fourteen."

"What point do you think you're proving?"

"I'm the one who found the letter."

"I realize that."

"You wouldn't even know about Bec's lie without me."

"I also realize *that*."

A little bit of my frustration at being constantly excluded and my disappointment at not having figured out yet who killed GG explodes in my dad's direction. I'm not shouting, exactly, but my voice is loud enough to wake if not the dead, then maybe Rob from his coma.

"I'm just sick of being kept in the dark about everything."

"Ruth, you're . . ." Dad takes a deep, slow breath, and I'm pretty sure he's counting to ten in his head, the way his anger-management book advises. Maybe even twenty. "I know you feel grown-up, and I'm sorry if I didn't give you enough credit for finding that letter."

An apology! Almost unprecedented.

"It's okay."

"Do you think Bec's telling the truth about Gertie leaving her in the will and not wanting to tell any of us about it?" Aunty Vinka asks Dad.

"Bec can be ruthless. But GG *didn't* tell us about the DNA test or any of it, even though she had the opportunity. So . . . maybe?" He looks at me, and I'm just waiting for him to send me away when he says this instead: "What do you think?"

"Me?"

"Yeah. What do you think, Ruth? Don't pretend you don't have an opinion."

I think about the Case of the DNA Letter and what Dad is really asking.

"I think it's possible that Bec and Shippy might have . . . hurt

GG to protect their secret," I say slowly. "Shippy is the only one of us who might have driven GG's jewelry up to Perth. He was also up late the night GG died, at least I think he was—I saw someone smoking in the garden."

Dad and Aunty Vinka swap a look, but I can't tell if it's of the *we need to get this kid to a psychiatrist* variety or if it has more of a *we are impressed despite ourselves* vibe.

"Bec and Shippy were both with Rob at the beach," Dad adds, and it's equal parts alarming and reassuring that his suspicions so closely align to mine. Possibly he's to blame, and not my diet of horror movies and crime novels, for my slightly disturbing brain. "We've only got their word for it that they left him there safe and sound."

"Why would they hurt Rob, though?" Aunty Vinka asks.

"Maybe he knew something about GG's death and they thought he was going to go to the cops," I suggest, feeling emboldened by the one-two combination of Dad's apology and his effort to include me in the conversation.

"But Shippy hadn't even met Rob when GG died," Aunty Vinka says.

"Actually, that's not true," I say. "Shippy said he'd met Rob in town before any of this happened. Rob offered to lend him a surfboard."

"Clever clogs," Dad says, the way he used to when I was learning my times tables.

"What about the whole missing-half-sibling thing?" Aunty Vinka says. "Do you think we'll ever get to meet them now?"

Dad gets a look on his face I recognize.

"That's another thing. Didn't you say Nick grew up in Yallingup, Vinx?"

Aunty Vinka frowns at the apparent change of subject, but with a sick lurch in my stomach, I have an idea of where Dad is going with this.

"What's that got to do with anything?"

"Nicky," Dad says. "Green eyes. Grew up in the south-west."

He waits. I wait. Aunty Vinka waits for more of an explanation. Finally, she gets there on her own.

"No," she says. "Don't be ridiculous."

"It really didn't occur to you?"

"There are a lot of people called Ni—" Aunty Vinka starts to say.

"Who have green eyes?"

"I think a lot of people—"

"*And* grew up in the southwest."

"It's a big place."

"It's not that big."

"He's *Korean,* Andy."

"So Dad's fling was with someone from Korea. Where did those eyes come from, anyway?"

Vinka stands up and starts to collect mugs. "Nick is not my brother, Andy, and this conversation is offensive."

"To you, or Nick, or Korea in general?"

"All three."

"If it makes you feel better, he would only be a half brother."

"He's not even a quarter brother."

"Uh-huh." Dad is, at least partly, playing with Aunty Vinka. Certainly, he seems to be enjoying himself. Aunty Vinka is not.

"There are probably dozens of people in Western Australia called Nick with green eyes, who grew up around here and are adopted."

Dad's face sobers.

"Nick's adopted?"

Aunty Vinka, realizing she's said too much, dumps the mugs into the sink and breezes out the door. "I'm having a bath!" she shouts.

Dad follows her (best-case scenario he's apologizing, but it's hard to say) and I take advantage of the moment to duck out the front door before anyone discovers the pile of wet towels in the bathroom. There's something I need to know.

Bec and Shippy are smoking in the garden, ashing into the lavender plants that wrap around one side of the house. Grandma used to dry the lavender and sprinkle it onto cakes.

"Ruth," Bec says. Shippy's stare should bruise my ribs, but with my family inside, he's lost the power to scare me. Mostly.

"You've come back for round two?"

"*Shippy*," Bec says, the same way she usually says *Dylan*. "What is it, Ruth?"

"I wanted to make sure you're okay," I lie. "I'm sorry." I'm not sure what they think I'm apologizing for—snooping in their room or indirectly accusing them of murdering my stepgrandmother are probably at the top of the list—but it does the trick, if the trick is to make Shippy stop looking like he's trying to decide between the candlestick in the conservatory and the revolver in the library.

"It's not your fault," Bec says, which is the truth, so I'm not giving her bonus marks for being classy in the moment.

"Is Dylan okay?" I ask, which isn't the question I want to ask but is the only one I can manage. Bec doesn't answer.

"Do you think they're going to call the police?" Shippy asks. I shrug, by which I mean *yes, probably* and also *what do you expect?*

"Thanks for checking on us, Ruth, but we're fine," Bec says. It's a polite way of asking me to get lost, but it's just polite enough that I can get away with ignoring it.

"I also wanted to ask something," I say. "Shippy, uh, I know this is a strange question, but were you smoking in the garden the night GG died?"

He gives me a look like he's considering that candlestick-versus-revolver thing again, but just as quickly his eyes slide to Bec and he looks guilty.

"It was a tough day."

"Right, right, that's always the line," she says.

"Staying with *this* family would be tough on anyone. I don't know if you've noticed, but they're a bunch of psychos. They probably all killed Gertie together, like that movie on the train." Bec and I meet each other's eyes, and it's a rare moment when I'm sure we're thinking exactly the same thing: *It was a book first.*

"Sorry, but is that a yes?" I ask.

"Sure. Why?"

"I saw someone smoking out here that night." So Shippy *was* out of bed and out of the house for sure on the night GG died. It would have given him the perfect opportunity to set up the ladder, but if he was planning on killing GG, wouldn't he go out of his way *not* to be seen outside? "Did you tell the cops you were out there?"

Shippy frowns at me, but not like he's angry. "I smoked a cigarette. I didn't kill your grandma."

"My *grandma* died"—quickly I do the math—"eight years ago," I tell him coolly.

"Shut up, Shippy," Bec says. "Ruth, I can see your mind working like it does, but Shippy only didn't mention it because he was trying to keep his smoking a secret from me. For good bloody reason. It's a disgusting habit. Ruth, don't ever start."

"I get it," I say, baffled by the idea that she might imagine that her schlubby boyfriend could make cigarettes appealing in any way.

"It's not like I'm the only one with a secret habit," Shippy says. "There's a bunch of butts in the driveway. In fact, if you're going full junior detective on this one—"

"Is Nancy Drew still a thing?" Bec asks me, clearly trying to take the edge off Shippy's anger. "Or, who's that girl in the TV show? The one where Henry Cavill is her hot uncle or something?"

"—then you should ask Vinka what she was doing taking a cup of tea into Gertie's room in the middle of the night."

I perk up at this. "What?"

"I saw her when I came inside from my smoke. She was going up the stairs."

"You couldn't have seen her go into Gertie's room from downstairs," I point out.

"I didn't see her go in," Shippy says, "but I saw her go up the stairs and then I heard her say something to Gertie and Gertie say something back." He looks pleased with himself. "Now go inside. I don't want to be accused of murdering you via second-hand smoke."

"One more question," I say.

"Oh, c'mon."

I ignore him and direct my question to Bec. This is the real reason I came out here. "Did Dylan know?"

She meets my eyes, and I wonder if I'll know the truth when I hear it or recognize a lie.

"No," she says. And, no, I have no idea if she's lying.

I start to go back inside because Dad is, surely, mere moments away from filing a missing-person report on me and the bathroom mess is probably mostly cleaned up.

"Hold on," Bec says.

"What?"

But then Shippy and I see it too: headlights coming up the driveway. (Lotta unexpected drop-ins for a supposedly remote farmhouse, I've got to say.)

"Seriously?" Shippy says, maybe thinking the same thing.

Bec raises her voice. *"Guys!"* she calls, her voice almost singsong. "We've got a *visitor*!"

21

WHEN SASHA GETS OUT OF HIS TRUCK, MY FIRST THOUGHT IS that he must have heard about Bec, before I realize how little sense that makes. For one thing, I'm not sure he was ever aware Bec was (supposedly) Dad and Aunty Vinka's half sister. For another, everyone who knows about the Situation is here, with no way of communicating with the outside world, short of semaphore, and I think I would have noticed someone up on the roof, thrashing about with flags.

Nobody looks happy to see Sasha, but I'm the only one who's actively rude about it: I bolt inside before he's even slammed the door of his truck.

"Go away," Dylan says when I bang on his door.

"Sasha's here!"

"What?"

"Sasha's here!"

"Why?"

"I don't know! Come on!"

Another pause. "I don't care."

Dylan's room doesn't have a lock, so I slide the door open, forgetting in the moment that I might not want to see what a teenage boy is up to alone in his bedroom. Fortunately for all concerned, what he's up to is scowling into his phone, which—in case you've forgotten—doesn't even have internet access. This is too tragic.

"Come on."

"I'm not coming."

"Are you going to sit here stewing about your mum lying to you and your girlfriend cheating on you, or are you going to find out why Sasha is here?"

That sounded better in my head.

But it works, because Dylan rolls off his bed and follows me back to the kitchen, although he makes a big deal of not sitting next to me.

"Ruth," Dad says, "do we think it's your bedtime?"

"We do not," I say. Then I add: "Please?"

Sasha is wearing the same clothes as this morning, but he's added an ugly sheepskin coat over the top of it.

"Thanks," he says, accepting a glass of water from Aunty Vinka, who is sporting a bathrobe and wet hair. "I can't stay long. I've just been struggling with something all day."

"Long division," Dad says, right into my ear so only I can hear it. I would laugh, but, as I keep telling Dad, nobody needs to know how to do long division anymore: That's why we have calculators. (He tried to show me using paper and pen once and it was like watching someone experience a psychotic break in real time.)

"What is it?"

"There's something I probably should have told you all about Gertie."

I know what you're thinking because it's what I'm thinking too: Is Sasha about to confess to killing GG? Unfortunately not, although wouldn't that be handy? For one thing, we've got a hundred or so pages to go here, so a murderer reveal would be a little premature. For another, Sasha's demeanor is all wrong for a mea culpa: He's a little apologetic, but not in a *sorry I murdered your relative* kind of way. Finally, while I've been keen to suspect the mysterious neighbor from the start, it's hard to see what he might gain from GG's death, unless he secretly seduced her in order to get name-checked in the will. It's a possibility, I guess, but ew, no.

"How much do you know about her condition?"

"Her illness, you mean?" Aunty Vinka asks.

"Yeah."

"Not much. She had medicine." Aunty Vinka waves one hand in the direction of the fridge, which, since Sasha can't possibly have any idea what she's flapping her wrist at, is probably more confusing than enlightening.

"It was serious," Sasha says, and his tone matches the words. "She was very sick."

"Oh."

"I told her she should tell you, but you know what Gertie was like: She never liked to bother anyone."

Dad and Aunty Vinka look at each other. I can see the word *seriously?* in a speech bubble over their heads.

"Are you saying Gertie was dying?" Bec asks.

"I think so, yes," Sasha says—apologetically, like GG's not already dead and his words might finish her off.

"Did you tell the police about Gertie being ill?"

"The police didn't really interview me." (I'll tell you right now, they should have.)

"What difference could it make?" Shippy asks. "Unless her illness involved a bad case of bashius brainius, Gertie didn't exactly die of natural causes."

"Shippy."

"The police will find out when they do an autopsy anyway," Dad says.

"Why would they do that?" Aunty Vinka asks. She sounds genuinely shocked.

"I think it's pretty standard in cases of violent death. Although, in fairness, most of my medical knowledge comes from *CSI* and Patricia Cornwell novels."

"But it's obvious how she died," Aunty Vinka says. "Why would they do an autopsy?"

Bec either doesn't hear Aunty Vinka or doesn't care for her question because she asks another one, more loudly. "Do you know how long she had?"

"Gertie?"

"Yeah."

"I don't know." Sasha looks down at his hands, which are big but look smoother than you'd expect from someone who presumably has to handle machinery and . . . till the field, or whatever it is farmers do now that they have automated tractors and drones. "The impression I had was that she was trying to tie up loose ends, get her affairs in order."

We all sit with that for a bit, wondering how (and why) GG got through the weekend without telling us any of this. Nobody would have called GG an oversharer, but concealing a terminal condition is next-level undersharing.

"There's another thing," Sasha says.

Isn't there always?

"Did she ever talk to you about her son?"

"A bit," Dad says. "He died before Gertie met our dad."

"Her son is still alive," Sasha says, delivering this knockout line with the gravity it deserves, by which I mean Darth Vader breaking the news to Luke Skywalker.

Dad, Aunty Vinka, and Bec all sputter out versions of "What?" and "Sorry?" and "Are you kidding me?"

"Her son is alive. That's what she told me."

"I thought Gertie's son was dead," Shippy says, two beats behind as usual.

"That's what she told everyone," Sasha says. "She was ashamed of him. He went to prison years ago, and she pretty much disowned him."

"That's so sad," Aunty Vinka says. She's right, but *sad* is not the word I'd have used. Not when a new suspect has entered the field.

"It was a long time ago. I think she regretted it, but she didn't know how to undo it."

"She never canceled the life-insurance policy," Aunty Vinka says. "She must have still cared about him, deep down. Don't you think?" I'm more tolerant of Aunty Vinka's tendencies than Dad, but even I feel like this might not be the time for a group-therapy session.

"Gertie's lawyer said they had no death certificate for her son and that she was still paying the premiums on her life insurance," Dad says. "I assumed it was a living-in-denial thing and maybe some slack filing by the insurer."

"There's one thing I don't get," Shippy says, understating reality significantly. "Why did Gertie tell *you* all this stuff? No offense, mate, but it seems odd to be going around confiding in some random neighbor and not in her own family." Everyone is too distracted by this surprisingly valid question to mention that at no point has Shippy himself legitimately been part of GG's "own family."

Sasha shrugs, and he looks, in that moment, like exactly the kind of guy in whom you'd confide your secrets. He's not smiling, but somehow his dimples are popping and he exudes the judgment-free vibe of a school psychologist who has seen it all and no longer has the ability to be shocked. Is it possible he's even making that stupid sheepskin coat work?

"Maybe it's easier to confide in someone who isn't family," Aunty Vinka suggests.

"That," Sasha says, "but also, something happened."

"What?"

"Gertie's son was getting out of prison. She asked my opinion on what she should do if he came here."

"Oh." Dad's mouth is a perfect circle. "Do you mean . . . was she worried about it?"

"She was nervous."

"Have you told this to the cops?"

"Like I said, the police never interviewed me. Plus, I wasn't sure Gertie would have wanted me to. The police haven't asked you about any of this?"

"Did the son ever show up here?"

"Not as far as I know." Sasha stands up. "I'm sorry for the interruption but thought you should know. Look, I have to go, but do you mind if I use the bathroom quickly?"

"What does this mean?" Aunty Vinka asks when Sasha's gone, lowering her voice in case he can hear from all the way down the hall and behind a closed door.

"Gertie knows how to keep a secret," Dad says grimly.

"I can't believe she never told us," Aunty Vinka says.

"Do you think Dad knew?"

"She *must* have told him."

"What do you think the son was in prison for?" Shippy asks. "If it's murdering someone with a typewriter, surely this is case closed."

"Shippy."

"I'm just saying, if it's a choice between us and some hardened criminal—probably an addict—the cops aren't going to be looking at us, are they?" When nobody answers, he gives a smug *I've made my point* look. "I'm going to the upstairs bathroom for a slash," he says, offering information no one asked for. He leaves the room and we all hear his yelp as he runs into Sasha.

"Sorry, mate."

"My fault. Just having a—"

Sasha comes into the room, pink-cheeked after his collision with Shippy.

"I don't know if the police know about Gertie's son," Sasha says, having quite obviously overheard our conversation (so maybe Aunty Vinka was right to worry). "But I wanted you to know."

Dad walks Sasha to his truck. When he comes back in, it's to send me to my room.

"We're not going to talk about this?"

"It's late," he says. "So, no. You too, Dylan."

My protestations are mostly knee-jerk at this point, because I want to be alone with my thoughts to consider everything we've learned: Bec is no longer my aunt! I have a criminal for a step-uncle! (Is that a thing?) Both of them had a motive to kill GG! Then there's the fact that GG was dying, which means there was no real reason for anyone to kill her, since she was going to die soon anyway.

I try to think this all through logically, scared that I'll drop the threads if I leave it till the morning. But exhaustion is all over me the moment I pull the blanket up, dragging me into mushy unconsciousness and what I hope is a dreamless sleep. It's just as I'm about to go under that a couple of rebel synapses fire off to remind me of the most important point: Nobody in my family seemed to know that GG was dying. Which means that everyone's collective motive remains intact and someone might simply have made a terrible miscalculation.

22

THERE'S A WOODPECKER OUTSIDE MY WINDOW.

Except . . . are there even woodpeckers in Australia? I've always thought of woodpeckers as existing only in American novels, where people get lost in the woods and there are bears to worry about instead of snakes. Certainly, I wish this one would go back to living in a fictional world and leave me alone when I'm trying to stay in my dream, which involved me playing in the Australian Open against Rafael Nadal (which, yes, I realize, makes no sense on a number of levels). I close my eyes, but the woodpecker is getting louder, and is it . . . talking? It's at this point I have to say farewell to Nadal and the cheering crowd and admit there is no woodpecker outside my window but instead somebody knocking on my door, with a frequency and power that suggests they're going to have bruised knuckles if I don't get out of bed soon.

I reach automatically for my phone to check the time and remember that I still haven't found it. How is that even possible in a house this size?

"Who is it?" I call.

"It's Dylan." He immediately opens the door, dramatically shielding his eyes. "I'm coming in."

"I see that."

"Get up, we're going into town."

"What?" I'm less surprised by the idea than by the fact that Dylan seems to be talking to me again, like nothing even happened, after last night.

"We've got to get out of this house." Dylan looks more awake than usual, with shower-damp hair and a T-shirt I haven't seen before, with what I'm pretty sure is a Pokémon on it. He sees me looking at it. "They're back," he says.

"Did they ever leave?" I mean it seriously, but he takes it for sarcasm.

"Shut up. Get out of bed. Your dad's giving us a lift into town."

"What?"

"Stop saying *what*. Your dad said we could go with him but only if we're ready in, like, ten minutes, and I hate to say it but he said that fifteen minutes ago."

"Do you want me to come?" I don't add the important bit: *Since I helped expose your mum and her boyfriend as huge liars and maybe prime suspects in GG's murder.*

"Yes."

"Why's Dad going into town, anyway? What time do they have to go into the police station?"

Dylan ignores the questions and lobs a dress from the floor at my head. "See you downstairs in five minutes."

I make it in four. So *there*.

"I thought you said town was just for tourists," Dad says into his rearview mirror.

"We *are* tourists. Also, we want to get out of the house."

"You sure you don't just want to check your messages and your TikTok?"

"Dad, I'm not on TikTok."

"I thought all teenagers had to be on TikTok. I thought there was a law."

"It's very loud."

"That's supposed to be my line."

"She's a lurker," Dylan says, a genuine betrayal. I forgot I'd told him that.

"What does that mean?"

"Exactly what it sounds like."

"Anyway." I talk over them both. "I think I've lost my phone."

"That's a shame," Dad says.

The phone's been missing since yesterday, and frankly, neither Dad nor Dylan seems as upset as they should be by this devastating development. I don't say it to them, but I can't quite get away from the idea that someone has taken it. The passcode protecting it is the year of my birth (I know, I *know*), which wouldn't exactly require an elite team of code breakers to solve. But why anyone would want access to my stupid texts and a series of embarrassing selfies in which I try and fail to master a smoky eye, I can't imagine. Or maybe I just don't want to.

We slow as the traffic backs up: SUVs full of Perth people, here to visit the allegedly famous bakery (it's only fine), shop in the general store (it's gone hipster chic), and pay six dollars for a lettuce at the supermarket.

"What are you getting in town?" I ask Dad.

"Bakery and supermarket run. If we're not leaving, we need fresh food. Plus: tampons for your aunt."

"Too much information, Dad."

"It's a natural bodily function, *Ruth*." He tilts the rearview mirror to give me a look. "How are those cramps, by the way?"

The mention of Aunty Vinka reminds me of something. Also, Dad's crack at my (fake) cramps feels unnecessarily loaded with suspicion and I'm keen to change the subject.

"Dad, weird question, but did Aunty Vinka go up to GG's room the night she died?"

"I don't know. Not that I know of." Dad's distracted, looking for a parking spot, or he'd be more suspicious about why I'm asking. "Why?"

"No reason."

"Ruth, you remember what I said about leaving this to the cops, right?" Okay, so maybe he's not that distracted.

"Yes, Dad. I just, uh, Shippy said something about her taking GG a cup of tea. Anyway, how much longer *are* we staying here?"

"The police want to interview us again today and Detective Peterson asked us to stay a day or two. I'd say tomorrow at the earliest, but we'll see."

"Do the police need to talk to me, too?" Yes, of course I'm having visions of swapping theories with Detective Peterson, culminating in her begging me to drop out of school early to join the police force, but what of it?

A parking spot opens up and Dad's focus switches to not sideswiping either of the Range Rovers hemming us in. We squeeze out of the car and Dad looks at his watch.

"Synchronize watches and meet back here in, what, an hour?" I wave my naked wrist at him. "Synchronize your phone, then. Okay, sorry, Ruth—synchronize Dylan's phone. Look, I don't care what you do. Just be back here at ten-thirty."

I wait until Dylan and I are alone to ask: "So, where should we go?"

"What about the library?"

"Do you even have a Dunsborough library card?"

Dylan is looking smug about something. "I thought we could talk to Laura."

"Laura?" The name sounds familiar, but I don't get there before Dylan fills me in, which I hate.

"My mum said she was a friend of GG's, remember? I thought maybe she'd know something about . . . well, I'm not sure, exactly, but something relevant?"

"That's not a terrible idea."

"I know."

"Have you ever heard of self-deprecation?"

"Of course not, I'm a moron."

"I see what you did there."

It doesn't take long to find the library, where a woman with LAURA pinned over one boob is handily right behind the desk.

Laura's way younger than I expected, not GG's age but late twenties, maaaaaybe thirties if she's hard-core about using SPF 50. She's too cool to work in a library, too, with a hi-top fade haircut and a nose ring worn where you'd put it on a bull.

"Excuse me?"

"How can I help?"

I wait for Dylan to step in but he just gives me a *go on* look, like we're kids again and Mum's sent us to the shop to buy our own ice creams. (Dylan never wanted to be the one to pay.)

"My name's Ruth. I know this is a strange question, but are you the Laura who knew my, uh, Gertie McCulloch?"

Laura's smile goes on quite a journey, from polite to genuine and then (don't ask me how her lips pull this off) melancholy.

"Ruth! Of course. Gertie told me about you. Poor Gertie. I'm so sorry for your family." She looks expectantly at Dylan.

"I'm Dylan. I'm a family friend."

"I like your T-shirt."

"Yours too."

That's when I notice Laura is also wearing a Pokémon T-shirt. (Seriously, *are* Pokémon cool or did Dylan just get lucky?)

"We heard that you were friendly with Gertie?" I say.

"That's right. She used to come in here a bit. She was great."

I avoid the temptation to ask what a cool librarian and a twice-widowed geriatric lady might find to chat about, but only just.

"We're trying to find out anything we can about Gertie to understand, I guess, why someone could have killed her.

She didn't talk about many friends, so we thought maybe you might know something?"

I'm floundering like a two-year-old in the deep end. We should have rehearsed this.

Laura frowns, looking genuinely concerned. (Fair enough, too.) "You're wondering if *I* know anything about Gertie's death?"

"Not like that," I say quickly, in case she thinks I'm accusing her of getting handsy with the typewriter. "I just mean, GG used to come in here a lot. Did she ever say anything about, uh, her health or her . . . family?"

"We talked about books, mostly. We were both into mystery novels."

"Anything else?"

"That's a pretty broad question."

"Did she ever talk about her health?"

"Not really."

"What about her family?"

There's a pause before Laura answers. "Sure. Like I said, she told me all about you and your grandad."

"Did she talk about her son?"

"She talked about him a bit."

"What did she tell you?"

"You know he died?"

"That's what Gertie said."

Laura gives me an impatient look. "Why don't you tell me what you want to know?" she asks.

"Did she tell you her son is still alive?"

"You found out about that, huh?" Dylan and I just nod. "I never really got whether she was ashamed because he was in prison or ashamed because she'd told everyone he was dead. Either way, it just seems so ridiculous, right?" We make non-committal noises. "I guess it's a generational thing because, like, who around here doesn't have a relative who's been done for dealing?"

I ignore the part of me that wants to ask about Laura's relative who has presumably been done for dealing. "Was Gertie's son in jail for drugs?"

"I don't know. But he was in there for a while."

"What's his name?"

"I don't think Gertie ever said. Or, if she did, I forgot."

"Do you know what he looks like?"

Laura frowns. "No."

"Did you know he was out of prison?"

The surprise on Laura's face looks genuine. "No. Is he?"

"Yeah. We think so."

"Did Gertie know?"

"Yeah."

"I'm surprised she didn't tell me. Although I have just got back from Bali." (I noticed the tan but entirely missed the opportunity to do a Sherlock Holmes bit where I inferred the location of her recent vacation because of it, combined with the fact that her Pokémon T-shirt is a cheap Balinese knockoff, not legitimate merch, which is a bummer, just quietly.)

"I told Nicola this, by the way."

"Who's Nicola?"

"Detective Peterson."

"The police know Gertie's son is still alive?"

"Sure, I thought they should."

A man holding a stack of books lines up politely behind us and Laura's eyes flick over my shoulder. We don't have long.

"Did she ever tell you about a life-insurance policy to benefit her son?" Dylan asks, and the customer's head performs an eavesdropper's tilt. *Way to be subtle, guy who should be using the self-checkout.*

"No. Did she have one?"

"We only found it after she died."

"She never mentioned it." Laura nods at the waiting customer. "Now, I'm afraid I'd better serve this gentleman."

"Okay, thanks."

We've already turned to go when Laura says, "Wait!" and the customer's book stack wobbles as he pretends he wasn't ready to take our place anyway. "There is one thing that was a bit weird."

(This is going to be good, right? You know it's going to be good because that's how it works in detective stories—the best stuff always comes when a suspect or a witness tells the detective *just one more thing*.)

"What?"

"Gertie was in here a few weeks ago. It was my last shift before Bali, so I remember. She said something about carrying a lot of cash on her. She'd just been to the bank."

"How much is a lot?"

"She didn't say, and I didn't ask, but she was nervous about carrying that much cash around, so I assumed it was at least hundreds."

"Did she say what it was for?"

"No, it was a busy day. I don't know if it's even relevant, but it was out of the ordinary." Laura turns to the man and motions for him to come forward. "Thanks for waiting, Michael." Our interview is over, and Michael has some C-grade gossip to take home.

"What do you think?" Dylan asks as we walk out of the library together.

"It's starting to sound like we've got some criminal mastermind son running around with the perfect motive."

"Can he be a mastermind if he got caught?"

"Is that the point?"

Dylan looks sideways at me. "Why do you look kind of depressed about this?"

"It's just, you know, up to the police now, isn't it? They've known this whole time about GG's son being alive. I wonder why they never told us."

"So thoughtless of the police not to keep the teen detectives up to date."

"Don't be like that."

"Cheer up," Dylan says, checking his phone. "This is good news. If the son did it, it means Shippy and my mum are in the clear." He says it in this awful faux-casual way that might fool someone who didn't know him or who had recently suffered a traumatic head injury, but nobody else.

"Dylan," I say, pausing in the hope he'll jump in and I won't have to figure out the second half of the sentence. When he doesn't, I go on, tapping his arm to make him stop and face me. "I'm sorry. You know I didn't mean to . . ." *Didn't mean to . . . what, exactly? Where am I going with this? I didn't mean to imply your mum might be responsible for GG's death? I didn't mean to reveal your mum as a grifter?* "I didn't mean to hurt anyone. I like your mum." There's no point pretending I liked Shippy, even before I thought he might be a murderer.

"Forget it," he says. "What about the money Gertie was carrying around? That seems like it could be important. Maybe she was being blackmailed?" The subject change is a little clumsy but I appreciate it.

"Sure, but don't blackmailers tend to be the ones that get murdered, not the other way around?"

"If you're going to bring logic into it."

"I wonder how much money was a lot to GG."

"We didn't find any cash in her room." Dylan's phone beeps and he checks it again, frowning. "I guess the police might have found some. Do you really think Gertie's own son could have come to find her and killed her?"

"He's got a better motive than anyone."

"Money and revenge for the mum who disowned him, you mean?"

"Exactly."

"I wonder what he went to prison for."

"It's got to be bad. Nobody gets disowned for unpaid parking fines."

Neither of us says the *M*-word.

"How old would he be?"

"I guess our parents' age, give or take."

"We've got some time to kill before we meet your dad. Let's do some internet research while we've got coverage. It might bring up something?"

It doesn't. Or, rather, Googling *McCulloch* and then *McCulloch + jail* brings up a lot of somethings, none of which appear to be related to GG or recent events. It feels wrong in the circumstances, but we actually have fun, sitting on a bench and eating jam doughnuts that Dylan buys. When we get tired of our useless attempts at research, we head to the secondhand bookshop.

"This might be my favorite part of this whole vacation," Dylan says, browsing the fantasy aisle, a small but growing stack of maybes next to him.

"Can you call it a vacation if someone gets murdered?"

"I think it still counts."

"D'you remember when my mum would bring us here at Christmas and let us each pick a book?"

"Of course. I used to wish I was part of your family. Just like my mum, I guess."

"And then you were." I hate this dumb thing I've said before I've finished saying it.

"And then I was not—again," Dylan says lightly.

It's then that I say the even dumber thing, in a failed effort to make Dylan forget that first dumb thing I said. Seriously, I'd take this part out if I wasn't committed to giving you all the facts, because you're going to die when you read it in three... two... one...

"At least we're not cousins anymore, so that's cool."

At least. We're not. Cousins. Anymore. So. That's cool.

There's truly only one way to interpret a comment like that and it's this: *I sometimes think about kissing you, so isn't it a lucky thing we're not related?* Dylan looks at me like he doesn't know where to start. Then he puts down the Garth Nix book he's holding and takes a step toward me, over in the mystery section trying not to vomit.

"Ruth," he says.

"Kids! I thought I might find you here." It's Dad, making the bookshop door jangle. His arms are full of paper bags, he smells like jam and sugar, and there's a suspicious crusting of white around his lips that suggests he's either started on the baked goods without us or developed a worrying drug problem (and also, maybe, doesn't know how to do drugs?). "What are you guys up to?"

"Nothing," we say, the way guilty people always do.

23

THE CAR RIDE HOME IS EXCRUCIATING. I'M SO DESPERATE TO avoid looking at Dylan that I deliberately provoke Dad into one of his favorite rants: why bakery vanilla slices (he insists on calling them "snot blocks") aren't what they used to be. The drive home is only twenty minutes and Dad can go on about custard-to-pastry ratios for twice that, so I'm not worried about awkward silences until he pulls into a gas station.

"I'll just fill up and then we can go home," Dad says.

Something occurs to me, probably later than it should have. "Don't you have to go into the police station?"

He shakes his head. "I called Detective Peterson in town and she said they'll come out to the house instead."

"Right." I want to prolong this conversation to avoid being alone with Dylan, but there's really nowhere to go.

"So," Dylan says when Dad is busy with the pump.

I jump in before he can come up with the second word in that sentence, twisting around in my seat to face him in the back.

"Can I ask you something?"

"Clearly, you just have," Dylan deadpans.

"Aren't you a bit young for dad jokes?"

"What is it, then?"

"You didn't *know*, did you?" I don't need to add *about your mum and Shippy*. I've already had the answer from Bec and I believed her. I think. Mostly. But I want to hear it from Dylan, and having *this* excruciating conversation is better than finishing the one we started at the bookshop.

"No," he says, without jokes. He doesn't even seem pissed off.

"Sorry to ask."

"I get it. We should be able to talk about this stuff if we're proper partners in crime. No, wait, that's the term for people doing the illegal stuff. Detectives in crime? That's not right either. There's a word for it, right? What do you call the two guys in a buddy-cop movie?"

"Cops?"

"Shut up."

"Buddies?"

"You know what I mean. And, just in case you're wondering: I know my mum would never hurt anyone."

"What about Shippy?"

"Straight-up psycho." We both crack a smile and I decide to just jump right back in and pretend the bookshop awkwardness never even happened (which maybe he didn't even notice and so, essentially, it didn't?).

"One thing I keep thinking about is how weird it is that GG was killed on the night that we were supposed to be back in Perth. Like, if Shippy—just for the sake of argument—did want to kill her, then why would he wait until *that* night? He didn't know Nick was going to try to catch that snake, so he didn't know we'd have to stay. He shouldn't have even been here. And if it was an outsider, like GG's son, is it just a coincidence he did it on the night we were supposed to have left?"

"Maybe whoever did it knew we were leaving. Maybe they'd been waiting for us to leave," Dylan says. We both sit with that for a beat, trying to unpick what it might mean. "There's another thing I wanted to ask you," he says, and my paranoid mind immediately leaps to my bookshop humiliation, so it's a relief when he goes on. "What was that about Vinka going up to GG's the night she died?"

"Oh, that. Shippy said Aunty Vinka took a cup of tea up to GG on the night she died."

"Is that it?"

"Aunty Vinka didn't tell us. Why would she keep it a secret?"

"Why wouldn't she? She might not have thought it was important."

"It's suspicious."

"How?"

"GG died that night."

"She didn't die from a cup of tea, Ruth." Dylan's voice sounds spiky, and his face has gone a little blotchy.

"What's wrong?"

"You're just . . ." His lips twist around like he's trying to find a nice way to say something not so nice. "You're just very quick to believe the worst in people."

"What does that mean?" It's not that he's wrong, but I sort of thought that was why we got along.

"My mum. Your aunt. Who are you going to suspect next—me?"

I look at him in surprise. "I thought that's what we're doing here. I thought this was about trying to figure out what happened, and I'm just being realistic. Until we learned about the existence of GG's son, the most likely scenario was that someone in the house killed GG, and the only people in the house were us. I don't want to believe it, but it's ridiculous not to admit that it's a possibility."

Dylan looks out the window, then down to the phone in his hand, which is lighting up with WhatsApp notifications. "I know, it's just . . . this doesn't seem so fun anymore. Does it?"

"Did I ever say it was fun? You're the one who *just* said this little excursion was your favorite part of the trip."

"You seemed like you were enjoying it."

"I'm just trying to keep my mind off my dead grandmother."

"Step-grandmother."

"That's my line. Also, you were the one who wanted to come into town and track down Laura. Then I say Aunty Vinka took GG a cup of tea and suddenly you're all over me."

"Sorry." Dylan looks uncomfortable. "It's not really about that."

"What is it, then?" When he doesn't answer, I put my hand on the door handle, ready to escape inside to peruse the gas-station candy selection with Dad.

"Wait, don't go. It's just, ugh, I don't know how to tell you this but I feel like I have to."

"You have to . . . what?"

"Tell you something."

"And that something is?"

"I'm sure it's nothing."

"Dylan. I swear . . ."

"I overheard your dad talking the other night."

"Okay?"

"I think he's having money problems."

"What do you mean?"

"Money problems. As in not enough of it. He was talking about selling the house, that's what I heard. Do you know about this?" My face clearly tells him that I don't. "I'm only saying this, you know, in the interest of considering all suspects." This is payback for daring to suggest Bec as a suspect, whatever Dylan says.

"What did he actually say?"

"Your dad?"

"Yeah."

"He said something like how the inheritance couldn't have come at a better time, but that he would still sell the house, something like that."

"Sell the house?"

"That's what he said."

"He's fine. We're fine." I try to think if this is actually true. Dad's never mentioned money being tight except, well, now that Dylan's being a jerk and making me think about it, Dad did say something about canceling our streaming services, although he's always threatening to do that, and he did sell one of his guitars, although he just said it was because he didn't play enough. He's definitely still going to work, and I'm pretty sure he's not sitting in a park for eight hours. He'd never have the patience.

"I'm just telling you what I heard."

"There's no way my dad had anything to do with this, okay. Just none."

"I'm not saying he did."

"You're paying me back for suggesting your mum was involved."

"That's not what I meant. Look, maybe we should just leave it to the cops. This whole son thing probably means we're all off the hook anyway. The cops will find this guy and we'll be in the clear."

There's another theory that's been bouncing around in my head that I haven't yet shared with Dylan, but I'm not sure if now is the time. It takes me a moment to decide whether Dylan and I really are a team, or if I'm going to treat him the way all fictional amateur sleuths treat their sidekicks and leave him in the dark until the last possible moment.

I go for option A, even if Sherlock would disapprove. "Has it occurred to you that Shippy is around the right age to be GG's son?" I see right away that it has not.

"That's crazy. We would know."

"Would we?"

"Shippy's been going out with my mum for years."

"Maybe GG's son's been secretly out of prison for years."

"Gertie would have recognized him, and why would they keep it a secret?" Dylan's pissing me off a bit, making multiple good points today.

"What about Nick, then?"

"What about him? Why would you think he could be Gertie's son?"

"I don't, I'm just saying he's the right age, and if we think GG's son had a motive to kill her..."

Dylan shakes his head. "Nick's one of the few people who couldn't have done anything. He's been in the hospital this whole time—he couldn't be involved. Plus, not to be weird about it, but wasn't Gertie's husband white?"

"Okay, good point." Another one? *This guy.* Still, my mind is full of scenarios in which Nick, faking his injuries, could have slipped out a window or through a back door, or Shippy, still assumed by GG to be in prison, has multiple facial surgeries so GG can no longer recognize him, then spends years getting closer to the family in order to...

"I don't know—" But I never do get to hear one of the many things Dylan doesn't know, because a burst of static and a beep from the car audio system make me jump. A voice is coming out of the speaker like a ghost in a Victorian horror story.

"... outrageous. How can you ask me that?" It takes me a beat to recognize Aunty Vinka's voice coming through the car speakers. "Hello? Andy?" Out the car window, I see Dad with his phone pressed against his ear (surely a total safety hazard?) heading back to the car. His phone call has been picked up by the car system. It's not the first time it's happened, but it's never been this... juicy? "You can't just accuse me of, what, trying to *drug* Gertie with her own medication?"

I watch Dad pull the phone away from his ear to glare at the screen. His lips are moving but I can't hear a thing.

Then the driver's door opens and Dad gets in, chucking a

bag of Licorice Allsorts onto my lap just as Aunty Vinka tries one more time. "Andy?" Dad's face makes it obvious that he's figured out what happened.

"Sorry, Vinka, I lost you for a second there. I'm in the car with the kids now, though."

"Oh." Aunty Vinka's voice smooths out immediately. "Sorry. Hi, kids. We can talk about this later, Andy."

"Sure," Dad says, hanging up. "So," he says to me, "how much of that did you hear?"

24

THINGS GO TO HELL SOON AFTER WE GET HOME.

You didn't miss anything in the car. If you're imagining for a moment that I'm fade-to-blacking over a heart-to-heart with Dad and Dylan in which we pool our suspicions and really bond over how messed up it is to speculate on whether your family members could be killers, you don't know my dad.

He refuses to answer any questions about what he and Aunty Vinka were talking about. Dad's official line is that I should be asking Aunty Vinka these questions, and then, when he finally gets pissed off with us, he says, "Gertie didn't die of an overdose, kids," in this really patronizing way, like the time I was ten and asked why he didn't have an iPad when he was young. Maybe he doesn't even realize that his choice of words has confirmed my suspicion.

When we get home, Dad makes a big show of calling everyone into the living room for a family meeting, and I'm pleasantly surprised when I (briefly) think it's about the whole

Vinka/drugs/tea thing. Instead he wants to discuss what they're all going to tell the police. Comparing notes ahead of a police interview is, I'm fairly sure, exactly what the police do not want possible witnesses to/suspects in a murder/attempted murder to do, but this is one conversation Dad can't exclude me from, so I sit down and wait for the revelations to start.

"I think we should tell the detective about Bec," Dad says, in a voice that suggests he's primed for someone to object. Bec and Shippy are sitting right next to him—grumpy but present—so this is kind of a ballsy thing to say.

But it's not Bec or Shippy who reacts. It's Dylan.

"You can't do that."

"Dylan," Bec says. "It's okay."

"You can't tell the police what Mum did," Dylan says. "It's got nothing to do with Gertie or Rob, but the cops aren't going to know that, and it makes her look so dodgy."

"Dylan, this isn't your choice," Dad says. "We'll tell the police the facts, but it's up to them how to deal with them. I'm raising this now so Bec can be the one to tell them the truth, instead of getting herself into more trouble."

"That's so kind of you, Andy," Bec says with such perfect sarcasm that it's hard to believe she and Dad really aren't related.

"I'm sure your mum has nothing to worry about," Dad says to Dylan, ignoring Bec.

"You're trusting the police to do the right thing? Sorry, aren't you a journalist?" Dylan says.

"Once the police have the facts, we can leave it in their hands." Dad's got his professionally sympathetic voice on but has unwisely added a dash of *I'm the grown-up,* which is never going to work with Dylan.

Sure enough . . .

"If you tell them about Mum, I'll tell them about your sister."

Who knew Dylan had it in him, right? There's a pause, while maybe we all try to remember just how many sisters Dad has these days (only one, in case you've lost track), and then everyone looks at Aunty Vinka. She gets it right away.

"What do you mean?" Dad asks, although he must get it too.

"I'll tell them about Vinka giving Gertie a drugged cup of tea on the night she was killed." Dylan has enough self-respect left to look embarrassed. "Sorry," he says in the general direction of Aunty Vinka but without meeting her eyes.

"Dylan, I don't know what you thi—"

"Once the police have the facts, we can leave it in their hands." Dylan's eyes flick to me and I reward him with a smirk. It's a good line and he knows it.

"I don't know what you're talking about," Aunty Vinka says.

"We heard you on the phone with Andy when we were in the car," Dylan says. "Shippy saw you taking a cup of tea up to Gertie's room. I guess that's where the missing meds went."

Not that anyone cares, but I reached the same conclusion.

There's a moment of what could be a dramatic silence, and it's unfortunate, if you like dramatic tension, that someone's stomach rumbles right at that particular moment. Everyone pretends they didn't hear it.

"Vinka." Dad sounds resigned. "Do you want to just tell us all the truth?"

"It's not what you think. I took Gertie a cup of tea that

night and I... I put her medication in the tea, but I wasn't... *drugging* her or anything like that," Aunty Vinka says quickly. "The Aztecs actually used to mix their medicine in a tealike drink, you know."

"*Vinx.*"

"I thought it would help her sleep, that's all. I was trying to help. Dad used to do it. My bedroom's closest to hers, you guys didn't hear her at night—she was in pain. I didn't mean to double her dose. She didn't even notice the taste." She adds this last bit like it might make everything cool.

"Why didn't you just tell us?" Dad asks.

"I gave drugs to a woman who died."

"I don't know why I have to keep saying this, but: Gertie didn't die from a bloody drug overdose."

"I panicked."

"You knew," Shippy says to Dad. "Why didn't *you* say anything?"

Dad looks betrayed, probably because Shippy has actually asked a reasonable question.

"I wasn't sure what I saw," Dad says, which is some kind of BS. "But we all know Vinx would never hurt anyone. She doesn't even eat honey because of the bees." He looks sideways at her. "It *is* the bees, right?"

"It's the bees."

"I'm sure the police will believe you once they have all the facts," Dylan says, trying to pull us all back to where this started.

"Dylan, you can't be serious. Just because your mum is

dabbling in fraud doesn't mean you have to leap into blackmail," Dad snips.

"If the stuff about my mum is relevant, why not the stuff about Vinka?"

"It's a fair question," Bec says. "Maybe the medication made Gertie so drowsy she couldn't call out for help or fight off her attacker." She's not looking at Aunty Vinka, so she doesn't see her face collapse at this.

"I could smell your cigarettes," Aunty Vinka says suddenly, ignoring the tear starting its kamikaze mission down one cheek. "When I took the tea up to her, the room smelled like cigarettes. That was you, I suppose, Bec, when you had your talk with her that night?"

"I already told you I was there," Bec says coolly. "Unlike your own nocturnal pursuits, Vinka, it's not a secret."

"And did you smoke one of Shippy's disgusting cigarettes?"

Bec's face answers the question and Shippy smacks his thigh.

"You took one of my cigs?"

"It was a stressful conversation."

"You quit ten years ago."

"It was one cigarette! Anyway, sorry to affect your nasal passages or disturb your chakra with my nicotine, Vinka."

"It's not that," Aunty Vinka says, and now both her cheeks are damp, but she's otherwise holding it together pretty well. I'm not sure where to look. "You opened Gertie's window—to let the smoke out, I assume."

"So what?"

"When I went in there with the tea, I asked Gertie if I should close the window, in case there was rain, but she asked me to leave it open a crack, to get rid of the smell."

"And you give *me* a hard time?" Shippy says, still on the cigarettes thing.

Bec ignores him. "Gertie didn't die of secondhand smoke, Vinka."

"Exactly." Aunty Vinka smiles grimly, the effect of which is only slightly blunted by the tears dropping over her top lip. "She died because someone came in through the window."

Bec frowns. She must understand what Aunty Vinka's trying to say, but she looks more irritated than guilty.

"Because it was left open and unlocked," Aunty Vinka says, for the slow ones in the class, "someone could get into the bedroom."

Dad interrupts. "That doesn't make sense. The window was smashed. Why would anyone smash a window if it was already open?"

Nobody has an answer to that, although I can think of one.

Aunty Vinka is properly crying now, and Dad pats her on the back distractedly.

"Chin up, Vinka. Unless you secretly offed Gertie, neither you nor Bec is any more to blame for her death than I am for the bloody typewriter."

"Typewriter?" Bec asks.

"Gertie asked me to take that typewriter downstairs," Dad says. "I got distracted and forgot, but if I'd done it . . . who knows."

"It's like she *knew*," Aunty Vinka says, and unfortunately for those of us who would rather scrub toilets with a toothbrush than watch grown-ups cry (just me? It's not like I'm going to use the toothbrush again, calm down), this makes her cry harder.

"So," Shippy says. "Between Andy with the typewriter, Vinka with the drugs, and Bec with the window—sorry, babe—it feels like you all had a hand in finishing the old girl off."

"Shippy," Dad says, "do f—" He remembers my presence. "Forget it."

"Does anyone want tea?" Aunty Vinka asks.

Do you want to know what *I'm* thinking during this whole weird showdown? Quite a lot, is the short version. Do I believe Aunty Vinka fatally drugged GG? Obviously not. But do I believe the cops might benefit from that information? I wouldn't say this to Aunty Vinka's face, but: absolutely. If reading, watching, and listening to (I love a good true-crime podcast) mystery stories has taught me anything, it's that you never know for sure what details are relevant. A throwaway detail on page 5 turns up in the final showdown and you wonder how you missed the importance of the car-seat covers being brown and not red. Laugh, if you want, but did you pick up the relevance of the clues on, say, pages 43 and 155? I wonder. (No, don't look now: That'd be cheating.) I'm also thinking I need to start carrying pen and paper like an old-school detective: At least three times through this whole drawn-out conversation I reach for my phone to make notes, before remembering it's still missing.

The mood in the room is restless and Bec stands up.

"Wait," Dad says; then, to the rest of us: "This is not the

family getaway any of us had imagined—the von Trapps had a better time en route to Switzerland—but the good news is, it's nearly over. I realize I've said variations on this *once or twice* before, but we can probably all head back to Perth tomorrow—Nick's health allowing—if we just pull together and agree what we're going to tell the police. Let's get our stories straight, give them the important facts, and leave them to it."

"You've changed your tune, Poirot," Bec says, but she sits back down.

"So, what, we don't have to tell them everything?" Aunty Vinka sniffs.

"I guess we can decide that together," Dad says.

"Guys?" Shippy says.

"Is that . . . legal?"

"Uh, guys?" Shippy says again.

"Vinx, why don't you put on some tea—some proper tea with caffeine in it, please."

"*Guys!*" Shippy finally gets our attention and we all look at him, then shift our gazes to what he's seen through the living-room window that overlooks the garden: a white sedan coming up the driveway.

"Is that the police?"

"They're early."

"Are we sure it's them?"

"Who else could it be?"

"I don't know—we seem to have randoms rocking up every two minutes."

"Shut up, everyone," Dad says, raising one hand to wave

at Detective Peterson, visible as she climbs out of the car. His party smile is in place, the one he and Mum used to put on when they'd just had a fight but still needed to be around other people. I haven't seen that smile since they separated, and I can't say I've missed it. When he speaks, it's in his party voice too, the one that means there's no point in arguing and the whole thing will just be done sooner if you roll over and submit. "The cops are here. That means we've got about ten seconds to figure out what we're going to tell them."

25

LET ME BE REAL FOR A MOMENT. THERE'S A SCENE HERE, A WHOLE bit that plays out when Detective Peterson comes to the house. I could tell you how Dylan and I eavesdrop from the bottom of the stairs, which we do (completely missing a clue right in front of our eyes), and how Dad catches us, which he does. I could tell you that nobody tells Detective Peterson about the whole Bec's-a-liar thing, the existence of a whole other "Nicky" love child who is not Bec, or the Aunty-Vinka-and-the-drugs thing, *and* that I don't say a word about GG's son being alive (is it just me or is this more missing mystery kids than one family deserves?), even though Laura reckons the cops already know all about it. But that's less because we're circling the family wagons to protect our many and varied secrets and more because it doesn't come up: The cops are here to talk about Rob, not GG. Specifically, they're having trouble tracking down his family, and also his phone, and want to know if we can help. We kind of can't. (Actually, we could have if someone had done a better job of cleaning the kitchen, but now I'm just being a tease.)

I could write all this down here and let you sift through the clues and see what little tidbits everyone let slip and all that business, but here's the thing: We're approaching endgame here, and, with so few pages of the book left between your hand and the back cover, you just want to know who did it and how I find out. I get it, I do.

So, the only important thing you need to know from this whole drawn-out *and another thing* encounter with the cops is that Rob's "accident" is being treated as an attempted homicide, thanks to some skid marks that make the cops think he was targeted. A big deal, yes, but aren't you glad I just kept it tight? You're welcome. Also, it might be relevant to note that there's a very good reason the cops can't find Rob's phone, but you won't find out why until a bit later—*I* don't even know about that yet.

Anyway, we've got bigger things to deal with in a sec.

26

HAVE YOU EVER WOKEN UP FROM A REALLY GOOD SLEEP WITH the feeling that your brain has been working on your problems overnight? It doesn't happen to me often (and never on the morning of a math exam, meaning I still don't understand integration), but it does happen. One day last year, just for example, I spent all day trying to come up with an embarrassment-free plan to figure out if Jade at school liked Libby or *liked* Libby, and I still had nothing by bedtime. The next morning I woke up with the perfect solution in my head, as though someone had whispered it into my ear as I slept. (Unfortunately for Libby, Jade turned out to be almost aggressively straight, but the *plan* was flawless.)

It happens that night when I wake up, just after midnight, suddenly sure I know where GG's missing box is. As with any satisfying mystery, the clues—three of them that I can count—have been in front of me, sometimes literally, but I haven't seen them. I get out of bed, as wide awake as if it's nine a.m. I *could* wait for nine a.m. That's definitely the sensible thing to do, since it doesn't involve thundering around a dark house recently linked to at least one murder. But if you think I can stay in bed without checking to see if I'm right, then I've completely failed to tell you anything about me at all.

The floorboards sag a little as I get out of bed, feeling for the slip-on woven flats I kicked under the bed last night. This house was built at a time when building standards weren't what they are now, and I wonder if anyone would even get in trouble if the floorboards collapsed beneath me and I plunged all the way down to the ground-floor bathroom to be impaled by the shower fittings. Given that Grandad built most of it back in the day, and he's dead, I'm guessing there'd be nobody left to sue.

The first flaw in my plan comes when I find my bedroom door locked. I never asked Dad if it was him who locked me in last time, and apparently, oh joy, tonight too, but it's got to be. Nobody else would care this much. There's a moment where I consider going out the window and shimmying down the drainpipe, except that seems like a not-so-fun way to break my legs. Also, there are two doors to my bedroom.

The door to Dad's room opens silently and I step through as quietly as I can, ready with a cover story about the toilet. I don't need it (the cover story, that is): He's asleep, face slack. There's another bad moment when I realize his door is also locked, but (of course) the key is in the lock.

At the bottom of the stairs, I stop. This bit is going to be tricky. It would be easier with Dylan here, for a couple of reasons, but I can't get to his room without going through Bec and Shippy's, and if there's one room I definitely don't fancy making a nocturnal appearance in, it's theirs. Shippy might use it as an opportunity to bludgeon me to death with his hiking boot first and blame it on thinking I was an intruder later.

The first thing I need to do, the hardest bit, is move the big standing lamp at the bottom of the stairs. When I noticed days ago that it had been moved from its usual corner position, I didn't think too hard about why anyone might move a lamp just a meter or so. Nor did I consider the significance of it having moved only after GG died. That should have been clue one. I drag the lamp back into place. It's not so heavy—the material covering all four sides of what's basically just a big column, lit from within, must be IKEA's lightweight best—but the metal feet it's standing on scrape against the floorboards, letting out a horrendous wail, reminiscent of when Mike got hit in the balls during school soccer training. I freeze, imagining a door opening, a light clicking on, a silhouette in the doorway. But nothing happens and nobody arrives, so I drag it again, and this time the wail seems more restrained, like when Ali tried to kick her school locker closed and stubbed her toe on her laptop instead. (Her parents don't really believe in technology, and as a result, her computer looks like something that might have been used to put man on the moon.)

When the lamp is out of the way, I can better see the patch of dust that sparked Dad's (thankfully barely developed and clearly insane) theory about dust working differently in the country. This weirdly localized patch of dust, mostly (deliberately) concealed by the lamp, was clue number two, by the way, but it was wasted on me.

Under that dust is the outline of a square in the floorboards, the entrance to the same crawl space where Dad once got stuck while trying to fix a problem with the lights. The square of wood comes away easily enough under my fingers, dislodging more dust as I set it down. The last person who did this must have wanted to hide the telltale dust that showed someone had been under the floorboards recently but didn't have time to go for a dustpan and broom and just yanked the lamp over a foot or two to cover it instead.

Beneath the floorboards is a snake's nest of wires. If you're wondering about clue three, we're there now: the flickering light in my bedroom, which, like the mysterious moving lamp, only appeared after GG died. Something happened that night to disturb the wiring in my bedroom, but I never slowed down long enough to ask myself the obvious question: *What?* Or maybe: *How?* Hell, even *why* would work, now that I think about it.

It doesn't take much rummaging to find the box, which has clearly just been dropped into the hole, and drag it out to confirm I got it right: the *for M* is written in marker on one side.

That's when I hear footsteps and look up to see a familiar face illuminated in the moonlight.

27

"WHAT ARE YOU DOING UP?" DYLAN WHISPERS.

"Same question," I hiss back, looking at the hardcover copy of *Anne of Green Gables* in his hand. "Is that supposed to be a weapon?"

He looks at it, a little embarrassed. "It's got sharp corners. Plus, I heard someone . . . howling out here? Was that you?" Then he sees the box and the cavity under the floorboards. "What *are* you doing? Wait, is that the box?" I nod, and, now that my heart has returned to its regular rhythms, I'm glad to have him here, partly for the company and partly to be a witness to my brilliance.

"It was hidden under the floorboards," I say as Dylan sits down next to me, placing *Anne* reverently on the bottom step of the staircase, where the next person to come down the stairs could slip on it and brain themselves on the floor. (This isn't foreshadowing, just an observation, but there's about to be so much more than a dangerously placed book to worry about.)

"How did you find it?"

I milk my moment, explaining to Dylan how I fit the pieces together (eventually) and (here's hoping) making him feel like an idiot for overlooking the same clues I did.

"Whoever put the box here must have knocked something loose that affected the lights in my room," I say, really spelling it out in case he got lost along the way. "Grandad's wiring is pretty dodgy. I guess they planned to come back for the box later, or maybe they just didn't want it to be found."

"Who?"

"The murderer."

"Right."

We both look at the box.

"What do you think is in it?" I ask.

"You haven't opened it?"

"It can't be gold bars," I go on. "Not heavy enough."

"Why would the murderer leave gold bars behind, exactly?"

"Cash, maybe?"

"This might be a crazy idea, but instead of speculating, should we just open it and find out immediately?" Sleep-deprived Dylan is no fun.

Now that I've found the box, I'm reluctant to crack the top in a way that must seem both ridiculous and annoying to an outsider. I don't know how to explain it except to say that it feels a bit like opening your end-of-year school report: You want to know, you *have* to know, but you're also very aware that the information is going to determine not just your immediate mood (and, crucially, that of your parents) but, potentially, your future.

I drum my fingers on the box and push it toward Dylan. "Do you want to do it?"

"You found it."

"We're supposed to be partners."

"Okay. Let's do it together." Dylan scoots closer, grabbing one side of the cardboard lid as I take the other, our heads bumping as we crane forward to see what's in the box.

What's in the box is . . . paper?

"At least it's not, like, a head," Dylan says, his mouth almost touching my ear. All those tiny little hairs on my neck I forget about ninety-five percent of the time stand up.

"Whose head would it even be?"

He ignores my question. "What did *you* think it was going to be, really?"

"Not a head."

"I kind of can't believe you actually found it."

"That's insulting."

"It's really not." Then Dylan does a thing that . . . okay, maybe it's embarrassing to be focusing on this right now when you just want to know *what's in the box, Ruth,* but this is how it happened. First let me paint the picture: The two of us are sitting close together on the floor, our arms are touching, and we're both leaning forward over the box, but supporting ourselves with one hand each on the floorboards. (I'm getting to the thing, honestly.) Then Dylan picks up his hand, the one on the floor, and I think he's going to dig inside the box, but instead he lays it back down on top of mine. He does it without putting his weight on it, so it's not so much that he's crushing my hand but that his hand is resting on top of mine. Take my word for it, it's so much better than it sounds (and he's *definitely not* my cousin, just in case you're starting to feel squeamish). Then he turns his head (remember, we're right next to each other, and also, chill out, you'll find out about the box really soon), so he's looking right at me.

"Seriously, Ruth, you're amazing."

His eyes have gone a bit soft again, and this is the point where if I was, say, Ali, I would lean in and kiss him. Or if I was Libby (and, in her case, if Dylan was a girl), I would stay right where I am and let him kiss me. Definitely, there would be kissing involved. I don't know how to explain it, but my best friends were born knowing how to make these things happen. I'm me, though, so, overthinking it, I ignore the hand situation and say, too loudly, "Let's take a look, then."

Dylan's face briefly drops, then rebounds. "Let's do it."

"Sorry," I say quickly.

"What for?"

"Nothing."

Unlikely as it seems, I've somehow made things worse because maybe the Moment was actually just a regular no-cap moment and I've imagined Dylan's accidental hand placement was a thing when it wasn't, and if the space under the floorboards was any bigger, I'd be tempted to throw myself into it. Then I sneak a look at Dylan's face and I'm pretty sure he's trying not to smile.

Dylan lifts out the top layer of papers and starts to go through them. I reach into the box for more and my hands hit plastic. It's a cheap sporting trophy with a softball player on top and BEST TEAM PLAYER engraved underneath. Not . . . quite what I expected. There's also a little drawstring velvet bag, which I weigh in my hand. This is more like it. Diamonds? Rubies? Some kind of microchip . . . thing, like in a spy movie? The thought exhausts me: I have seriously not got the energy for international intrigue/espionage/fighting anyone on top of a train, or whatever.

I tip the contents of the bag onto my hand, then immediately let them drop through my fingers to scatter on the floorboards.

"What?" Dylan asks in response to my stifled shriek.

"Teeth," I say. "It's full of teeth."

We look at the small pile of beige-yellow teeth lying on the floor, and then at each other.

"So, Gertie was, like, a serial killer and these are her trophies?" he asks, joking but maybe not completely joking.

"I think they're baby teeth," I say when we've both calmed down.

"That's worse, isn't it?"

I pick up some papers.

"I'm scared it's going to be a huge anticlimax. Like GG was secretly a tax dodger and this will be forty years' worth of pay slips."

"Well, let's find out if the tax office needs to get involved."

We spread the paper out on the floor and it doesn't take long to get the picture. Here are the birth certificate, school records, sports trophies, and, yes, presumably baby teeth of someone called Martin Robert McCulloch. GG's son. It's got to be.

"So," I say, wanting to be the one who puts it all together but also not sure what the hell I'm putting together. "GG kept all these mementos of her son—that makes sense. But why did her killer not want anyone to find them?"

"There must be something in here."

"Like . . . what?"

Neither of us says anything. I go back to the box to see what else I can find, and I'm sifting through swimming certificates when my hand strikes something hard. It's a phone. It's old but not ancient—an iPhone from maybe four or five generations ago. It's dead.

"I've found photos," Dylan says, glancing quickly at a couple of them. "They look like some kid: Gertie's son, I guess." He looks up. "You found your phone."

"It's not mine."

"Are you sure?"

"Yes, Dylan. My phone is my fifth limb. This isn't mine."

"So, whose is it?"

"I dunno. It looks familiar, though." I turn the dead cell phone over in my hands. "It could be GG's, because Dad gave her one of his old ones. I think I recognize the chip on the screen."

"What does that mean?" Dylan asks.

"I don't know."

We abandon the box for the kitchen and plug the phone into the charger.

"I'm so dusty," I say, holding up my hands, and Dylan, oh so casually, like it's not even a thing, takes one of them and turns it over in his.

"Filthy," he says, dusting my hand with his own. It tickles but I don't laugh. When it's clean(ish) he doesn't let go but laces his fingers through mine. I could write another whole chapter about the hand-holding, but I am aware you've come here to see a mystery solved (and we're so close), so I'll try to be restrained. Just take my word for it that it's . . . something.

"Ruth," he says. "This is probably not the time, but there's something I wanted to tell you."

Then the phone beeps and we step apart, Dylan banging against the microwave so hard it skids across the kitchen bench.

"Crap," he says, grabbing his elbow. "Hold up," he says a moment later as he pushes the microwave back into place. "There's something here." Then he's holding another phone that's a few generations younger than GG's. "Here's *your* missing phone. It fell down behind the microwave when it was charging, I think." He hands it to me.

"That's not my phone either," I say, although I have to double-check because not only is it the same model, but the lock screen has a photo of what I'm pretty sure is Yallingup Beach—the same as mine. When Dad took me there not even a week ago, the water was too cold to swim in, but it was chock-full of surfers. The combination of that beach shot and the fact that the phone's screen is crammed with missed calls and messages makes me sure I know who it belongs to.

"Seriously? How many lost phones can one house reasonably contain, do you think?"

"Seriously."

"Well, whose is it?"

For now I don't tell him. Instead I pick up GG's phone, which is now asking for a passcode.

"What's her passcode?" Dylan asks.

"I don't know. Do you know?"

"How would *I* know? What year was she born?"

"I'm going to try 1234," I say, stabbing it in.

"How old do you think she was?"

"GG wouldn't have bothered putting on a proper security code—she would have left it with the default one or something she could remember." I say this more confidently than I feel. It doesn't work. "Nope."

"9876?"

"Nope. I'm going to try four zeros. That's what my mum has on hers; she says it's the only one she can remember."

I think we're each as surprised as the other when it works.

"Now I'm impressed," Dylan says.

"You weren't impressed when I discovered the phone?"

"Can we call it *discovered* if it was just sitting in a box?"

"What happened to 'oh, Ruth, you're a genius'?"

"I literally never said that."

"You thought it."

Dylan laughs. "Come on. Let's start with her messages."

It takes minutes of scrolling through GG's messages (hardly any), calls (minimal), and apps (she's not on social media, what a shocker) before we think to check out her photos. It's right there: a video, recorded the night she died. I tap it to play, then tap it again to stop.

"Do we watch it now?"

"Obviously, but wait." Dylan grabs my hand to stop me before I can tap the screen again. "Just, before you do, that thing I wanted to tell you."

"Tell me later," I say, wanting and not wanting to know.

"It's just, uh, Lisa and I broke up."

I cover my face with my free hand. "Do we have to talk about this now?" I say, talking as much to Dylan as to my own brain, which is filling up with questions. When did he find the time to do this in a Wi-Fi and phone-service dead zone? Was a carrier pigeon involved? Did he hire a skywriter on the DL? Is Lisa right now answering the door to a singing telegram prepared to use music and dance to break the bad news?

"Just thought you might like to know."

"Thank you for the update. Can we watch the video now?"

"I just didn't want you to think—"

"I am up to speed."

"I'm glad we had this enlightening talk."

I mostly manage to hide my smile. Dylan doesn't even try.

The video starts, and the moment it does, I forget about Dylan and Lisa and even about the hand-holding because I'm looking at GG's face, speaking straight into the camera.

"Hello," she says.

28

THIS IS THE PART WHERE I SHOULD CUT TO DYLAN AND ME AT THE police station, handing over this crucial bit of evidence (the phone), telling them what we've learned from watching the video (who killed GG), and going back to Perth safe, sound, and with one hell of a What I Did on Vacation essay up our sleeves. That would be the smart thing to do. But it doesn't happen like that.

Instead let me cut to the next morning (don't worry, you'll get to see the video soon, and it'll be better this way), to the living-room couch where Dylan and I fell asleep the night before, only after putting everything but GG's phone back into the box and returning it to its hiding place so we could be the ones to reveal its existence to our parents, rather than Dad discovering all when he trips over it and breaks his neck en route to the bathroom. We're smooshed head to toe but with just the one blanket over us and Dylan is holding one of my socked feet like it's a comfort toy. All of which makes it kind of weird when Dad finds us half asleep.

"Good morning?" he says, making it a question. I sit up and Dylan's foot kicks my boob, while GG's phone drops out of my hand to the floor. I pick it up and the time on the phone tells me it's late, nearly ten a.m., and I have no idea how we slept through the family having breakfast in the next room except that we were up until three a.m. watching that video of GG and talking about what it meant until our throats were sore and even the idea of disappearing to our respective beds felt like too much.

"Dad!"

"Correct. What's going on here?"

"We couldn't sleep."

"You seemed to be doing a pretty good impression of it."

"Insomnia," I insist, still thick-headed. "We thought TV might help."

Dad and I both look at the TV, which is off. Resisting the temptation to prattle into the silence (always a classic giveaway of a lie in progress), I smile my blandest no-teeth smile. The one thing Dylan and I agreed on last night was that we'd show the video to our parents together, but Dylan is either still asleep or pretending to be.

"Where is everyone?" I ask, kicking Dylan lightly. "There's something Dylan and I want to talk to you about."

"They're all outside—Vinx and I are going to bring Nick back from the hospital and Bec and Shippy are going to go check the bus timetable back to Perth."

"They can't drive home with Aunty Vinka and Nick? Or us?"

"I'm not sure they feel good about being in a car with any of us for three hours. Shippy said he'd rather risk motion sickness."

"Fair enough."

Dad does that peering-into-my-soul thing he whips out sometimes, and, clearly, he doesn't love what he finds there, because his expression gets very focused. "I was going to go with Vinka to help with Nick, but I can stay here if you'd rather."

"We'll be okay. How long will you be?"

"Not long. Are you sure it can wait until we get back?"

"Sure."

Dad kisses the top of my head and goes out the front door. I lie back down on the couch, wondering if I've made a mistake not showing him the video right away. (On balance, probably yes: A lot of things might have gone differently if I'd just told Dad the truth.) But I'm tired and my thoughts are mushy.

Dylan sits up as soon as the cars drive away. Faking, then.

"Man, my head hurts," he says. "I think I got about three hours' sleep. You wriggle."

"You could have gone to your own bed."

"And leave you scared and alone?"

"Whatever. You snore."

"I do not."

"You do." This is a lie, by the way, but how would he know? And how dare he say I'm a wriggler when what I was really doing was constantly readjusting my body in an attempt to not fall off the couch entirely or knee Dylan in the balls. Maybe I shouldn't have tried so hard.

"You didn't tell your dad."

"I knew you were faking. Should I have?"

"I don't know. I'm not sure I'm awake yet."

"We should tell everyone together. Nick's getting out of the hospital, so we'll tell them when they get back." (If you're getting a bit tired of Nick's whole deal, let me assure you he really is coming home, just in time to . . . well, you'll see.)

"Sounds like a plan." Dylan closes his eyes again.

"Then we take it to the cops."

"Uh-huh," he mumbles.

"Are you seriously going back to sleep?"

"Are you seriously not?"

I am not. I get up, put on the kettle, wash my face, brush my teeth, and put bread in the toaster. The moment he smells hot toast and cold butter, Dylan decides he's hungry too, and we wind up having quite a pleasant little breakfast at the dining table, GG's phone between us like a gun in a play.

"Should we watch it again?" he asks.

"I sort of don't want to."

"I know."

"But maybe? I'm still not sure I have it straight."

"It made sense last night."

"I know."

Dylan swears.

"Yeah."

"No, I mean—" And he swears again but he also nods over my shoulder, and I turn to see a familiar-looking truck coming up the driveway.

This time *I* swear.

"Exactly."

"Doesn't anyone ever call first in this town?"

"No reception."

"It was a joke. What do we do?"

"Hide?" Dylan says, looking around the room.

"Why?"

"He'll think nobody's home and go away?"

"He doesn't know we know anything."

"How do you know that?"

I take a massive slug of my tea. "Or maybe we do the opposite of hide."

"What's the opposite of hide? Expose ourselves?" Dylan makes a face.

"We invite him in." I drain the rest of the cup. The tea is too hot and burns my throat, but I don't care. I'm too busy pulling Dylan's phone out of his pocket. "What's your code?" He tells me, not asking why, and I have to enter it twice because my fingers have gone shaky and useless. "We put this up here." I tap the screen a few times and lean it back against the kitchen backsplash so it's facing Dylan but mostly concealed by a stack of cookbooks (all Christmas and birthday presents from Mum and Dad to GG, and all pristine). "We talk to him."

"Ruth, *no*."

"When are we going to get a chance like this?"

"A chance to be murdered? Hopefully never." He stands up. "I'll get rid of him." We both hear the slam of the truck door.

"Don't be dramatic. Has anyone even *been* murdered?"

"You don't think—"

"That's only a theory."

"You seemed pretty confident last night," he says. "Let's just leave it up to the police."

"The police don't have any evidence."

"Ruth, no."

"Dylan, yes."

There's a knock at the door, and Dylan and I look at each other. We can each see what the other is thinking. Dylan doesn't want to do this. I do want to do this. I know that I shouldn't do this and that wanting to solve a puzzle isn't worth the risk. But, also, how long can it take to discharge a man from the hospital? Dad and the others can't be far away.

"Okay," Dylan says, standing up. "But let's at least try to leave Rob out of it." I don't agree to this, but maybe he takes my silence as assent because he says: "I'll get the door; you put on a bra."

I'm touched he noticed.

When I come down, Dylan and Sasha are drinking coffee at the kitchen table. Dylan gives me a little nod, which I interpret as *We've got this*. (Do we, though? Do we *got this*?) The plan that seemed reasonable five minutes ago now seems childish and ridiculously dangerous, like the time I was ten and tried to buy a wireless spy camera over the internet using Dad's credit card. Okay, I was twelve, but I got cold feet and told on myself.

Sasha's smile is friendly enough. For now.

"Hi, Ruth."

"Hi, Sasha."

"Sorry to drop by. I was hoping to see your parents, but David tells me they're out."

"Dylan," Dylan and I say at the same time.

"Right. Like I was saying to . . . Dylan, I think my credit card might have fallen out of my pocket last time I was here. Okay with you two if I have a quick look about?" His smile is impossible to disbelieve, unless you've recently seen that video on GG's phone.

"Actually," I say, before Dylan can change his mind and get rid of this guy, whose muscles are taking up too much room in his shirt, "we have something to show you first." I try hard not to make my voice go up on the last word and turn it into a question. I smile, all too aware that Dylan and I are exuding the vibe of a nervous young couple inviting the boss over for a dinner party. Except Sasha should be the nervous one; he just doesn't realize it yet. (Have you figured out what he did? Better yet, have you figured out *why* he did it?)

"What is it?"

"A video." Is that a flicker in one eye?

"Of who?" He's given himself away, whether he realizes it or not. The obvious question to ask here would be of *what*?

"Why don't we just play it?"

"What's this about?" he asks, and there's something in his voice that wasn't there before. He knows, or at least he suspects. I want to risk a glance toward the backsplash, but that would defeat the whole purpose of this (awful) plan. How much of a comfort will it be, exactly, if I get murdered but it's all captured on video?

"This is about Gertie's death. Dylan and I know what happened."

Two pink splotches grow on Sasha's cheeks. He doesn't have to ask the question—he knows the answer, just as we do—but he's still trying to work out how much we know, and so he asks it anyway. "Who killed her?"

"To answer that question, we really have to go back to when GG found out she was dying," I say.

Dylan's face asks if we're *really* doing this, and, okay, maybe my delivery was a little Daniel Craig at the end of *Glass Onion* (minus the accent), but I'm trying my best.

"Right," Sasha says, smiling like he's not panicking.

"When GG got her diagnosis, she started to reevaluate her life choices. In particular, I think she regretted her estrangement from her son—his name's Martin. She'd always told everyone he was dead, but the truth is that Martin's been in prison for years."

"*I* told *you* that," Sasha points out.

"You did. You were the one who told us that GG's son was still alive and that she knew about it. I assume you did that because you wanted to throw him out there as a possible suspect, just in case?" No response. "Or maybe you just wanted an excuse to come over that night, so you could find out if we knew anything and go hunting for, what was it, a missing credit card?" Again: nothing. "But it's not so easy to go hunting under the floorboards with a house full of people, is it? I *heard* you bump into Shippy outside the kitchen, but *Shippy* was on his way to use the upstairs bathroom, so how would he run into you if you were coming back from the downstairs bathroom, which is in the opposite direction? I didn't pay attention to it and Shippy didn't ask the question. Well, he's not that bright."

"Ruth," Dylan says, trying to bring me back.

"Anyway, the point is that GG was feeling pretty bad about her son, but what she didn't know was that Martin had recently been released."

"I told your parents all this already: She knew he was getting out."

"I know that's what you *said*," I say, enjoying this a bit too much (another check in the psychopath box?), "but I don't think that's what really happened, because it doesn't make sense." I pull GG's phone out of my pocket and turn it around to face Sasha. His hand twitches like he wants to reach for it, but he doesn't move. "I think GG wanted to make amends with her son, and I think she wrote to him in prison, probably begging his forgiveness, at the very least saying she was sorry."

"So?"

"I think that letter was seen by someone who should never have seen it: Martin's friend, or maybe his cellmate—are cellmates a thing in Australian prisons or is that just an American TV thing?—and that guy got the idea into his head that there was a rich old lady out there who was desperate to be forgiven and might make a good target."

Sasha's mask of polite interest barely shows a ripple. But barely isn't nothing.

"I think Martin's cellmate—or maybe they were just acquaintances in the exercise yard or something; most of my knowledge of prison comes from *Orange Is the New Black*, so—"

"*Ruth.*" Dylan is barely audible.

"Right, right. So, Martin's . . . whatever gets out of prison first. He comes to find Gertie, representing himself as a friend and a confidant of Martin's. This bit is mostly guesswork, but I, we"—I gesture to Dylan to make it clear in what direction that *we* extends—"think he convinced Gertie that he had Martin's ear and that Martin was still angry at Gertie, but that perhaps he, as an intermediary, might be persuaded to smooth over any unpleasantness."

Still nothing. I flick a glance at Dylan, who gives me a tiny, encouraging smile. My body is surging with adrenaline now. I don't think I could stop if I tried.

"Maybe Martin's dodgy mate—no offense—also knew about the life insurance and had a plan to get his hands on it. I have no idea."

"Is there a point to this?" Sasha says, and he's (finally) stopped smiling, which is a relief, because the whole thing was getting a bit Jokeresque. "You said you wanted to show me something."

I waggle GG's phone in my hand.

"This video," I say, "will show us—and the police—who killed GG."

Sasha's face suggests we're discussing how many calves he expects to sell this year. He really could have been on *Farmer Wants a Wife:* He's a good enough actor to feign interest in half a dozen women ostensibly looking for love.

"Who *did* kill your grandma?"

"Step-grandma," I correct him. "And: nobody." Then I hit play, and it's such a shame there's nobody here but me and Dylan and Sasha to see, because it's about as cool a moment as I'm ever likely to have.

29

GG IS SMILING INTO THE CAMERA, AND I DON'T CARE HOW MANY times I've seen this, it's still creepy as hell. She's sitting on the edge of her bed, twisted to face the phone, which must be propped up on her bedside table. The cardboard box that so intrigued me is sitting beside her. Also, just in frame, sitting on top of the wardrobe behind her, is the killer typewriter, and once you see it you can't *unsee* it, lurking there the way a famous actor in a TV crime procedural never quite blends into the background: You just know they're going to be outed as the killer in fifty minutes. If you listen hard enough, there's the grumble of distant thunder in the background.

"This video is for my son, Martin," GG says. "I'm filming it now because I'm not sure how much time I have left. I don't think I'm well enough to visit you in prison, Martin, even if you would agree to see me, which I'm not sure I deserve. I'm so sorry that I've wasted so many years not being in your life. I was ashamed by what you'd done. But now it all seems so very petty and ridiculous. I hope one day you'll forgive me. I hope one day you'll be able to build a life for yourself.

"Your friend Sasha has been delivering my cards—I couldn't trust them to the mail, and I'm sorry it's not more—and he has promised to deliver you this message, along with some other things I want you to have. You'll probably think I'm ridiculous for having held on to some of these things, but if you ever become a father yourself, perhaps you'll understand."

I look at Sasha, who is leaning forward so far, he's in danger of toppling out of his chair.

"I'd better finish this now; I'm not sure how long this phone can record for," GG says. "I wanted to leave you something to remember me by, in case we don't get to meet again."

GG stands up, with some visible effort, and walks toward the wardrobe. "There's one more thing I want you to have," she says, her voice getting quieter as she walks away from the camera. "This typewriter was given to me when I was a girl by *my* mother. I don't know if you remember the way you used to love to type on it when you were little. I always told you it'd be yours one day."

The three of us watch, transfixed, as GG reaches up to grasp the typewriter in both hands. Even knowing what's going to happen, I'm tense, like this is a choose-your-own-adventure book where a happy ending is still possible. This time GG survives! But, no, instead I have to watch (again) as GG lifts the typewriter down. The angle of the camera makes it impossible to say if she trips over something on the floor or merely staggers under the weight of the machine. (I'll never suggest as much to Aunty Vinka, but it's also occurred to me this might be the drugs in her tea, rendering her limbs unreliable.) Either way, GG goes backward and the typewriter slips out of her hands, following the most gruesome possible arc to crash against her head. The whole thing is made ten times more gruesome because, just as the typewriter strikes her, there's a massive clap of thunder. A moment later a flash of lightning illuminates GG as she falls out of frame to the spot where Aunty Vinka will find her the next day.

At this point I pull the phone back from Sasha, who lifts one hand to suggest he's going to stop me, then puts it back in his lap.

"How . . . do you have this?" he asks.

That's maybe not the question I'd be asking, especially given he must know the answer.

"We found it hidden under the floorboards in a box of things GG wanted her son to have. I guess whoever was here that night stashed it in a moment of panic—maybe they thought they heard someone in the house? Maybe they didn't want to risk being caught with it?—and planned to come back for it when everything had died down."

"What do you mean someone put it there the night Gertie died?" Sasha says. "This video proves that what happened to Gertie was just an accident."

"It was," I say, turning the video back around to face him. "But you might want to see this bit."

Sasha must know what's coming—we've seen this already, but he's *lived* it—but still he cranes toward the screen again like it's the sun and he's a neglected houseplant.

We all watch the video on the phone as the door to GG's

bedroom swings inward and stops. There's a long wait before Sasha's head appears around the door, staring at something on the floor. I think we can all agree what he's looking at, and, in my personal opinion, his face doesn't look nearly horrified enough.

"Can you just—" Sasha reaches for the phone, but I'm ready and pull it back.

On-screen Sasha is already at work: looking under the bed, through the drawers in the wardrobe, rifling through GG's dressing table. He's clearly looking for something, but carefully, replacing items as he goes rather than leaving things strewn around behind him. He finds what he's looking for at the back of the dressing table drawer: a blue velvet box containing GG's jewelry collection. The box goes into the pocket of his vest as he looks at the writing on the side of the cardboard box and grabs that too. Then he looks up in triumph to notice the phone and his face filling the phone screen. Sasha's hand looms large, folding over the phone, and everything goes black.

I slip the phone back into my pocket as fast as I can, but Sasha doesn't even reach for it.

"Did you mean to put GG's phone in the box or was that a mistake?" I ask. Sasha ignores me, probably because he's doing an hour's worth of thinking in about five seconds.

"I want to know about the phones too," Dylan says, possibly feeling left out. "Did you tamper with the landline and hide Gertie's phone bill or something, so there was no chance she could call the prison, or was that just a coincidence?"

"I don't know what you kids think this proves, but that video only shows that Gertie's death was an accident," Sasha says.

"It was," I agree. "Which makes it really weird that you were there at all, not to mention that you stole Gertie's jewelry and smashed the window and dragged the ladder up against the house." I imagine it: Sasha trying to figure out what he's just walked into. I see him spotting the ladder on his way out of the house and coming up with a (let's be real: bad) idea that would make the police look for an outsider and definitely not look too carefully at the ex-con already in GG's life and living next door.

That's the best I've come up with and it's an objectively dumb plan, but who hasn't acted on one of those?

Sasha shakes his head. "I didn't touch the ladder or the window," he says.

"You wanted to make it seem like this was an outside job," I say, and if this was court, which it definitely is not, I can imagine some American-accented judge accusing me of leading the witness. "You were scared that the police might look a bit too closely at the people in GG's life. Of course, if you'd been thinking clearly you would have left everything as is and hoped that the police wouldn't notice the missing jewelry and would dismiss it as an accident, which it really was."

"I didn't do anything to her. You saw that." Sasha has recovered some of his confidence. "You can't prove anything. I didn't even break in that night: Gertie and I were supposed to meet up that evening, but, well, everyone was supposed to be gone and you were all still here. I just came a bit later than we'd planned."

"In the middle of the night?"

"It's not a crime to be a night owl."

I'm only half listening. Mostly I'm trying to figure out if what Sasha has said is the truth: Was he standing out there, waiting for the house to fall asleep that night? GG certainly seemed like she'd been getting things ready for Sasha's arrival, between the box and the typewriter. But she hadn't said anything about expecting a visitor.

"Do you smoke?" I ask, and Sasha looks caught off guard, which is quite nice, actually.

"What?"

"Do you smoke?"

He hesitates, not wanting to give me even this, then shrugs. "Sure."

Another couple of pieces snap together as I think of the cigarette butts Shippy noticed out in the driveway. Maybe Sasha isn't BSing and he really was supposed to meet GG earlier that night but stood out there instead, waiting and smoking, not knowing what about the plan had changed but still wanting his chance at getting GG's money and whatever valuables he imagined she planned to pass along to her son.

"You must have come back to try and get the box," I say, thinking as I talk. "That was you in the garden on . . . Tuesday night"—I think I've got that right—"I guess. Was the idea to break in and get it? You must have been so stressed about that phone, which proved your innocence in GG's death but also that you were up to some seriously shady stuff."

"This is ridiculous," Sasha says, crossing his arms, and

as the muscles in his biceps bulge menacingly, I'm suddenly aware of how big he is, and not in a charming *Farmer Wants a Wife* way so much as a not-much-else-to-do-in-jail-but-lift-weights kind of way. "You kids are ridiculous, and you have no idea who you're even talking to."

Letting Sasha into the house was insane; showing him the video was worse. I'm suddenly sure I've made a colossal mistake. I want him out of here.

"Why haven't you shown that video to the cops yet?"

I wait a beat too long. "We have."

He shakes his head. "Nah. I think you only just found it. I think you haven't had a chance. I think maybe you haven't even shown it to your parents." He stands up. "I think I'd quite like to take that phone, actually. Just in case."

I push back my chair and stand up, trying to angle my body so that Dylan's phone, recording all of this from the kitchen backsplash, will be able to take in the whole scene. It's supposed to be one part evidence, one part insurance policy, but it won't do me much good if the phone captures Sasha bludgeoning me to death. He could so easily drive straight to the beach to throw the phone (and our bodies?) in the ocean, wash the blood from his hands, and maybe pick up a coffee while he's at it.

"Like you say, this video only exonerates you, so what's the big deal?"

"Come on, kid," Sasha snorts, and I can't believe I ever thought he belonged on reality TV. What an insult to the *FWAW* franchise. "Do you think you're in a movie or something? Give me the phone. I'd love to stay and chat, but I'm sorry, I've got to go. You've got nothing and I didn't do anything wrong."

"You took GG's jewelry," I point out.

He scoffs. "It wasn't even worth anything. And who's to say she didn't ask me to give it to her son?"

"You tried to kill Rob." It's the thing I shouldn't say. The thing Dylan definitely didn't want me to say. The thing I told myself I'd only say if and when I saw my dad's car coming up the driveway. My dad's car is not coming up the driveway.

"You think I tried to kill your friend?" Sasha has a stab at putting a wryly amused expression back into place, but he's not quite pulling it off and he doesn't sit down. "Why would I do that? I didn't even know the guy."

Dylan stands up, and Sasha half turns toward him, one hand sliding into the pocket of his coat. Surely if he had a gun he'd have produced it by now? Do all farmers have guns? Is he even a proper farmer, though, or was he lying about that too?

"Do you really live next door?" I ask, more to take his attention away from Dylan than anything else.

"Nah," Sasha says slowly, turning back to me but keeping his hand in his pocket. "I just wanted an excuse to come by. Didn't you guys ever wonder how one person was supposedly running a whole bloody cattle farm?"

I knew his hands were too smooth and pale. Farmers' hands get messed up.

Dylan shuffles away from Sasha, and he'd better not be going for that knife rack because Dylan is tall but Sasha could bend him around his arm like a warm pretzel. Why didn't

Dylan's stupid dad ever tell him the stats on weapons being used against him?

"The police will be interested in hearing that you pretended to be GG's neighbor," I say. "They already know Rob's hit-and-run wasn't an accident."

"It's not a crime to give someone the wrong home address. If I had tried to kill your mate—Ross, was it?—that *would* be a crime. Why would you say that I had?" His voice is casual, but I'm starting to recognize his expressions, and I'm pretty sure that Sasha is scared. If I hadn't been sure before that he'd tried to kill Rob (and, real talk, I wasn't), I am now.

Dylan takes another side step, and I want to tell him with my eyes not to be a hopeless show-off and to stay away from those knives, but I don't want Sasha to see what he's up to and get any ideas. So I talk.

"Rob was GG's son. His real name is Martin, but he was calling himself by his middle name, Robert, when we met him. I don't think it was a coincidence that he befriended Shippy, of all people. I think he knew his mum lived here and wanted to see her. Maybe he was nervous about the kind of reception he'd get. Maybe he wanted to surprise her. Maybe he even wanted to pay her back for ghosting him for so long." I try not to think about how awful it must have been for Rob to turn up and learn of his mum's death through casual conversation with strangers. I try even harder not to think about how close GG came to getting to see her son again before she died. There's a tiny tragedy in there, among all the rest of it.

Sasha just shakes his head. "You're a creative kid."

He's not wrong. The list of things I *think* could be true is a lot longer than the list of things I *know* to be true. But Sasha doesn't need to know that, and I just need to keep him talking long enough for the others to get home, so he doesn't have a chance to get away with GG's phone.

"You must have been shocked when Rob walked into this room that day." I try to think back to the awkwardness of the moment, which I'd put down to Rob's lack of clothes. "He knew who you were, and you knew who he was: You'd been in prison together. You were the one who saw that letter from GG and took an interest in this guy with the rich mum. That day, when he said he wanted to check out your truck—what did he say to you? Did he know you'd been taking money from his mum already? Did he want it back? Did you arrange to meet up at the beach then or did you just swap numbers so you could text him later?"

"That's a lot of questions and not a lot of answers," Sasha says lazily, but he's not convincing.

"You got out of prison first and came here to track down his mum." I keep going. "GG believed you when you presented yourself as a friend of her son, and she believed you when you said you'd give the money to him. That thing she says in the video about you passing on her cards and how she's 'sorry it's not more.' That doesn't make sense unless the cards had money in them. Money for prison, maybe. Or money for when he got out. Laura at the library said GG had been taking out big sums of money from the bank. How much was it?"

Sasha doesn't answer.

"Did Rob *know*, or were you just scared that he was going to figure it out? Maybe you thought there was a way you could get your hands on more of her money. Rob, Martin, whatever you want to call him, must have told you she was rich. How disappointing to learn that her idea of an inheritance was an ancient typewriter and a bag of baby teeth." Sasha looks genuinely confused at that last bit and I realize that he probably didn't have time to look in the box very carefully before stashing it. I don't bother to fill him in. "Why *did* you hide the box, anyway? Did you hear something and panic?" I'm spitballing wildly, but there's a moment where Sasha almost looks like he wants to answer. He doesn't, of course, so I keep talking.

"I should have known it was you when you turned up with that story about GG being scared of her son. Is a terminally ill woman seriously going to be scared of being confronted by her estranged son? It never made sense."

"You've got no proof for any of this," Sasha says as Dylan takes another big step away from him. Bloody Dylan—he never quite thinks things through. There's a noise from outside, but maybe it's all in my head because nobody else reacts and I can't look away from Sasha. I have to keep his attention off Dylan. "Are you going to give me the phone or do I have to take it? Because this is getting boring."

"You made a mistake, though, when you hit Rob with your car." I reach into my pocket, and Sasha, misinterpreting my move even though he *just asked for GG's phone,* pulls his own hand free from his jacket to reveal, oh crap, an actual gun. It's not a farmer's shotgun but the kind of shiny small gun I've only ever seen in the movies. The scale of my miscalculation swamps me: an act of pure recklessness and arrogance that's going to take the body count to three or four (Rob/Martin's life also still being very much in the balance at this stage) and leave this mystery unsolved.

"Wait!" I yelp. "It's the phones! They're in my pocket."

"They?"

"There's two of them."

"Get 'em out."

I take out the two phones and lay them on the table. "The other one is Rob's," I explain.

There's movement outside the living room window, but I'm the only one facing that way, so, again, I seem to be the only one who notices. It makes me brave.

"You must have thought you killed him when you hit him with your car. You stopped just long enough to take his phone and, I assume, destroy it. Except you destroyed *my* phone, which is actually such a pain in the arse. Rob and I had the same phone. We even both had photos of Yallingup Beach as our lock screen. Rob probably wasn't looking closely when he grabbed mine the day he went to meet you. I didn't realize why my phone was missing until I found his. But I do now. And this phone has proof—the message you sent Rob to tell him where to meet you that day."

This is me bluffing. Can you tell? I can no more open Rob's phone to read his messages than I could find a phone signal in this ridiculous house. But the only time Rob and Sasha were ever alone, so far as I know, was a minute or two outside our house, which doesn't seem long enough to arrange a rendezvous. So much easier to swap numbers.

"There's nothing incriminating about sending a text message."

"There is if you arrange to meet someone and a car turns up to run them down."

"Give me the phone," Sasha says, almost conversationally. "Or I'll shoot you and your boyfriend here." He swings his arm so the gun is pointing at Dylan, still meters from the knives, which is something. At least he's not going to accidentally behead himself with a bread knife.

"He's not my boyfriend. Until recently we thought we were related."

"*Ruth,*" Dylan says.

"Probably not the time."

"Both phones now, please."

"Don't do anything. I'll give them to you." I push the two phones across the table to Sasha. What else can I do: karate-kick the gun out of Sasha's hand? Throw the phone at his head and overpower him while he's distracted? Dylan and I combined don't weigh as much as this guy, and my deadliest weapon is my sarcasm. Sasha keeps the gun steady as he puts the phones into his pocket. The adrenaline that got me this far has burned out and my legs are spaghetti. Or is that relief that this is nearly over? I'm still the only one with a view of the front yard.

"The police," I say.

"They can't prove anything," Sasha says.

"That's not what I mean."

"Then what?"

"They're outside."

How's my timing on this? Sasha turns his head just as the front door busts inward and Detective Peterson stands silhouetted in the doorway. It's straight out of an action movie and my legs immediately give way, which is convenient because I fall just as she shouts, "Police! Get on the floor!" I don't see Sasha shoot but I hear the shot and see Detective Peterson fall backward.

I think I might be screaming as Sasha runs for the door, hurdling the body on the ground with more speed than you'd expect a big guy to have. I get to my knees and see Detective Peterson saying something into her radio, but everything is muffled. I do nothing but watch as the brake lights of Sasha's truck come on and then he's bumping toward the driveway, but I can't bring myself to care all that much that he's getting away because a Sasha at large still beats a Sasha with a gun in my face.

"Ruth, are you okay?" It's Dylan's voice. He's on the floor next to me and I start to answer, but anything I manage to get out is lost to the sound of a tremendous crash outside. I look out the window and feel like I'm going to throw up.

Detective Peterson is back on her feet and her face is weirdly calm.

"Stay where you are!" she shouts as I stagger toward her, but she's running too and in the same direction as me: toward the crash and the two cars, one of which is my dad's. *Dad, Dad, Dad. No, no, no.* None of this is supposed to happen this way. I was supposed to get Sasha's confession on the phone and go to the police and he'd be put away and I'd be a hero and now Dad is in his car, which Sasha has smashed right into and . . .

The door to Sasha's truck creaks open before I'm halfway across the yard and he stumbles out, looking dazed but still on his feet, moving away from the car and toward the trees that line the driveway.

Dad is in the driver's seat of his car, looking shocked. I can't tell for sure whether that's shock to see me, shock at Sasha's flight into the trees, or shock from the crash. Maybe a little of all three. I don't care much because he's climbing out of the car, and that's not a thing dead people do. I fall against him, not yet sobbing but wanting to.

"What the—" he says. "Is that *the farmer*?"

I shake my head, although he's only half wrong. "He's not a farmer" is all I can say, which must confuse him further.

Aunty Vinka climbs out of the back seat, rubbing her head just as Dylan arrives at my shoulder. She has a cut on her forehead but seems otherwise okay. "What was that?"

Detective Peterson appears beside her.

"Is everyone okay?"

"Yeah, I'm fine." Aunty Vinka inadvertently smears blood across her cheek as she pushes her hair off her face, but she doesn't seem to notice. She's too busy looking at Detective Peterson. "We have the same eyes," she says, sounding dreamy or mildly concussed.

"Uh-huh," Detective Peterson says in a way all cops must learn in police school when dealing with unbalanced perps or witnesses. "I've called an ambulance, ma'am."

But Dad is there too, and I'm sure he and I are looking at

the same thing: with Aunty Vinka's hair swept off her face and the two women side by side, there's a sudden, obvious physical similarity between my aunt and this policewoman. Detective Peterson is (just) taller than Aunty Vinka and she doesn't jingle when she walks, but, beyond that, they have the same cool green eyes, the same shade of brown hair. They could be . . . they could be . . .

"Detective Peterson," Dad says slowly. "Nicola, right?"

"That's right."

"Does anyone ever call you Nicky?"

Before Detective Peterson can answer a question that must sound, to her, like Dad has also suffered a serious head injury, Aunty Vinka remembers where she is and what's just happened. "Nick?" she says, running around to the other side of the car, and I realize who must be in the front passenger seat.

"Stay here and wait for the ambulance. I'm going after the suspect," Detective Peterson tells us, sprinting into the trees in the same direction as Sasha.

Nick is moaning but he's conscious, which is something, and he doesn't seem to be screaming in pain, which is even better. He looks a bit pale and unwashed, but it's hard to say where hospital grime ends and car crash malaise begins. One leg is encased in a thick white cast from the foot to the knee.

"I hate to say it," Nick says, closing his eyes with pain. "But I think I've broken my arm."

"Course you have, mate," Dad says, and he starts to laugh.

There's a shout from the trees and we all turn to look, Dad's arms tightening around me. I don't know about the others, but

I'm braced for a shot and wondering if I should have grabbed that bread knife from the kitchen after all.

But there's no shot and nothing happens for a few seconds until Detective Peterson emerges, absolutely legging it toward us, shouting something I can't understand. She's probably still twenty meters away by the time she's audible.

"First aid kit!" she shouts at us. "In my car!" Still holding me, Dad stumbles in that direction, but he's moving so slowly she'll overtake him before he gets there. "Better make it two ambulances," she says into the radio held in one cupped hand. "Our suspect has sustained a snakebite."

30

THERE'S NO TEA. SOMEHOW OVER THE COURSE OF THE PAST FEW days we've drained the farmhouse dry, not just of proper tea but of Aunty Vinka's disgusting herbal stuff too. This turns out to be a good thing, since one of the policemen summoned by Detective Peterson boils up a batch of hot chocolate on the stove, using a jar of chocolate powder that's been hiding at the back of the pantry all this time. Everyone takes a mug, and a packet of gingersnaps (seriously, there were *gingersnaps* in the house?) is passed around. The double sugar hit feels restorative.

We're mostly all here, gathered around the table, including Bec and Shippy, who arrived in the other car two minutes too late to be of any help at all. Detective Peterson has stayed behind to take some preliminary statements (her words) from us all. She's not such a badass that she's doing this while bleeding all over the floor or anything: She was wearing a bulletproof vest when Sasha shot her, and so she has only a gross red lump just under her collarbone that will rule out spaghetti-strap sleeves for a week.

Sasha was last seen in the back of an ambulance, which turned on both its lights and sirens this time. Do people still die of snakebites, I wanted to know only a few days earlier. I don't know it yet, but they do, and Sasha is one of the unlucky ones. He's that Body Number Two I promised you, or he will be pretty soon.

Nick and his suspected broken arm took the second ambulance, and he waved Aunty Vinka away (figuratively, not literally) when she offered to go with him. The paramedics were buddies from his last hospital stint, apparently. "Alex and Sarah will take care of me—we're watching *Yellowjackets* together" were his last words before the doors shut (not last words as in he's going to die—don't worry, he'll be fine).

"You must be wondering why I turned up," Detective Peterson says to Dad, who looks blank because he really hasn't had time to think about that: He's been too busy apologizing for leaving me and Dylan alone. I'm trying to enjoy it because he's not going to be nearly so sympathetic when he learns I tried to bait a would-be murderer into a confession.

"Did you find out about Sasha being in prison with Rob, I mean Martin?" I ask, for once not showing off but genuinely curious. All the faces in the room turn in my direction, embarrassingly catching me trying to dunk the last chunk of cookie into my hot chocolate and losing my grip.

"That's right," Detective Peterson says, giving me an X-ray of a glance. "I came here to ask you all how much you knew about Gertie's son and got a bit of a surprise when I looked through the window and saw Sasha holding a gun."

"A *gun*?" says Dad.

The X-ray intensifies. "But how did *you* know about Martin and Sasha, Ruth?"

The blush starts at my neck, but I ignore it. I figured this out and I'd like to get some credit for it.

"I knew that GG's son was still alive, so—"

"Sorry, GG is Gertrude?"

"Yeah, that's just what I called her."

"Go on."

"So, uh, I knew that GG's son was still alive because Sasha told us he was and Laura at the library confirmed it."

"I know about that."

"We didn't figure out that Sasha was in prison with GG's son until we saw the video, but it makes sense."

Silence. Then: "Sorry, did you say video?"

Oops. I meant to save that bit for later. Or maybe I should have opened with it.

"GG recorded a video the night she died," I say, feeling exhausted at the prospect of trying to explain it all and (almost) wishing Dylan would step in and take over. "It actually, uh, I was going to tell you all, of course, but it shows everything that happened that night." I explain about the video GG made for her son and the money she'd been sending him via Sasha, all over a chorus of "What?" and "Are you kidding?" and "How am I just hearing this now?" When I do the big reveal about how GG died, there's a long beat of silence. Obviously, now, I can see I should have opened with this.

Aunty Vinka starts to cry with what I assume is relief.

"Where is this phone now?" Detective Peterson asks.

"She was trying to lift the typewriter down?" Dad says, and there's not really anything I can say to him about that. Too late I realize my dad might be the most responsible of any of us for what happened. If he'd taken the typewriter downstairs like GG had asked, presumably so she could give it to Sasha to pass on to Rob/Martin, GG might still be alive. I let him put his arm around me, but that's as close as I get to telling him it's not his fault. Parents get to lie to kids all the time, but I don't think it really works in reverse.

"Where *is* this phone?" Detective Peterson asks again. "And why didn't you bring it to us immediately?"

"We only found it last night," Dylan says, and heads whip around to him too.

"You knew about this?" Bec asks her son.

"You're really going to give me a hard time about keeping secrets?"

"*Where is the video?*" Detective Peterson asks again, and even though she's not talking all that loudly, somehow her voice shuts everyone else up.

"We gave the phone to Sasha," I say.

"How did he know you had it?"

"We showed it to him."

"You *what*?" That's Dad, catching up.

"He just turned up," I say, which is not a super-solid defense. "I had the idea that we could, uh, you know, that he might give himself away about having tried to kill Rob."

"Sasha tried to kill Rob?" Dad asks.

"Sorry, yeah, I should have said. Rob is GG's son. His real name is Martin." I thought I'd love this, but I'm already tired of telling this story, which I'll spend months telling and retelling.

"What?" Detective Peterson says.

"Are you serious?" Dad chimes in.

"Dylan, were you involved in this too?" Aunty Vinka demands.

"I'm going to need you to explain, please."

Since that last question comes from Detective Peterson, I decide that's the one I'll deal with first.

"Along with GG's phone, we found a bunch of photos. Most of them are GG with Rob/Martin when he was really young, so we didn't recognize him at first. But some show him when he's older, before he went to prison, I guess, and it's pretty obviously Rob, so we figured Rob must be Martin. That's why Sasha tried to kill him." The room is silent: Everyone is hooked, except Shippy, who, rather than meditating on this string of revelations and contemplating his own role in bringing about Rob's potential untimely death, is reading a two-day-old racing guide from the paper.

"There's other stuff too: The date of birth on Martin's birth certificate was a week ago, and when we met Rob, he said the surfing trip was a birthday present to himself, so that lined up too." I try to get this bit out modestly, but, seriously, I'm smug about having noticed this. Unfortunately, nobody else seems impressed. "Plus, Martin's middle name was Robert, so, you know, once I saw that . . ."

"*Ruth*," Dad says.

"I don't know why Sasha wanted Martin's birth certificate and stuff," I say. "It's not like it's worth money."

Detective Peterson nods. She's the only one who seems to be taking this even slightly in stride, and if I could crack open her skull (which I wouldn't, gross), I think I'd see the bits of this mystery clicking together. "It's possible Sasha's original plan was to assume Robert's, which is to say Martin's, identity."

"But Sasha couldn't have convinced GG that he was her long-lost son," I say.

"No. It's not plausible that Gertrude wouldn't have recognized her own son. It's just a tragedy that she never got to see Rob. He only missed her by a matter of days."

This is basically the moment I'd hoped for, when Detective Peterson and I get to pool our theories, but I'm barely able to enjoy it because I've thought of something else.

"If that was his plan, it would only have worked if GG was dead," I say, thinking aloud. "Did Sasha plan to kill GG and assume Martin's identity to inherit?"

Detective Peterson doesn't pat me on the head and urge me to enroll in the police force, but she doesn't laugh, either. All she says is: "We don't know what he was planning."

I sit with that for a moment, wondering if Sasha had planned to kill GG and Rob/Martin all along. If we'd gone back to Perth as intended, and he'd bumped her off that night and Rob/Martin another time only to turn up later as Martin, GG's long-lost, surprisingly alive son, would there be anyone to say otherwise? Or were we being too harsh on Sasha and he never had murder on his mind, just some light fraud and theft? The number of questions to be filed under Never to Be Known is really annoying for someone like me, whose preference is to have every loose end double-knotted into place.

"Sasha said he and GG were supposed to meet that evening at the house, but he got put off when he saw that we were all still here," I say, remembering. "I think maybe GG got all the stuff out for that meeting but she didn't have a phone to call and cancel." I try to think back to that night and replay it in my head. Was GG waiting that whole evening for Sasha to rock up and trying to figure out what to tell the rest of us when he did? Could it be that she didn't want to take her meds for fear they'd knock her out, or was she just being stubborn? "Did Rob come here to see his mother, or was he trying to track down Sasha?" I ask, probably pushing it, but, hey, I have basically solved a non-murder and a near murder today. The most surprising thing about this whole exchange is not so much that Detective Peterson seems willing to chat but that my dad is letting it happen.

"Given that we found this address on Robert, it seems likely that he came here to see his mother," Detective Peterson says. "Matthew mentioned that Robert befriended him on the beach one day." She nods at Shippy, which is good because I forgot his real name again. Matthew just doesn't suit him; he's got a Shippy face and there's nothing to be done about it. "It seems possible that meeting was engineered to gain him entry to the house."

"Why was Martin calling himself Rob?"

"He's not in a position to talk yet," Detective Peterson says. "He might have been going by his middle name simply to distance himself from his past."

"It's so hard for the formerly incarcerated outside jail, isn't it?" Aunty Vinka puts in, and Dad gives her a look that's only slightly more polite than the one on Detective Peterson's face.

"Maybe not now, Vinx."

"I'm just saying. There's a lot of prejudice against people who have been incarcerated. Not just Rob, I mean Martin, but Sasha, too."

"Sasha *did* try to murder a guy." Dad looks at Detective Peterson. "Right?"

"It's really too early to say," she says automatically. Then: "If, as seems possible, Sasha arranged to meet Robert or agreed to meet him with the intention of hitting him with his car, we could go for a murder charge, although how much of this we'll be able to prove, I don't know." There's a moment where maybe she remembers that Dad's a journalist and that she's being pretty loose-lipped in the moment. "This is all off the record, by the way," she says, looking right at him.

"Oh!" Dylan, who's been letting me have the spotlight here, stands up, then sits right back down again. Maybe his legs, like mine, are still feeling a bit wobbly, even with a hot chocolate and cookie in him. "Rob's phone!" he says, looking at me. "Sasha took it after you told him it had proof that Sasha and Rob had arranged to meet the night that he died."

"After you told him *what*?" Dad almost shouts at me, and Dylan mouths *sorry*.

"I was bluffing," I add, quickly and a little lamely. "But Sasha believed me and he really wanted that phone, so there's probably something incriminating on it."

"Sasha had this phone on him?" Detective Peterson asks.

"He should have."

"Ruth, we're going to need you to come into the station to make a full statement about this. You too, Dylan."

"Oh!" I say. *"Dylan's* phone." Belatedly I realize that this is one more thing I really should have mentioned before now. And if you're rolling your eyes at me, why don't you try confronting an attempted murderer, witnessing a car accident, and possibly locating a long-lost aunt in a half-hour time period and see how sharp you're feeling at the end of it?

"We were filming the whole time with Sasha, when we asked him about GG and Rob/Martin and all of that."

I look up at the kitchen counter but the phone is gone. *How?* This house straight-up *is* the Bermuda Triangle for phones.

"What?" That's Dad.

"It was Ruth's idea," Dylan says, and I can't tell if he's trying to avoid getting into trouble or trying to help me out. He pulls the phone out of his pocket and hands it over to the detective. "I grabbed it when you ran outside," he says to me.

"Sasha didn't know about this one," I add.

"Right." Detective Peterson doesn't look as pleased with this development as I feel she should be. Gushy invitations to join the police force to put my detective skills to use may prove thinner on the ground than I'd like.

"Just to clarify: Are there *any more phones* I should be aware of that contain *crucial video evidence*?" She has the kind of voice that could make me confess to crimes I didn't commit.

"I don't think so."

"Michaels," she says to the hot-chocolate-making policeman,

who is brewing up a second batch and looks annoyed at being distracted just as he's sprinkling in some cinnamon. "Bag this phone as evidence and radio the hospital. See how many phones were found on Sasha when he was taken in. If there weren't two on him—no, three; he'd have one of his own—grab some gloves and check the truck."

Michaels (presumably) nods and turns off the stove, but he doesn't look pleased about it. (Neither am I: Cinnamon in hot chocolate, who'd have thought it?)

"Let me clarify what happened," Detective Peterson says. "You filmed the suspect without him knowing it, even though you believed he had tried to kill a man, in order to confront him about that attack? That was seriously dangerous, kids. This isn't an episode of *Scooby Doo*."

"What's *Scooby Doo*?" Dylan asks.

Detective Peterson meets Dad's eyes. "Kids don't get a real education these days," Dad says.

She nods. "All my daughter wants to watch is kids unwrapping presents on YouTube." Then she snaps back to being a cop and gives Dylan and me a look that would have told me she's a mum, even if she hadn't mentioned it. "You're both very lucky things worked out the way they did."

Dylan and I look at each other, ostensibly contrite, but I suspect he's thinking the same thing behind that façade of apology: that, whatever the grown-ups feel about it, we did something pretty awesome. While I'm watching, the corner of Dylan's mouth twitches up, and I know I'm right.

"We didn't know he had a gun," Dylan says.

The police radio on the kitchen table buzzes, and Detective Peterson snatches it up, stepping away from the table to talk into it.

"You got pretty deep into this detective stuff," Dad says, tipping his untouched hot chocolate into my empty mug. It's lukewarm but still pretty good, so I'll forgive him for (deliberately or not) stopping me from eavesdropping on the police-radio call.

"Sorry."

"I wish I'd realized how serious you were. Maybe I could have helped."

Well, this is some dictator-style rewriting of history right here. "You would have just told me to stop."

"Maybe."

"Definitely. But I suppose you could have told me where you were that night."

"When?"

"The night GG died and you were out of your bed. You said you were checking on GG, but you weren't because I heard her talking to Bec. You weren't in the bathroom because I was there, and you weren't out in the garden because Shippy was smoking. So where were you?"

Dad looks like I've spat in his face. "You didn't think that I—"

I shake my head. "I never thought that."

"I went out to the paddocks late that night to make a phone call."

"Okay."

"To a friend. A woman."

I think I'm starting to get it. "Oh."

"Ruth, I was going to tell you about her, but—"

I put one hand over my face so I don't have to look at him. Murder I can handle, but an insight into Dad's love life is too gruesome for me. "Dad, it's fine, I get it. You don't have to tell me." It would be childish, under the circumstances, to be annoyed that my detective skills so utterly failed to detect the presence of a girlfriend in my dad's life.

"I hope you don't think it's too soon."

"Dad, Mum is already *married* again—how can it be too soon?"

"Maybe when we get back to Perth you can meet Jane. That's her name, Jane." Detective Peterson is back at the table and looking at the floor like there's a blood-spatter mystery to solve there.

Another puzzle piece drops into my hand. "How late were you out there?" I ask.

Dad looks confused. "A while, I guess. I was on the phone for a bit—we had some things to talk about."

"What about the storm?"

"I had my jacket, but there was hardly any rain and the lightning didn't get that close."

I want to ask Dad if he'd be this Zen about *me* being out in a paddock with lightning flying around, but I've got other things on my mind. "Was anyone up when you got home?"

"No, I don't think so."

"And you came in the front door?"

"Yeah. I dropped my keys right on the doorstep and had to

hunt for them in the dark." He frowns, like maybe he's trying to remember. "I thought I heard something, like somebody might have still been up, but there was nobody there when I finally found my keys and came inside."

I think about what it was that made Sasha stash the box under the floorboards—a dumb move, however you want to spin it—and whether it could have been as simple as the sound of Dad coming home. Of course, if I'm right, that means Sasha had hidden the box and was lurking in the house when Dad came in. He wouldn't have wanted to risk retrieving the box with someone awake in the house and a dead body upstairs; he'd have slipped out as quickly and quietly as possible. It's a theory and one Dad's not going to want to hear (*I* barely want to hear it), but, much as I'd love to impress Detective Peterson with my deductive skills, for now I want to take advantage of Dad's chatty mood. I also really don't want to think about what might have happened if Dad had run into Sasha that night.

"What about the money problems?" I ask.

"What?"

"You canceled the streaming services and sold your guitar. Dylan says you want to sell the house. Is there something going on?"

Dad gets a bit more uncomfortable. "I've been thinking about buying a new place, that's all. And you know I haven't touched that guitar in years."

"Oh?"

"A bigger place." He doesn't add *for Jane*, but that's got to be the subtext, if I'm going by the fact that his cheeks are on fire.

"What about the streaming services?"

"We have too many streaming services. Human brains weren't made to have this much choice." He does a very un-Dad-like thing and puts his hands over his face. "This is not how I wanted to have this conversation."

"Forget I said anything," I say, wishing this could literally happen.

Nobody speaks, and then Detective Peterson inserts herself back into the conversation. "Are there any more romantic revelations to disclose, or do you think we can get back to the criminal investigation?" she says brightly.

There's a bit more back-and-forth about who said and did what. Dylan and I do most of the talking, tripping over each other. At some point Michaels reappears with news that three phones were found on Sasha and have been taken as evidence. Detective Peterson stands up, closing her notepad.

"It's been a big morning and I should head back to the station. Ruth, Dylan, you both look exhausted. Maybe we'd better have you in tomorrow for an official statement instead of today."

(At the risk of confusing the timeline, it's worth noting that what Detective Peterson also learned on that radio call, but doesn't tell us right away, is that Sasha has died. She already knows there's not going to be a big trial, just a sad little inquest that Dad, Aunty Vinka, Bec, Dylan, and I will attend, so a lot of the urgency has drained out of this whole thing.)

Dad doesn't look thrilled. "We were hoping to head back to Perth."

"Really?"

"Detective, no offense, but we've been trying to get out of this town all week."

"Nick's back in the hospital," I point out.

"If we wait for Nick to stop injuring himself, I'm going to die in this farmhouse."

"We really do need the kids to come in, in person," Detective Pearson says in a way that it almost sounds like she's asking a question, although she definitely is not.

"Okay, but we are leaving *first thing* after we've been into the police station tomorrow, then," Dad says, way louder than I think he means to. "You need to go to school. I need to keep my job. I also need Wi-Fi, my coffee machine, and I really, really need some clean boxers." Nobody responds to that last one because: ew. Also, there's a washing machine here that Dad could have been using, so that one is kind of on him.

Dad and Aunty Vinka walk out with the cops and Dylan and I trail behind. I'm carrying the last two gingersnaps. It's only lunchtime, but I'm shattered, held together by sugar and whatever adrenaline leaves behind when it goes away.

"Detective Peterson, can I ask you a personal question?" Dad asks.

"You can ask."

"Are you adopted?"

It can't be what she's expecting, but Detective Peterson must have an amazing poker game because, from what I can see of it, her face doesn't change. "How did you know that?"

"It's a long story."

I know why Dad asks and I assume you do too, unless you're seriously not paying attention. Sure, it's a pretty long shot that this Detective Nicola Peterson could be the half sibling "Nicky" who was adopted out, but also, well, here she is with the right name, the right eyes, and living in the same town where Dad and Aunty Vinka grew up. Personally, I'm already gaming out what it would be like to have an actual cop in the family. She could be the cop source-on-the-inside every amateur detective needs... assuming she's both unprofessional and reckless enough to let a kid get involved in proper criminal detection, which seems pretty unlikely. Still, it's a start.

I look at Dylan to see if he's listening and he raises both eyebrows. I raise one back, just to piss him off.

"Stop for a sec," he whispers, and I do reluctantly, wanting to eavesdrop on the rest of the conversation.

"Didn't you hear what they were saying? Dad thinks the detective could be Grandad's love child."

"I'm going to wait for the DNA test on that one," Dylan says. "I've been burned before."

"You have a point."

"We need to do something, quickly, while your dad and Vinka are out here. Please?"

There's an urgency in his voice that stops me from asking logical questions like *Why? What for?* and *Haven't we just solved the whole case like a pair of child geniuses?* Instead I follow him inside and back to the kitchen table, where Bec and Shippy are still sitting.

"... completely different to Bitcoin," Shippy is saying. They look up.

"There's something I want to ask you, Mum," Dylan says

before Bec can speak or Shippy can elaborate on what Bitcoin-adjacent scam he's about to lose money on. We sit opposite the adults and I keep my expression neutral, wishing there'd been time for any kind of background briefing so I could adjust my face accordingly.

"You can ask me anything," Bec says.

"Will you tell me the truth?"

"What is it?"

"Just answer: Will you tell me the truth?"

Shippy gives me a *what's all this about* look that I ignore. Mostly because I have no idea what all this is, in fact, about.

"I'll tell you the truth."

"Did you smash the window and put the ladder against the house the night Gertie died?" Dylan asks.

This is . . . not what I was expecting. If Dylan had asked me, real quick, to jot down a list of my top ten ideas of what this was about, that wouldn't have made the cut. It's not what Bec was expecting either, if the southerly location of her jaw is any indication.

"What?"

"Just tell me. Did you do it?"

Shippy licks the tip of one finger and runs it through a line of gingersnap crumbs on the table. "Don't be ridiculous, Dylan."

But Bec doesn't look like Dylan is being ridiculous. "Why would you ask me that?"

"Just tell me the truth, Mum." For a guy who usually operates somewhere between a two out of ten and a four out of ten on the intensity scale (one being comatose), Dylan has jumped all the way up to nine, and it's freaking his mum out as much as it is me. Plus, what is he talking about? Did he miss the whole confrontation scene with Sasha, who, sure, denied breaking the window and setting up the ladder, but also confirmed himself to be a straight-up psychopath who cannot be believed?

"Yes," Bec says, but quietly. "How did you know?"

Dylan looks at me, presumably to make sure I'm paying attention, as if something more interesting than this bizarre eleventh-hour confession (to what, exactly?) might have distracted me.

"I didn't *know*," he says. "But you had a cut on your hand the morning after Gertie died." I look at Bec's hand and see a faint red line across one finger in the spot where I'd noticed a Band-Aid covering what I'd assumed was a burn from the stove. She immediately covers one hand with the other, as though this isn't a bolting-the-barn-door/horse-on-the-loose situation. "I heard you get up early the morning Gertie died, but you never said anything about it. Plus, Sasha said it wasn't him, and why would he lie about that, of all things? The window was unlocked and open, so the only reason it could possibly have been smashed was to make the police believe someone outside the house killed Gertie. It never really made sense that Sasha would bother trying to divert suspicion from people in the house."

Um, rude? It made sense to me when I accused Sasha. Sometimes criminals have dumb plans.

"What's this about, Bec?" Shippy asks.

"I did it, but that's all I did," Bec says quickly, her eyes on the front door. Through the window I can see a couple of police officers photographing the crashed cars. Dad, Aunty Vinka, and Detective Peterson are in conversation. "It was so stupid." She puts her hand on top of Dylan's and he doesn't immediately pull it away.

"What happened?" he asks.

"I woke up really early," she says. "Nobody else was up. Gertie was an early riser as well, and so I went upstairs to see if she wanted anything. I wanted to talk to her too. You might not believe this, Dylan, but I wasn't sure if keeping up the lie about me being part of the family was the best idea." She's looking at her son but getting nothing in return. "I found her on the floor. I thought she had been killed. There was no sign of a break-in or a forced entry. I thought . . . I didn't know. The last conversation we had, she basically confirmed I'd get a lot of money when she died."

Nobody says anything because *yikes*. I can only think of one reason why Bec might have done such a reckless, fairly stupid thing.

"You thought Shippy had done it for the money?" Dylan asks.

"You thought *I* killed Gertie?" Shippy, it appears, has finally caught up.

"I wasn't thinking straight," Bec says, now turning to Shippy. "I'd just told you that I was in Gertie's will and then she died. You'd been out of bed that night and you took a shower before you came to bed."

"To get rid of the smell of smoke."

"I know that now. After I found Gertie, I went outside for a walk, just to clear my head—I was probably in shock, but I was planning to hike across the field to call the police. Then, when I walked around the house and saw the ladder right there, I thought, well, I thought I could make it look like someone came in from the outside. I smashed the window with a rock for the same reason. It was an insane thing to do, obviously."

"Right." Shippy looks into her eyes, which are big and pleading and, gosh, she really does manage to look so pretty, even in a crisis. I'm sort of bummed, just for the moment, that we're not related so there's no chance I'll age like her. "You were trying to protect me." (Is it just me or does Shippy seem . . . flattered?)

The front door opens, and Dad and Aunty Vinka come in.

". . . chakra," Aunty Vinka is saying. "I felt it from the start."

"Vinka, you're so full of it," Dad says. "Let's save it for the DNA test. No online tests either. I want to talk to someone wearing a white lab coat." He pats me on the head. "What a day. Ruth, how are you?"

"I'm okay." I'm seriously *not* okay. I'm trying to process this latest development that (a) Bec thought that Shippy might have murdered GG, (b) she tried to cover it up to protect him, and (c) he seems *cool* with it? And (d) Dylan figured it out without me.

Dylan looks across the table at me and I try to decode the message in his eyes. Is he asking me not to tell Dad what his mum did? Is he telling me I can if I want to? Is he just, like me, utterly exhausted and trying not to face-plant into the dregs of the hot chocolate and drown?

"I think I'm going to lie down," I say.

Dylan catches me on the stairs. "Thanks," he says.

"For what?"

"Not saying anything to your dad."

"The cops might still figure it out."

"Maybe."

"Do you think Sasha will survive that snakebite?"

Dylan shrugs. "Is it bad that I don't really care? You solved it—our part in this is over."

"We solved it."

"Sherlock never gives Watson any credit."

"So, you admit you're the Watson in this relationship?"

"I've always been the Watson." Dylan gives me a sideways smile as we reach the landing outside my bedroom. "About the Lisa thing," he says.

I put my hands over my face. "I'm too tired to talk about this. I just want to go to bed." I listen back to what I've just said. "To sleep! Alone!"

"Ruth!" Dylan sounds like he's laughing, but I'm not moving my hands to find out. "It's okay. Go sleep. We can talk about this later. If you want to."

A pause. "I want to. Later."

"Good." I'm not sure exactly what I'm agreeing to. More hand-holding? Kissing? A define-the-relationship conversation? It all feels only marginally less intense than solving a not-quite-murder mystery and helping to bring an attempted murderer to justice but also a perfectly acceptable task to put off to another day.

In my room I ignore the creepy figurines (I've faced so much worse) and crawl into my bed, closing my eyes. When I wake up it's evening and my eyes feel gritty with sleep. Dad has woken me with news: Dinner is ready, Rob is out of the ICU, and Nick has broken not one but both of his arms.

Acknowledgments

Many hands have touched this book since I typed *THE END* for the first time, and every one of them has made it so much better, transforming it from a nice but shaggy idea into a book that people who aren't related to me actually want to read.

That includes the entire team at Knopf but particularly my brilliant US editor, Nancy Siscoe. I knew Nancy was the perfect fit for the book from the moment she sent me the house floor plan she'd sketched out, based on my vague, frequently contradictory descriptions. If I'd known then that she likes to send homemade biscuits to her authors at Christmas, I probably would have proposed on the spot.

I'm so grateful for the chance to get this West Australian crime story into the hands of readers on the other side of the world. WA's South West is such a special place and normally surprisingly low on murders, I promise.

Thanks also to my Australian publishing team at Allen & Unwin, especially my editor Sam Forge, who let me slide into her DMs like a creep; my publisher Anna McFarlane; and rights guru Carey Schroeter.

This book is all about family, so it would be weird to ignore them here, especially as I have such a good one.

Shout-out to my grandad George Emery for giving me an appreciation of old typewriters; my sister, Ruth, who is not my muse, whatever she tries to tell you; and my brother, Marty, because I can't acknowledge one sibling and not the other. I'm including my brother-in-law Shannon too because he thinks I don't like him. See, Shannon, I think you're great.

My parents, Hett and Geoff, raised me in a house full of books, for which I'm very grateful.

Thanks to my husband, Andy, for helping me dig my way out of that plot hole and to our daughters, Agatha and Christobel, for being the best. Nothing means anything without you two.

No parent writes a book unless they get help with the kids, and I had oodles. Special thanks to V-Dog, who offered to look after the girls so she could make it into the acknowledgments of this book but did not—and I really can't emphasize this enough—actually look after them at any point.

Final acknowledgments must go to the greatest pub quiz team the Paddo has ever known, The Beagles. Some of you will recognize your names on these pages but not, I hope, your personalities. Especially not you, Shippy.